To Mary & John — Enjoy the history — and the pictures

Al Gould

Millions of GHOSTS Plead...Don't Forget
ISBN 0-9659081-8-6
Copyright 2003 by Al Gould
Distributed in the United States and Canada by Hartley Press, PO Box 2657, Gearhart, Oregon, 97138
No part of this book may be reproduced without written permission except for brief quotation in books and reviews.
Design by Erica Gibson
Additional copies of Millions of GHOSTS Plead...Don't Forget, may be purchased for $17.95 plus $1.65 for shipping and handling. In Canada the price is $25. Send your request and check or money order to Hartley Press, PO Box 2657, Gearhart, Oregon 97138.

FOREWORD

It was George Santayana who said:
"Those who cannot remember the past are condemned to fulfill (repeat) it."

Did this nation vindicate the words of this Spanish-born philosopher when it did battle with the people of Iraq, who lived under a punishing regime of perhaps the most heinous of genocidists since the reign of the Japanese murderers?

What the Japanese did to humanity throughout the world known as Asia or the Orient should not be forgotten. But has it been forgotten? Is that why we found ourselves embroiled in a desperate fight to repel another despot? Because these despots don't believe we will remember the past?

Santayana told us. But we forgot, so were condemned to repeat the frightening phase of history which has long needed complete telling. This story relates some facts that haven't been told. Then it adds some fiction to suggest what should have happened but didn't.

As the director of the editorial department of one of the nation's largest and most influential publishers wrote after a cursory look at this manuscript: "It's certainly an interesting story and one that should be more known."

This is the effort to tell it.

DEDICATION

This historical accounting of the years of torture inflicted by the Japanese on defenseless men, women and children, is dedicated to the men and women of the military who overthrew this empire of cruelty.

Millions and millions of humans, in and out of uniform, men and women, adults and children, died. None was spared by the marauders.

Years of research to insure fidelity to history, coupled with conversations with personal friends involved in that area presents in a single volume the truth concerning horrors inflicted by the followers of the Emperor.

A fictional part of the story tells of dedicated soldiers and a young boy who attempted to gain some measure of vengeance. This action was more factual than fictional.

Surviving generations should learn of the medieval treatment of the multimillions who were slaughtered by the Japanese wherever they were sent by the Emperor. May these millions rest easier as more people learn of these sacrifices and appreciate them.

May those horrors never be forgotten. Others who would test the mettle of the avengers' successors should not be given encouragement by some who would pacify rather than punish those who created the murderous climate of the past.

SECTIONS

Locale--Date	Page
San Francisco -- 1939	1
Honolulu -- 1940	9
Ashland, Oregon -- 2009	37
Manila -- 1940	45
Portland, Oregon -- 2003	55
Manila -- 1946	69
Ashland, Oregon -- 2009	91
Tokyo-Manila -- 1946	177
Southern Oregon -- 1947-2009	221

SAN FRANCISCO -- 1939

Larry Clew was a young guy who'd wanted to be a sports writer since the days he was the press box boy at Seals Stadium at 16th and Bryant in San Francisco. That's when he was attending University of San Francisco. And long before New York Lawyer Walter O'Malley had sunk his fangs into the Pacific Coast League, extricated its two most valuable properties, Los Angeles and San Francisco, and removed baseball from Brooklyn forever.

At that time O'Malley slyly introduced Expansion by Extortion to baseball in America.

But the kid Clew knew nothing of that. It hadn't happened yet. It was long down the road. He'd gone to high school in Eureka, but freqently watched St. Marys and Santa Clara play Sunday football at Kezar Stadium in the City, as San Fran was called. That was the pre-49er era.

Clew got his job helping out in the press box through a friend of his father. He loved the free spirited guys in the press corps. From that grew his love of the newspaper game.

In those days there were four newspapers in San Francisco. Bobby Stevens, with the Chronicle, Harry Borba, Examiner, Bucky Walters, the News and Jack McDonald, Call-Bulletin were the baseball writers. Now and again Prescott Sullivan, the Examiner's columnist, would show. Clew thought these guys were great.

He could handle the usual night duties without much interference with his studies.

His parttime work at Seals Stadium gave him a chance to catch on as a go-fer boy in the United Press bureau in San Francisco, while he was still at USF. Even though his introduction to the newspaper guys had been via baseball, he was constantly seeking answers to a flock of burning questions. Most of them had nothing to do with baseball or sports in general.

Actually, the center of his curiosity was the militaristic Japanese, their plundering of the Far East and the expansion of their hostile dominance over a vast territory.

He had at least one asset of inestimable value to a reporter, whether male or female, or interested in sports writing or general assignment or whatever. That asset was a burning curiosity.

He frequently pondered this question: "How was this small island nation, Japan, able to move so decisively against nations seemingly far more capable?" Or, as a young man whose friends in Honolulu at the time openly voiced their fear of Japan's intentions, "How were the Japs able to instill such fear in citizens of a major nation?"

His thoughts continued. How did the forces of Japan build their strength to such a level? Furthermore, what sort of selfconfidence must be instilled in them as individuals and as a nation to think they could dominate the Far East and much of the world beyond without inviting annihilation?

When he caught on at United Press the facilities there gave him access to much of the intelligence which was available to the American military. There were intensive programs acquainting the military with Japanese customs as well as the primary belief of that race; the belief they enjoyed total superiority to all other peoples of the world. He absorbed as much as he could.

He learned one of the principles, a national doctrine of the Empire of Japan, was the fact that Emperors long ago had established the doctrine of superiority. This belief of superiority by the people of Nippon to all other peoples was based on philosophies which had been set forth centuries ago.

There were many other beliefs which dominated the Japanese and their thought process. Most important of all was the credo, don't surrender. To surrender was an act of treason to the Emperor, sitting in divine authority as the Japanese scathed all in front of them. This thought of dying before surrendering to insurmountable odds just wasn't acceptable. Clew said, "I'm not sure I could accept their philosophy. Not for an emperor or anyone else."

But the Japanese fighting man approached every battle with an edge based on his suicidal philosophy. He didn't have to worry about his death. To die was to acquire status of hero. Clew learned of this blind refusal to surrender. The need to die was prime. Surrender wasn't considered. It wasn't bravery. Just foolish and fatal fanaticism.

Away from the news bureau, he managed to become acquainted with a couple of young recruits stationed at the Presidio. The Presidio was the garrison in San Francisco which was on constant alert in those days. The young soldiers freely discussed the trepidations of the military regarding the obvious desire of the Japanese to expand.

"We figure it's bound to come. We just don't know where or when. But they've been building for this for a long time."

Clew nodded agreement with what his buddies had told him and asked the obvious questions. "Why don't we stop them now? Before they attack us?"

"Can't do that. Then we'd be the aggressor. Hell, we just aren't in that mode at all. Not ever. Look what happened when the Japs sank that gunboat in China a few years ago. We didn't do a damned thing."

Clew knew what he was talking about. It was the sinking of the Panay, a gunboat on the Yangtze River. That was in 1937 and here they were in 1939 still not certain what the government planned to do, if anything, to halt the obvious expansion plans of Japan.

Someone spoke up. "Oh yeah, we did something about that boat. We took a check for a couple of million dollars from the Japs and called it even for two men and a boat."

His Army buddy added, "Remember, there was a foreigner on the boat who died too. He was in your business," the private said, looking at Clew. "A newspaper guy but not American."

All of them remembered one detail precisely. There was never any reprisal. The U.S. took the check and closed the issue.

Clew was, quite frankly, puzzled. "If we know we're in their sights, why don't we shut them off on raw materials? I mean, that's a small island. They don't have the raw materials, do they? To build tanks and all that? No iron ore there that I know of?"

The two Army youths looked at each other and smiled knowingly.

"There's a lot of people in this country who are more than happy to do business with those guys. They're the ones who've made it possible for the Japanese to put together a machine that's capable of attacking anyone. Hell, the Japs have already attacked and ripped everyone in their own backyard and you know damned well they'll be coming our way soon."

He quickly learned what they meant by people 'doing business' with the Japs. One of the others came from a small town in the Pacific Northwest and he said, "Everyday I'd walk through town, cross the railroad tracks, and I'd see these big gondola cars on the sidings. They were loaded with scrap metal of all kinds. Know where they went every week?" He went right on. "Japan, that's where they went. My dad used to growl at dinnertime, 'that stuff'll be fired back at us one of these days' and he was right on."

Clew was a small-towner too, and chimed in, "You know, I remember now what you guys are talking about. Back in early days, I've heard of old men who'd have their horse drawn carts going through the streets of the city picking up all the scrap metal. And that's where that crap was going too. Straight to Japan. Hell, some of those people got rich by selling that crap to the Japanese, who were able to build up their armament stores with no problems."

Much of this information the young recruits had received in indoctrination earlier. It was startling to them, as it was to Clew, to realize that some Americans were, in effect, supplying a foreign military machine. A military machine that could potentially stretch out to attack American strongholds.

Clew was right. Many American junk dealers had no qualms about growing wealthy selling these raw materials to the Japanese, by now a potential enemy and a dangerous one. And scrap metal was raw material to the mineral-poor Japanese. These people did business with a potential enemy right in America's back yard. Many Americans either didn't know, or didn't care they were helping to build the strength of the Yellow Peril and its war machine. They were people who had eyes only for the almighty dollar.

Partially because of this illicit scrap metal and its violent Far East attacks, Japan was viewed in the U.S. as the Yellow Peril in those days. Many freely predicted Japan planned to strike the United States.

Despite all the indications of impending doom, the lure of easy money was too strong. They did business with Japan.

Most of the military personnel, even these young men at the Presidio, learned far more of the fully-bloomed Japanese hostility. Even in the unemotional wording of the War Department's Educational bulletins, it was truly a shocking eye-opener.

For example, the suicidal tendencies of the Japanese fighting man. The blind refusal to surrender. The need to die rather than surrender. The realization that surrender was an act of treason to the Emperor.

In one of the first bulletins they studied they learned the basis for that philosphy was called BUSHIDO. That's the Japanese name for an accepted moral code. Bushido was the moral code of chivalry in Japan.

In the Japan of World War II and long before, it was the guideline for a warrior and as a precept, Bushido left no doubt that the greatest honor a warrior could attain was death for the Emperor.

"You fight enemy of our Emperor. You kill enemy of our Emperor. You will never surrender to any enemy of our Emperor. You die, yes. You surrender, NO."

The truth of the philosophy, when coldly stated, was chilling. It was even more frightening when strangers to the code realized the Japs lived by those words. Many died by the same code.

Bushido, simply stated, demands a fighting man must continue his fight to the death. Surrender simply wasn't an option. The Japanese, swarming throughout Asia in their crazed forays, told prisoners their dead comrades were the lucky ones. For prisoners, it was a slow, painful death.

"It doesn't make any difference who they're fighting or where they're fighting," offered one of the young soldiers. "They tell us that no matter where the Japanese fight it's always the same."

"And they've fought all over. They've fought on the mainland of China since late in the 19th Century. Hell, that's where they ground out their scary vengeance against the Chinese populace because they had battled so long.

"It goes back further than that, too. As early as 1895 the Japanese grabbed off Formosa and the Pescadores from China. They're now known as Taiwan and Penghu, and the Pescadores Channel lies between the two. East of Penghu is the Formosa Strait.

"From what we've learned, it's just gone on and on. The little bastards annexed Korea in 1910 and that was after they'd taken over as a protectorate of Korea in 1905."

All of this was new and overwhelming to Clew who had no inkling of the ferocity and far-reaching plans of the lustful Japanese.

From the aspect of China, the first positive step in the unification of the country to aid in defense of all, occurred when Chiang Kai-shek, Commander of Dr. Sun Yat-sen's Kuomintang Army, achieved a military success against the Chinese warlords in 1926.

The Communists had gained strong footholds in China as the Chinese Nationalist Government alternated conflict and cooperation with the Communist rebels. The Nationalists had only a shaky command of the provinces of the old Chinese Empire on either side of the Great Wall.

Finally, Chiang Kai-shek captured the old imperial capital of Peking and established a centralized and unified government in that city. But nothing could save China from the continuous attacks of the Japanese. The Army's political espionage agency was located at Mukden, and a fight erupted there, starting a war that would last ten years.

During that time Japan absorbed almost all of China's economically valuable provinces and a population of more than 10 million. It was then the Japanese occupied Manchuria and renamed it Manchukuo, establishing a puppet government there. In 1932 Manchuria fell and two years later Japan abrogated whatever was left of the Washington Treaty System, intended to curb unwanted expansion.

But what was known as the China Incident in 1937 provided the springboard for Japan to move from an incident at Marco Polo bridge to capture Peking and launch a total invasion of China's heartland with its 500 million citizens.

Less than a month following this July invasion of China, General Matsui Iwane was designated Commander-in-Chief of the Japanese forces in China. He concentrated on Shanghai which fell in November to the Japanese forces.

Before the year 1937 drew to a close, the Japanese had advanced up the Yangtze River and seized the capital city.

That's when the storied attack on the American gunboat spotlighted the extreme arrogance of the Japs in America's world. When they sank the Panay, killing the two American seamen and the foreign journalist, it opened some drowsy, unseeing eyes in America.

This international explosion was settled when the U.S. received a check for $2,214,007.36, in exchange for the used gunboat, two American sailors and a foreign journalist.

Immediately after this attack, the infamous Rape of Nanking began. Marauding Jap soldiers, encouraged by their commander, Matsui Iwane, began this horrible slaughter. It was concentrated bestiality at a magnitude never witnessed in the world, civilized or otherwise.

Sadly, the sinking of the Panay seemingly caused more upset in the West than the slaughter in Nanking.

A helpless Chiang Kai-shek had no choice but to move his forces from Nanking, moving West to Chungking.

It was about this time that Larry Clew had been graduated by USF and he was able to use his background with the United Press folks in San Francisco to get an offer for a job as a rookie in the bureau in Honolulu.

He didn't think twice. He took the job. He bid goodby to the Seals press box, Kezar stadium, the loves of the city such as Lefty O'Doul's, DiMaggio's Restaurant and the thrill of watching Joe DiMaggio play before he went to the Yankees. The DiMaggio who hit in 61 consecutive Pacific Coast League games in 1933.

These were all thrills for a young person from a Northern California coastal community of Eureka.

But it was easy for him to thrust those thrills aside as he made ready to visit Honolulu, the capital city of Hawaii. More than just visit, he reminded himself. It was his new home. His first fulltime employment of serious nature.

He could hardly wait.

HONOLULU -- 1940

The tremendous change in climate from the Bay Area to Honolulu was a welcome change for Clew. He made no secret of the fact he looked forward to the sunshine of the Islands. The style of life was something else. He wasn't quite ready for that abrupt change of operating speed at work or otherwise.

No longer was there the hurry-hurry-hurry attitude he was accustomed to. It was more a downright leisurely lifestyle. He quickly got the message the locals figured if the task in front of an individual got finished today, or tomorrow or sometime next week, that'd be okay.

The Island people simply didn't hurry.

At the bureau it wasn't like that, of course. The United Press bureau here was a focal point. It was the relay point, for stories originating anywhere in the Far East and destined for the mainland, usually Los Angeles or San Francisco. This was in addition to the local stories involving military installations such as Hickam Field and Pearl Harbor.

The situation in China, coupled with Japan's military strikes throughout the Far East on an almost daily basis, kept the bureau a beehive busy place.

Clew loved it, thrived on it and learned something every moment.

Although Honolulu didn't have a baseball team in the Pacific Coast League there was plenty of other sports action. As he related to his parents, the surfing was out of this world.

"And the weather." He expanded on this. "Sure, sometimes it rains. But an hour after the rains stop the tennis courts are dry and you can get back on them to play. You should come out here and have a look. It's really something."

Aside from the weather, the surfing and the ample supply of restaurants of all types, Clew found his work in the bureau intriguing.

Just a couple of days in the office gave him more knowledge of the situation in the Far East and Japan's involvement in it, than all of his studies and frequent talking of it back on the mainland.

One of the longtime bureau men, and now the bureau chief, a Bob MacFarland, seemingly could answer any question a person could offer on the subject of Japan and what might be expected from Nippon in the future. Failing that, MacFarland could always tell a staffer where the subject could be researched.

Clew thought himself honored when MacFarland included him in his small group of newspaper types, and some not, when they met for a post-work beer and BS session. At the Times Grill, next to the Honolulu Advertiser newspaper offices on Kapiolani Boulevard, one of the busy streets in Honolulu.

It was in such a session that Clew received confirmation of his belief that Japan's efforts to expand and strengthen its control on the Far East started as long ago as 1895; concerning the Emperor's people seizing Formosa and taking Pescadores from China. The Japanese continued their expansion as they established a 'protectorate' over Korea 10 years later and ultimately, in 1910, annexed Korea.

He also learned that after the first World War ended, the Treaty of Limitation restricted Japan's naval power. Japan's power was tethered momentarily.

Some of his colleagues at the bureau spoke of these developments as they might discuss some current baseball game scores and Clew was impressed. As he told friends, "It's easy to keep my mouth closed in those sessions. Hell, I don't even know what they're talking about. I couldn't add anything to it if my life depended on it."

He also confided in these friends away from the bureau, and some of them were still in college, that "I just listen. If I hear of some spot, or hear of a name I've never heard before, I make a note of it and then look it up.

"Like the Pescadores. I'd never heard of it before. But I looked it up the next day and found out it was an island between Formosa and the mainland of China."

He looked around at his buddies and said, "Those people know what they're doing. It's easy to see why the Japs wanted Formosa. "It sealed up that whole section of the China coast. And they needed China for the iron ore there. And the forced labor supply, of course."

When away from the office and the bureau staffers he hung mostly with young folks from the University of Hawaii who were just working parttime in Honolulu. So they didn't really connect to the serious status of this Island outpost. They certainly weren't privy to the same view of the entire situation which was made available to him since he began work at the UP. But they seemed more than casually interested as they listened to Clew's words on what appeared to him as the next logical place for the Japanese to strike.

He told them, "If they keep calling the shots as they have up to now, it seems a cinch the next they hit is the Philippines and then Hawaii. You don't have to look at a map to figure out that one.

"They've got no chance to go all the way to the mainland. Right now they don't. Not with surface ships or subs, either one. At least I don't think they can."

He paused and looked closely at his friends who were now hanging on his every word. "Right now I just don't think they have the capability to hit the mainland in force. But I'll bet anything that's exactly what they have in mind," he said, looking around for agreement or dissent.

A suddenly quieted group offered not a sound.

And back at the office of the UP he discovered most of the staff believed exactly the same as he did. They cited the actions of the Japanese elsewhere.

"Look at their actions in Manchuria. They'd always eyed and coveted Manchuria. All the minerals that section had and Japan didn't have. Minerals, coal and iron reserves. Just the things Japan needed to build a sound economic foundation," the bureau chief stated.

"Or to build a war machine," one of his listeners blurted out.

"And it was easy," MacFarland continued, nodding agreement. "Japan's Kwantung Army in Manchuria had secretly assassinated Chalin, who was then the warlord of Manchuria.

"This was easy because the area bordered on Korea and Japan had annexed Korea clear back in 1910. So now Japan didn't have to rely so much on the money-hungry Americans who gladly traded all the scrap they could find for money from the Japanese. They had a source of raw material close at hand now."

Clew looked carefully at his collegues in the bureau as the chief was talking. He was curious to know whether these words were as surprising to them as they were to him. They really gave him no indication.

But he knew the Japanese incursions were many in the Far East. They had spread far and wide from the home island. His interest in MacFarland's words on the philosophy of the Japanese was intense. The words made it clear Japan's philosophy held that the nation's destiny was to rule the world.

"There was a Dr. Shumei Okawa, and I haven't any idea if I'm pronouncing his name correctly, but he wrote a book in 1924. The militarists followed his ideas. This Okawa wrote that since Japan had been the first state in existence, it was Japan's divine mission to rule the world. And that's just about verbatim," MacFarland declared.

"Japanese civilians have always been told the Japanese were the master race and their mission was to end the tyrannical rule and oppression of the westerners. Again, that's just about the way, he, Okawa, wrote. Looks to me as if Adolph Hitler copied a page or two from Okawa's book, both in that 'master race' bit as well as some of the brutal treatment of civilians and anyone else who disagreed. The Japs just weren't as methodical in their genocidal tactics."

MacFarland also enlightened the group regarding a couple of other principles of Japanese conduct which contributed significantly to the militaristic expansion policy of Japan during this period.

"One of those principles was HAKKO ICHIU," and he emphasized the two words. "That means making the world one big family. His second principle was KODO. That simply means the first could only be obtained through loyalty to the Emperor."

He tossed his hands in the air and said, "There you have it. Those who made military aggression the national policy also made HAKKO ICHIU the moral goal. KODO was the only way to achieve it.

"Again, these militarists were following the writings of this Okawa," MacFarland concluded as he reached for his beer.

There was quite a buzz around the table as he stopped talking.

Most of it centered on the terminology which advanced the belief, as Okawa had written, that the Japanese were the master race. All those in the group were quite mindful of the well-publicized beliefs of Adolph Hitler who was constantly drumming into the heads of all Germans, whether they were his followers or not, that they were the chosen race. That the Germans were the master race. Superior to all.

As the group in Honolulu listened to some of the facts they were startled. Startled as they readily recognized there was no difference in the philosophies of the two countries. None whatsoever. It was suggested one had been louder about it.

Clew couldn't speak for the others but as he heard these philosophies related, he recalled some of the the stories he read of Japanese soldiers, describing their wild animal-like behavior in China.

Particularly in Nanking. Several years ago, the reports told of Gen. Matsui Iwane's forces involved in a brutal four month campaign as they smashed their way from Shanghai to Nanking.

They captured it and sealed it off. Once that was done, they inflicted horrible, sadistic terror on the helpless Chinese. This was in 1937 and male Chinese were machine-gunned en masse.

One day it was reported 20,000 fell. Clew had heard of Japanese soldiers wagering on the number of Chinese they could kill with daily tallies carried in the Japanese newspapers.

"Like it was a fucking sports page, reporting on a tournament and the number of runs, or points scored, for God's sake."

That's about all the dazed Clew could whisper when he heard of the many defenseless soldiers and civilians, captured, and then mercilessly slaughtered.

Rapes were never-ending, with probably 15,000 women and girls savaged before they too were slaughtered in a variety of particularly hideous ways. Reports he read stated the Yangtze River was a logjam, created by the masses of bobbing and bloated bodies. The drunken and howling Japanese soldiers were everywhere.

According to one report Clew had noted, the death toll was somewhere between one hundred and two hundred thousand. Almost 50,000 of that number were civilians.

Clew soon learned the UP bureau was a wealthy reference library right at his elbow. He could detail the rise of Japan and highlight what were indicated as the crucial milestones in the bloody advance.

Based on what he read in the office files, the Japs had intensified its strikes in Manchuria in September, 1937 and they never lessened the intensity of their offense. Shanghai was slammed by the Japs all through October.

Finally, in November of 1937, Shanghai fell to the Japs. It was from that date the invaders expanded. Clew was amazed. To think this tiny island nation had a one and a half million man army in China.

It was also about the time he moved to Hawaii, in 1939, that the Jap troops occupied Hainan in the Gulf of Tonking, directly off the coast of Vietnam. They kept moving along as they claimed sovereignty over the Spratly Islands, disputing the claim of France.

The Japanese next deployed a task force to Palou, at the end of the Marianas chain of islands and just South of the Philippines.

They also occupied bases in Northern Indo-China.

All this happened in 1939, so Clew was on the scene in Hawaii now.

But of all the events which took place after he arrived in the Islands, one stood out in Clew's memory.

That's when the U.S. finally put a halt on the booming business certain calloused and uncaring American citizens had struck up with the Japanese in the scrap metal industry. He didn't expect any military action and there was none but he was tempted to clap his hands literally when the government finally stopped these 'patriotic souls', as he caustically labeled them, from filling their cash pockets as they fed the military needs of Japan.

Simultaneously, the U.S. banned all export of aviation fuel to Japan. At long last the warring forces of Japan lost one of their prime sources of crucial war materials. In July of 1940, as the actions by the U.S. increased the tension further, the Japs responded by declaring a joint protectorate over all of Indo-China. When that happened, the U.S., Great Britain and the Netherlands jointly froze all assets under their control and also imposed a total trade embargo on Japan.

Even a newcomer to the situation, which Clew admittedly was, could read these signals with ease. An explosion had to happen.

He got together with MacFarland on a regular basis, and valued these confabs as a means of updating himself on some of the background of the Asian situation. He also valued them because the guy was the boss.

Bob MacFarland was nearly twice the age of Clew at 42 and had been with the UP in the Islands for almost 10 years. "I'll tell you something right now. Your guess is every bit as good as mine as far as what's gonna happen.

"Roosevelt's sitting over there right now playing footsie with the Jap envoys. What's that tell you? On one hand we're stopping all aid to these guys and yet he's sitting there in Washington dealing with them as if they're honorable people."

He looked up as he noticed Clew giving him a rather questioning stare. He hadn't yet been exposed to Clew's humorous quirks and asked, "What's it? What're you questioning?"

"I just wondered. You said FDR was playing 'footsie' but aren't I correct? Am I wrong? Didn't Roosevelt have polio and he wouldn't be able to play footsie, would he?"

MacFarland looked as if he'd like to throw his beer at him but carefully and quietly enunciated two words: "Fuck you."

He laughed and continued.

"Anyway, as they say, you know what I mean."

"Yes I do know what you mean and it's scary. Like we don't know what's goin' on at all. But if they don't know in Washington what's happening out here, I sure don't. Here it is already December. I feel like a native. Not quite.

"But I've been out here almost two years now. Actually, I was hoping to get home for Christmas but I don't think so now. There's just too damned much happening out here. I think I'll write the folks tonight and tell them it's going to be later."

They broke it up, MacFarland to go home and Clew to the office to knock out a quick letter.

"Dear Mom and Dad,

"I really thought I'd be home by now but you can't imagine how busy it's been out here. The darling Japanese are everywhere. Everywhere they're not supposed to be. It must be impossible for you to imagine the immensity of all the territory they've gobbled up.

"And there's probably some we don't even know about.

"That's a rather long way to say I don't see how I can get home for Christmas. I'd actually been tentatively planning on that but the tentative's out of it now. I just can't leave right now.

"Who knows what might happen tomorrow. It's just a crazy world out here in paradise.

"There's one thing about them raising so much trouble — makes for busy days here at the bureau. As you probably know, there are a lot of Japanese people here and the tourist traffic is heavy with them too. And as the saying in the Philippines goes: Where there's a Japanese, there's a Japanese spy. So we're always a little uneasy.

"But almost everything that happens out here is big news.

"As I think about it, I'm sure it's big news in Eureka, California too, but obviously and fortunately Eureka's never seen some of the terror these people have brought to the entire Far East. Trust me, no place has. Let's hope so anyway.

"Well, that's it for now. If I don't write or talk before Christmas, I hope you all have a Merry one.

"I'll be thinking of you all day, in between work here at the bureau.

Love,"

He signed off with "Larry".

Once again he was back talking to himself as he exclaimed, "Wait a damned minute. This isn't going on the wire. No telling how long it'll take to get home. I'd better date it."

He moved to the top of the page, taking great pleasure in typing Honolulu, HI, with the date, December 6, 1941.

He dropped it off at the post office before he made his way over to check the action at the Times Grill before heading home that night.

There wasn't much going on but he sat at the bar and had a beer, yakking it up with the bartender. "You know what. There's not a person in here I know. That's amazing. Wonder what's going on?"

"You never know. Saturday nights here can be pretty active. " But that's the bar business. Slammed one minute and blooey the next minute. Always a surprise. It's sure dead tonight."

Clew agreed and quickly downed his beer and left, saying with tongue in cheek, "This excitement's too much for me. I've got to get out of here and go to a real calm spot. Like my bed's gonna be tonight. This is weird. Like the calm before a storm but there's no storm expected."

He waved goodby and walked out into a still and balmy evening.

Not surprisingly, it was a pleasant evening in Honolulu, what else, as the 22 year old Clew strode briskly along Ala Wai Boulevard to his little skimpy apartment. It was on Leahi Avenue, not far from the Honolulu Zoo. Actually, his apartment was in an alley behind the avenue and he was close enough to the zoo he could hear the animals on restless evenings. The elephants, lions and such. He loved it. Couldn't get enough of it.

As far as he was concerned, this was his life. He had no desire to leave. He'd already met a young Hawaiian girl who was trying to convince her parents that this young Hauli, as they called the non-natives, was a respectable young man.

They weren't convinced yet.

Meantime, Clew wondered whether the draft was going to start making exceptions and some medical shortcomings might be overlooked. He'd drawn an exemption in the first go-round in San Francisco because of an ear drum problem he'd had since childhood. He didn't relish being in the military service, but he also knew that if the country became involved in this terrible mess out here, he'd be in the middle of it. He wouldn't be kept out.

These were some of the thoughts which went through his mind as he strode along Ala Wai Boulevard, one of his favorite walks. It ran along Ala Wai Canal which always offered some interesting sights. Darkness had pretty much overtaken the canal but during the daylight hours, one could look across the canal to the Ala Wai Golf Course.

The area wasn't the most up-scale in Honolulu but it was certainly well above the average. Lots of tourists, who wanted to avoid the busy and touristy atmosphere of Waikiki, enjoyed staying in some of the units available along the canal. They were still within walking distance of the beach but they didn't have to pay the top dollar they'd have to pay if they were fronting on the sand.

His mind wandered through all of this information he'd acquired since his trail had led him happily to the island of Oahu. He could find no fault with Oahu and freely told his associates he became more fascinated with the place every day.

Sure, he remembered what MacFarland and the others drummed into him when he started talking of his love for Hawaii. "Wait'll you've been here a few years. You get the feeling that you're trapped. Remember, it's an island. You can't just go out in your car and buzz into the City, as you say. Or, you can't drive up to Oregon and see your friends up there. You're on an island. You fly out of here or take a boat. That's a feeling you'll probably get sooner or later."

It wasn't a matter Clew could debate but he didn't think it would happen.

"I'll tell you one thing, guys, I'd love to visit the City or my friends in Southern Oregon but I think I could figure this place is my home and everything else is a vacation trip."

That night, as he arrived back at his apartment, his mind had turned to more pressing matters. Such as the devastating path of destruction and cruelty the Japanese had hacked out in the lands west of Hawaii.

What puzzled Clew the most was the reluctance of the U.S. to attempt to corral these devils. "We've always taken the lead in shackling the belligerent countries. Look what we did to Germany after World War I. And probably that's part of that crazy man Hitler's motivation. To try to get back some of the land the League of Nations took away after WWI. He sure used it to sell himself to the people of Germany. But why don't we do something about Japan?"

He said softly, almost whispering what he was thinking.

"A man named Adolph Hitler comes to power in when, 1933, and America's all opposed to him. Rightfully so. Roosevelt does all he can to help Great Britain and that's all right too. But he does nothing to put the clamps on the Japanese.

"And how about the Russians? Josef Stalin has killed millions of his own citizens. They say more than 20 million Jews were killed in the intelligentsia scourge of Stalin's. But the Russians have done more to help the Chinese against the Japs than anybody. And we've done nothing against Russia. I don't dig it.

"I guess we like Russia. Even though they've got a non-aggression deal with Hitler. And I know President Roosevelt doesn't like Hitler. Who does? Just enough people in Germany to let him become chancellor, I guess."

The thought of Hitler reminded Clew that Germany had begun supplying China with aircraft and aviation experts. Chiang even got Hitler to send Hans von Seeckt to China as a military adviser.

He had only today read of von Seeckt. He was the former chief of the German army command.

What Clew was reviewing in his mind was all true. He'd seen it all in the UP files. Japan objected strongly to Germany's support of China but Hitler ignored it. Germany seemed to be the only country willing to defy Japan in sending substantial assistance to China. Of course, the Communists in Russia welcomed the strong support they received in China so it was easy to understand their reaction.

But in the U.S. President Roosevelt's entire focus seemed to be on Great Britain, the only European country still showing defiance and battling the Germans.

Roosevelt's prime concern, other than Hitler, was endeavoring to end the country's economic depression. As one writer expressed it, he had no desire to become "bogged down" in China.

Even though Russia and Germany had signed a non-aggression pact, it seemed to Clew the Russians had been forgiven of all their sins. They recognized the Nanking government in 1932. The Russians themselves were even recognized by the U.S. and in 1934 the Soviet joined the League of Nations.

In short order Clew had learned more of the mysterious workings of international politics than he ever expected to know.

He wondered where it would all lead.

Finally, his senses dulled by his non-stop mental journey through history, he flopped into bed. He had the day off but his day coming up was busy. He'd never taken a day to explore Pearl Harbor, Pearl City and all that area out there. He wanted to get up early, catch an early bus heading west and spend as much time as he needed to satisfy his curiosity about this huge naval base.

After a long yawn, Clew slowly moved and groaned these sarcastic words, "After such a riotous night on the town, how in hell am I able to wake up at 5:30 in the morning, wide awake?

"Well, that's okay. I wanna grab a bus and get underway to Pearl anyway."

Soon he was perched in one of the front seats on the bus which would take him past the downtown area of Honolulu, in front of the Aloha Tower and on out to Pearl City.

That was west of the city of Honolulu, but using the native directions, it would be Ewa, but he reminded himself, pronounced EVA as in never. The opposite direction got its local name from what perhaps was Oahu's most well-known natural landmark, Diamond Head, east of Honolulu. Clew quickly learned, east was Diamond.

North, or toward the mountains, was called mauka. And south, toward the ocean, was named maki.

It was a lovely morning, the distance was about ten miles plus, and he was totally at ease. The entire day was his to use as he so desired. Deadline was a word that demanded constant attention at the bureau but was meaningless today.

With his press credentials he had no trouble gaining access to any of the otherwise-restricted areas at Pearl Harbor. Everyone was relaxed and extremely friendly.

At one of the gates he passed through, Clew chatted briefly with the young sailor on duty.

"How's it going today?" asked Clew, "The Japs up to anything? Anything happening?"

"Nah. Pretty quiet here. They had some big parties around here last night. Don't know what the deal was but they were heavy into it."

"You mean you weren't invited?" laughed Clew, who'd seen enough back at the Presidio to know the rank and the file, and as one of his friends said, "Never the twain shall meet."

"Nope. I'm not on the admiral's list I guess."

"Well, I'm gonna stroll around here. First chance I've had to take a look at the base. I'll see you later," said Clew as he walked on.

The young man went back into his guard cubicle.

For someone who'd never been around these monstrous ocean-going military vessels, to be able to get so close and eyeball them all by his lonesome was exciting. But before he really started thinking about the tremendous naval might collected here, his thoughts turned to something else.

With all the action by the Japanese, he was first of all curious to see if there were any signs of mobilization. To see if there was any preparation to support with force, if necessary, the embargo and the ensuing freezing of their assets.

He saw none.

That little chat at the entrance somewhat prepared him for what he thought was a nonchalant attitude on the base, so he was less shocked by the lack of alertness than he might have been.

Despite the tensions generated in Hawaii by the Japanese and their hostilities throughout the South Pacific, all was tranquil at Pearl Harbor. He looked out at the Arizona but saw only a few members of the crew on deck. It was downright quiet.

Clew wasn't sure just what he expected to see but said, "Hell, it's getting on toward eight in the morning," He reminded himself. "You'd think someone'd be up and at 'em."

As if to reassure him, the sounds of approaching aircraft were suddenly heard. "That's a little better," he said, assuming the sounds came from American planes out on morning patrol of the general area. Hickam Field was nearby and it was packed with airplanes.

He turned to catch a glimmer of the planes. His love of flying sent excitement surging through him but when he saw the planes, he cringed. They were dive bombers. That wasn't the reason he cringed. It was something else. All of the planes had the unmistakable markings of the Japanese. They each had huge red circles painted on the wings and fuselage. The first two he spotted were definitely Japanese.

"My God, they're Japs." He knew there must be some bigger planes nearby. He'd heard others. Realization struck him. Here he was, watching the strike everyone had expected. Apparently everyone, he thought wryly, except the military.

Completely without opposition, the dive bombers flew in and released their deadly missiles. Although Clew wasn't aware of it, as the dive bombers struck, torpedoes hit the Arizona, fired from subs just off shore.

As all this happened, Clew was speechless. Only a few seconds later, he was silent with good cause. Like thousands of seamen aboard the Arizona, he was dead.

But at the United Press bureau the Sunday man quickly recovered his composure after learning of the strike at Pearl. He was on with MacFarland by telephone immediately. The bureau chief's first question was, "Where's Clew? Seen him?"

Because he remembered. This was the day Clew had decided to have a first hand look at Pearl Harbor. He'd chosen the same day the Japanese decided to follow up the looks their spies had taken for them on previous days.

"Sonuvabitch. No, not you," he quickly told an astonished young staffer on the phone. "Keep going in there, I'll be right there."

MacFarland didn't know it at the moment but simultaneously with the dive bombers and submarine attacks, the high level bombers were attacking nearby. They hit Kaneohe and Ford Islands.

It wasn't yet nine in the morning at the MacFarland household. Bob MacFarland went into the bedroom and found his wife in the process of getting herself going in order to start their two children, a boy and a girl, on their way to Sunday school.

"I think we can probably forget all about Sunday school, Amy."

Accustomed to MacFarland's rather bizarre sense of humor, she looked up at him and said, "What is it this time? The Japs bomb the church?"

His head snapped around. He looked closely at her and said, "Not quite my dear. But not too far off."

It was her turn to look and ponder his response as he continued, "They've bombed Pearl Harbor and probably a couple of other targets out there. So you'd better plan on keeping them home today."

His wife clutched at him and the two embraced for a second before MacFarland held her close but looking into her eyes said, "I really don't think we have any reason for great concern. So don't get all upset. But until I can get to the office and get a better reading on what's happened and what's predicted to happen, I think we'd be smart to keep both of them in sight. I'll get back to you on the phone as soon as I can get some up-to-date scoop. Okay? I love you and just take it easy."

Amy was verging on tears but tightlipped, nodded and grudgingly released her hold on MacFarland. He shouted a farewell to the two children and was out the door.

Driving to the office gave him a half hour to listen to the radio and ponder the fate of Larry Clew. If he'd actually made it to Pearl Harbor, that's probably all she wrote for the budding young bureau member. That was MacFarland's immediate conclusion and it sadly received support from the radio reporter.

"No news of any survivors in the immediate area of the targets which the Japanese struck have been received," the announcer intoned.

"The ships have been sunk and no survivors have surfaced in the slightly more than two hours since the attack. There were others in the crucial attack zone who were not aboard ship and there's been no news of any survivors from that group either.

"It is emphasized these are preliminary reports and certainly shouldn't be accepted as conclusive. But it doesn't look too promising for anyone who was there this morning, at eight o'clock, when the Japanese completed their sneak attack on Pearl Harbor."

Softly MacFarland snarled, "Not too damned promising for our guy Clew. The bastards. God, what a day for Larry to pick to go out there. Kee-rist, I can't believe it. The guy's been here damned near two years and doesn't get out there. He picks this day, of all the days he could've picked, to go take a look. That's really the shits."

As he pulled into the parking lot at the office, he refused to give up hope. He'd check everything out but he had a hunch he was only kidding himself. Putting off the inevitable. Sooner or later, and he knew it really had to be sooner, he'd have to send a telegram to Clew's folks.

He clomped into the bureau and quickly picked up all the hot stuff off the wire. There was nothing positive. It all looked bad.

He called out to his two man staff, "What's the situation? Do they figure it was a carrier attack? Any talk of an invasion? Any land troops mentioned?"

The anxiety in his voice was quite obvious.

"There's been no mention of an invasion. Looks as if it was a one time shot here, and on the islands, Kaneohe and Ford."

"OK, have you had any luck catching up with Clew? Do we know for sure he was out there?"

The answer was negative. Impulsively, MacFarland decided to go out to Clew's apartment. There was nothing he could do here that the two staffers couldn't handle and although he was pretty sure Clew had bought it, he had to go out there and try to make certain. "He'd have called in by now, if he was alive," he reasoned to himself. "I'm afraid he's had it."

His quick trip and brief chat with the adjacent apartment dweller confirmed his negative thoughts.

"I heard him head out early this morning. Little after six. Is he missing?" his immediately concerned neighbor asked.

MacFarland silently nodded his head and walked to his car.

Back at the bureau he was informed a public information officer had called. "I don't know whether he was Army or Navy or whatever but he said there were some civilian casualties at Pearl this morning. Doesn't know who or how many. Most of them ended up in the drink. It's one big mess out there."

MacFarland was silent for a moment after receiving the official information which he had pretty well figured out in advance. "Well, I think I'd better get a note off to Clew's folks. And listen up, if his folks get lucky and are able to get a call through trying to get some information, just tell 'em he's missing. He was there and there's little chance of survival. No point dancin' around the facts of life. Or death," he added dismally as he realized what he'd said.

As he looked through his address scroll in his office, he came upon the name of Clew's sister. "Might be a better idea to give news like this to someone younger and let them carry the lousy message."

He soon found the address. Clew had told him his sister, slightly older than him, worked at a state college in Ashland, Oregon. It wasn't all that far from Eureka, California, where his parents lived. It would be a simple matter for her to contact the folks.

He sent the telegram to Marjorie Clew, Faculty, Southern Oregon State College, Siskyou Boulevard, Ashland, OR.

It read:

"Sad news for you and your folks. Larry was at Pearl Harbor this morning when the sneak attack occurred. It's been reported there are no survivors of any of those who were on the premises this morning. They are all presumed dead. If we hear any different, we'll advise immediately. Please forward this information to Larry's parents. All of us here at the bureau feel this deeply.

"Again, accept our most sincere regrets. He was a good man."

After finishing that he thought: Man? Like probably 90 per cent of the fatalities out there today, it was more likely boys rather than men.

Then he turned to the task at hand. Responding to queries the world over regarding Pearl Harbor.

A Declaration of War was only hours away.

America's President, Franklin Delano Roosevelt, knew the treacherous attack by the Japanese would melt the opposition of the isolationists in the nation regarding the war in Europe. Those who had opposed his vigorous efforts to get involved with Great Britain would quite likely accept his beliefs after that attack, regardless whether it was justified or provoked.

He thereupon launched his single most melodramatic presentation of many during his extended political career. The nation listened to the official declaration. But the Japanese didn't. They didn't have to. They were already at war.

On the eighth of December, delaying by only 24 hours, they launched their attack on the Philippines. Spearheading this invasion was the attack on Manila. Elsewhere they attacked Hong Kong.

Meantime, along the coast of America, submarines lurked in the waters, just off-shore from the major cities and ports, in position to assist in attack if needed, but not taking action.

A heavy population of people of Japanese descent lived in all the cities of the Pacific coast. Outright rioting erupted in these cities because of the presence of the Japanese. America too had heard the Philippine philosophy which stated, Where there's a Japanese there's a spy.

Finally, the situation became so tense along the Pacific seaboard, the Federal government made a decision to move all those of Japanese descent away from the coast. Far inland, encampments were constructed where the Japanese were held for the duration of the war.

This decision was accepted because it eased the tension. There was no way to determine when the Japanese warlords would choose to strike again, killing all in their path.

And none knew who might be helping them on America's shores.

Honolulu's bureau of the United Press was never busier as the Japanese military forces moved quickly all over the map.

Two days after invading Manila and Hong Kong they struck at Guam. A mighty busy bureau chief, Bob MacFarland, gulped as he saw the Japanese had sunk the British battleship, Prince of Wales and the cruiser, Repulse in the Gulf of Siam. This was the same day they invaded Guam.

The next day Japan attempted to invade Wake Island but they were repulsed. MacFarland told his staff, "They won't quit. They'll stay in there."

And they did. Just two weeks later Wake Island's forces surrendered to the constant pressure of the Japanese. "Hey, don't you love this. In the Philippines they've declared Manila an 'open city' so the civilians won't suffer because of the battles in the city's interior. And the Japs ignored the Open City status. Our military must have known they would."

On and on the Japs plundered their way through the Far East.

On Christmas day Hong Kong surrendered. Sumatra was captured and Darwin, the Northern-most principal city of Australia was bombed, bringing the conflict to the Aussies.

The carnage continued.

MacFarland and his staff had trouble keeping up with the course of conflict, it moved so rapidly. In February of 1942 Singapore surrendered and Rangoon also surrendered. Finally, a flicker of optimism was offered when carrier planes were moved close to Japan and actually brought the battle home to the aggressors. They bombed Tokyo with minimal damage but the mission, as many ascertained, was to boost morale.

The next action by the Japanese was one which created much unrest in Hawaii. That was the invasion of Kiska, the westernmost island in the Aleutians. It added to the uneasiness of the mainland defenses too.

Where are they going to strike next? Everyone talked of that. Why weren't they stopped?

If there were any answers they weren't offered. And the advances continued. In August more than 8000 soldiers were landed by the Japs at Buna, on the East Coast of New Guinea. From here, on the shores of the Solomon Sea, they began a trek through Kokoda across the Owen Stanley Mountain Range to reach Port Moresby, on the East Coast of New Guinea.

MacFarland always tried to get his skimpy staff together for a meeting, as much for morale as anything else. Today he had something of a positive nature. "The Marines have landed."

His guys looked at him and each other, wondering, What's this?

He continued. "Listen, the Marines have invaded Guadacanal. They've told us this is for real. America's in a position now to strike back and start taking some land away from them. Yeah, yeah, I know, I saw that note the Japs had reinforced Guadacanal with 60,000 veteran troops. They've told me that, yeah, it's now August, and it's gonna be a long battle, but the Japs will be stopped on the 'Canal. It's turnaround time."

It helped everyone's morale when that did happen. The Japs were defeated. They didn't surrender but they departed the island with only remnants of a force left.

That night at home, and MacFarland had spent a lot more time at home since the Pearl Harbor debacle, his wife Amy asked him whether this was it. "Seriously Bob, do you really think we're now going to take care of those people? I mean is this really it?"

"Amy, this is really it," he said earnestly. "Twenty, thirty or hell, more than 60 years from now, I think people will remember the victory at Guadacanal as good a signal point as any for the turnaround in this damnedable mess. You and I may not see it, but the kids will," and he hugged her until it almost hurt.

At the time they didn't know that a couple of parachute bombs, carried by Jap subs to release points near the Oregon coast, had been released, The 'chutes carried the bombs over the mainland,

One of them exploded harmlessly on the Northern Oregon coast and another in Southern Oregon.

Now the Red Alert was on in earnest for Oregon and other coastal points. But it had been before and this type of attack appeared unstoppable.

Fortunately, there was no repetition of these bombings.

More than 65 years later, the same general area was visited by the death of a man whose passing revived some memories of the major tragedies which had occurred during that costly period of history. A period of inhuman behavior by one nation, Japan, against anyone in the world the Japanese decided to attack.

The death of this man in Southern Oregon reminded many that little if any vengeance was ever brought to these purveyors of death in all forms and to all persons, military enemies or poor unfortunate women, children and civilian males.

He was known for many good deeds. His compatriots applauded everything he ever did during his long life, which ended on a lonely hillside.

Wallace Robinson, IV, was back in the classroom of the sixth grade at his school in Lake Oswego, Oregon much sooner than he preferred. His break from school had been for a mission concerning the death of his great-grandfather in Southern Oregon. Nonetheless, the circumstances of Robbie's time spent away from school were so interesting he was downright reluctant to return.

But there he was. He was physically, at least, back in his seat in school. Mentally, he was undoubtedly many miles away.

He sought desperately to concentrate on the words of his teacher. Frankly, it was a losing struggle.

He'd been on a cleanup mission at his great-grandfather's house in Ashland, almost as far south as one could travel in Oregon and still stay within the state. It was only a few miles, perhaps 15 or so, from the California border.

It wasn't the boring trip and chore he'd expected. Quite the opposite. The cleanup process of his great-grandfather's material he encountered in the cleanup, made him aware of some of the defects or oversights in the historical education he'd received thus far in his brief life as a student.

He knew he had learned more of history in those few exciting days reading his great-grandfather's memoirs, than he had in his six years of schooling.

Now he was besieged with an overwhelming urge to ask his teacher why they hadn't learned some of the things that he'd been exposed to as he read of the era in which his great-grandfather had lived. Because that was history. Right?

He'd like to have his teacher confirm his now-solid conviction that his history class studies of that era during which his great-grandfather lived and served his country, were woefully lacking.

His puzzlement was logical. Quite simple. If what he'd read was history, why weren't they learning of it right now? Why hadn't they been required to study it?

Young Robby had the cold, uncluttered logic sometimes possessed only by the very young. And he wanted some answers to the questions his visit to the era of his great-grandfather had roused in him.

Because he now knew his great-grandfather, a doctor in service to his country, had suffered and witnessed and cared for other victims of horrible atrocities by the Japanese of the early 1940s. He'd cared for one young Chinese boy who had witnessed the death of his entire family.

This had taken place in 1937 in Manchuria. That's where Emperor Hirohito sent a pair of diabolical doctors with orders to conduct an unbelievably cruel experimental station. The subjects used for these experiments were living helpless humans.

Why hadn't they, Robbie and his classmates, learned of that?

Why did some cities, such as nearby Portland, Oregon, proudly speak of its 'sister city' in Japan? Didn't they know of these atrocities in that country? A country which brought death to multi-millions of innocents.

Robbie had now learned this. Didn't anyone know? Or care?

He suffered through that first school day, anxiously awaiting a chance to talk to the teacher alone. Miss Bjork was his favorite grade school teacher and he knew she'd explain the situation.

When the bell sounded for the end of the day, he scurried up to her desk.

"Miss Bjork, may I ask you a question?"

"Why of course, Robbie. And welcome back to class. What is it?" his teacher asked. She certainly wasn't anticipating the question.

With little preamble, he blurted out his question: "Why aren't our history lessons telling us anything of the millions of people the Japanese killed in Manchuria? And the millions more innocent civilians they killed during the war they started?"

"Well, now, that's a surprising question. I'll try to answer it the best I can. But I don't think you'll be satisfied with the answer.

"We are guided by the school district, and the school board. That's what they've provided as our course of study and we really don't deviate from that."

Robbie quickly blurted the inevitable, "But why? All we hear about or read about is what the Germans, or Nazis as the books all say, did to the Jews. And that was terrible. But my dad says we can't figure bad by the numbers of dead people. But look at the difference. Four or six million Jews put to death by the Gestapo or their SS or whatever. Like there's more like 30 million by those guys. The Japanese."

"Robbie, I certainly agree with your father. And I agree with you it's a terrible thing. It's something that happened and we would like to forget it although we're constantly reading of what the Germans did. And I know the Russians killed 20 million innocent people just because of their religion. But we don't read of that either. I'm sorry but I'm just afraid I don't have an answer for you."

Robbie, who'd been expecting more from his favorite teacher, was disappointed.

His shoulders sadly slumping, he grabbed his books securely and said, "Okay, Miss Bjork, I'm glad to get back. I wish we'd learn more of the truth. I don't understand. But thanks and bye."

Miss Bjork didn't understand either. As a history student herself, she knew they weren't teaching the facts. Why? She didn't know.

ASHLAND, OREGON -- 2009

Deep in Southern Oregon, in the small community of Ashland, the staff of this town's daily newspaper was hurrying to the point of panic. Telephones were ringing, people racing from the newsroom to the backshop and questions resounding on the intercom. They had a big story in this small college town.

Ashland was the last stop in Oregon before the California state line and big stories were more rare than usual.

Clarity came to the confusion as they focused on the question that was shouted from the city desk, "Larry, do we need to shoot a picture of the area where they found the body of that old guy? Or do we have a file shot that will do?"

That question came over the intercom to the photographer's offices. Back came the response.

"That's Rabbit Rock up there," returned photographer Larry Hunter, twisting his lips and scowling as he looked at his colleague. He shared his opinion of the man on the news desk, in fact an opinion of all such 'immigrants' brought in from the Midwest by the newspaper chain now operating the local daily.

Hunter, longtime chief photographer at the paper, muttered, "Working on the desk of the paper and he still doesn't even relate to Rabbit Rock. That's one of the few landmarks around here, not counting the college.

"Here it's two thousand and nine and that damn rock's only been up there all those years."

He stopped his muttering long enough to say, "Yup, we've got plenty of shots of the Area," having his fun with the newsroom man, placing undue emphasis on the first syllable as he mimicked the man's pronunciation.

"That's great. Let me take a look at one, okay?"

"Shall do," said Hunter as he switched off the intercom.

"Yup, we've got plenty of file shots of that area," he repeated for the benefit of his colleague as he continued to imitate the import's speech. 'Import' was his word for the staffers brought in by the chain which now owned the paper.

Turning again to his fellow laborer in the land of pictures, he shook his head and slowly phrased a serious question, "Can you figure this? That old timer they found today up at Rabbit Rock? Clambering all the way up there. That's quite a climb even for the kids. I remember we used to hang up there all the time. But this guy's about a hundred years old. How'd he ever make it?" As he talked, the photographer grabbed a print and left the room to let the man look at it.

His partner thought about his departing colleague's statement. He too was a native of Easy Valley as the area was occasionally called by those who had spent their lives in Rogue River Valley. He knew the terrain and was young. The peak was a challenge even for him.

He mused aloud. "Take that old guy, at an age when most humans are propped up by cushions someplace or already planted, he's out trotting up the side of Grizzly Peak. He musta been in damned good shape. Unless someone carried him up there and dumped him. But the cops didn't indicate any rough treatment."

It's true. The police report stated, in effect, what the photographer mumbled to himself. It also added a Jeep was located down by the dirt road, probably a mile or so below the area of the rock itself.

Rabbit Rock was nothing more than a jutting of rock from the side of the mountain known both as Grizzly Peak or Mount Grizzly, named after the bears which once inhabited the vicinity. Had there been any chukars in the area, they'd certainly have been nesting there because those imported birds loved a setting such as that. An occasional eagle floated by in search of an unwary squirrel or other morsel of food on the ground.

The rock was visible from almost any vantage point in Ashland. After the name was mentioned, directions to Rabbit Rock were usually easy to obtain. From almost anyone.

Identification of the deceased took a little longer.

The reporting policemen were puzzled. "The man had no papers on him. I mean nothin," one of the cops reported as his partner nodded agreement.

Before the question could be asked, the second policeman spoke up and said, "The Jeep was registered to some medical clinic in Medford. And we've got the number for the temporary license. We just don't have the name on it yet. It'll be at the station."

By using the registration and the temporary license the police soon established the identity of the dead person, having had no luck in getting anyone from the clinic to make the ID.

Wallace Robinson, MD, was the man. Officers also noted a card identifying him as a retired member of the Regular Army, Medical Corps.

Subsequently, they learned he had opened a clinic in Medford, just 11 miles or so North of Ashland, many years ago, after the conclusion of World War II. He maintained his home in Ashland. The reporters soon established that house pre-dated WWII days. It had been built by his wife's family, and the reporters also determined the wife had died just before the outbreak of World War II.

Ultimately, with the help of the doctor's clinic staff, the police located the man's son. He was a resident of Sacramento, California. It was the state's capital and about four hours drive south of Ashland. But if the police had hoped for a family identification from this man they were disappointed. Instead, he volunteered to contact his son, who lived in a suburb of Portland, about 280 miles north of Ashland.

He apologized, saying, "He'll be able to get there quicker and take care of everything. I'm almost in my seventies but I haven't been able to get around too well lately. My father lived up there in Ashland and I haven't been there for years."

The police then contacted Wallace Robinson, III, of Lake Oswego, advising him of the death and of his father's desire for him to handle the ID.

He was loaded with questions. "When, how and did they just find his body up there? What happened?" he asked in a torrent.

Before they could respond, he volunteered, "The old man was an independent guy and didn't rely much on anyone. Ran his own operation and actually had lived alone for all the time I've known him. His wife, my grandmother, died while he was in the service."

The police had few additional details for him and Robinson said he'd get under way immediately.

In his Lake Oswego home, Robinson the Third leaned back in his chair after replacing the phone. He attempted to recall some segments of his grandfather's life, although he knew blessed little of it.

He knew his grandfather was a graduate of the University of Oregon medical school and had interned in Portland, at the newly established medical school hospital, before he entered the service.

Long ago he had learned the sad news of his grandmother's death soon after Wallace Robinson II, his father, had been born. As a result of his grandmother's death and his grandfather's absence during the war, his father had been raised almost exclusively by his aunt, who lived in Northern California.

He did learn his grandmother had spent her pre-college life in Ashland, Oregon and that she'd gone to nurse's school, had been a registered nurse and met his grandfather while he was an intern at the University Hospital in Portland.

They married and his father was born only a year or so before the Japanese had killed thousands with their treacherous attack at Pearl Harbor. Prior to that, his grandfather, a Captain in the Medical Reserve, was already stationed in Manila. When war became reality for the United States, his grandfather was in the middle of it.

One thing his grandson had learned, even though he'd seen little of his grandfather during his early years; he knew his grandfather had utter dislike if not absolute hatred for the Japanese. His skills as a medical man had enabled him to assist some of the horribly mistreated, starved, tortured and beaten people who had fallen into the hands of these marauders. His skills undoubtedly helped him survive what he had referred to as the March, and his subsequent life in a Japanese Prisoner of War camp.

The Third researched the Bataan Death March, which was what the grandfather referred to as the March, the best he could. Little was supplied to him or his classmates in school. When Manila and Corregidor, and subsequently, all of the Philippines, fell to the invaders, the Japanese had forced the thousands of military survivors in one area of the Philippines to walk from the southern tip of Bataan to San Fernando, about 100 kilometers. Those sixty miles were later littered with bodies as the Japs committed murder after murder of helpless men, already weakened with disease and by their starvation rations. These facts he gleaned from the school's librarian, an older woman whose nephew had been an officer in Manila.

Finally he asked a teacher, "Why don't we learn any of this history in school?"

This one at least seemed willing to discuss the matter. Others wouldn't talk about it. This teacher answered bluntly, "The history we teach in school was and is fraudulent. That's why children know nothing of the Death March. Certainly nothing of the atrocities committed by the Japanese. World War II's history has a complete void regarding the treatment of the defenseless in the South Pacific before and after the fall of the Philippines. All children learn is the selected material in the general category of the "Nazis", a political party headed by despicable Adolf Hitler and a term incorrectly applied as a pejorative since that time to all Germans, apparently to lump them all together for blame in the treatment of the Jews in Germany by Hitler and his SS and his Gestapo."

When he told his grandfather the teacher's answer it received his hearty approval.

As the young man learned more of the facts of the war in the South Pacific, it was easier to understand his grandfather's undying hatred of the Japanese, starting with the Emperor and working on down from there.

More pleasantly, he remembered his father talking of the family visits to the big house on a steep hill in Ashland. It was his grandmother's family home and had remained in the family after her death. This house offered a panorama of the entire valley, down to the little Bear Creek meandering through the floor of the valley and then on up to the mountains on the other side.

For his father, a young boy accustomed to much smaller houses or apartments, it had been a magnet.

Part of the allure was in the barn which held a marvelously intriguing machine, the incubator. The doctor raised a few chickens and he developed his own supply with the incubator.

Naturally, when the magic time arrived, young Robinson watched the incubator by the hour, waiting for that great moment when it was time for the young chicks to begin pecking their way out of the egg shells. That was a memory which remained with him for a lifetime.

Down the hill from the house, the sharply sloped acres were covered with cherry and peach trees. When the fruit ripened, the baby chickens were relegated to second place.

Thoughts of those long-ago days filled his mind. Now he was going to renew that life of long ago, in company with his 12 year old son, Wallace Robinson, IV. They'd open up the house again.

"No telling what we'll find in there," he muttered as they drove the freeway, "Prob'ly a lot of dust and spiders."

"Wha'd you say, dad?" asked his fellow traveler from the rear seat.

He glanced in the rear-view mirror of the rig they were driving, smiling at his son who'd barely heard his mumbled thoughts concerning the condition of the old home.

"Well Robby, I was just thinking out loud. 'Bout what we might find down there. Probably pretty dirty. But I know I liked it a lot the few times we got to Ashland. When I was about your age."

But young Robby was back concentrating on his portable computer game by this time and if he heard his father, failed to respond. His father was left to his recollections of the life and times of the now-deceased doctor as he continued his driving.

Actually he knew little of his grandfather. When his son began helping in the cleanup of the old house and poring through his grandfather's boxes of memorabilia, he learned more. More than he ever would have imagined.

The doctor's experiences in World War II obviously had been devastating, even for a man professionally prepared to take care of physical tragedy. But these experiences were rarely discussed by the doctor. He simply didn't respond to curious relatives' inquiries regarding that phase of his life.

From his own father, Robby No. 3 had discovered his grandfather had returned from the Philippines almost two years after cessation of hostilities with Emperor Hirohito's hordes. It was late in 1946 or maybe 1947. Although Robby No. 3 was driving south in Oregon, his thoughts had been carried far afield. He could recall the doctor's disgust with General MacArthur and loved Dr. Robby's response when people would innocently approach him after the war. Many had to ask him what the devil MacArthur was thinking of as he permitted so many of those horrible scoundrels to go unpunished. Not even held for trial. "I fear the good General was preoccupied at the time."

Privately he would confide MacArthur was concerned regarding the welfare of his property in Manila, although the Allied troops had ample advisories to avoid certain buildings as they recaptured the Philippines.

And also his line concerning MacArthur's obvious conceit and self-satisfaction. His grandfather freely admitted stealing the line from the caustic pianist, Oscar Levant, who used it to describe George Gershwin:

"MacArthur's in love with himself and he has no competition."

Dr. Robinson had seen too much of the drastic results of the fall of the Philippines and the subsequent tortures inflicted on millions by the Japs all through Asia to have kind thoughts of anyone who was less than severe with them.

Although all of Robinson's experiences had been in the Philippines, he had spent many hours nursing shattered humans who had suffered throughout Asia at the heartless hands of the Japs.

In the Philippines the invasion by the Japanese was awaited with great forboding. They were ready. As was MacArthur. The general and staff flew off to Australia, leaving General Wainwright to carry the load in the Philippines.

MANILA -- 1940

Dr. Robinson's life in the Philippines would never become a forgotten chapter. As he once put it in a frank discussion with a college friend he encountered after World War II:
"It's a part of my life I've not forgotten. It's part of my life I have no intention of forgetting. But it's part of my life I must put behind me because we all have our lives to live.

"When my wife died no doubt a part of me went away too. It was difficult to handle her death. Ironic, isn't it. A man trained to deal with death admits his inability to handle it. But it was after all the death and suffering I saw in the Philippines I seemed able to face my wife's death more easily.

"I have many guilts because I was in the Philippines when my son was a youngster. He was lucky my sister was able to provide a home for him. Maybe it was a better life than it would have been had it been just the two of us and me always on call. Day and night.

"It's difficult to come up with a definitive answer to that question. I always remember what that old-time Kansas City Monarch pitcher, Satchel Paige, said: 'Never look back. Something might be gaining on you.'

"That's really what I try to do. Don't look back."

His friend nodded silently and dropped the subject entirely. He knew no amount of prying would bring forth any additional information. It was 1940 when Capt. Wallace Robinson landed in Manila. He wasn't long removed from medical school but any internship he'd served would soon pale to insignificance when matched against the years in front of him.

At first it was fun in Manila. It was peacetime.

He was through at the garrison usually by mid-day so he was able to avail himself of whatever social life the city had to offer. His peace-time hours at the clinic inside the walls of the old Fort Santiago were such that his life was pretty much his own after twelve noon.

His responsibility was to the 600 or more soldiers of the garrison. He rarely faced a serious challenge. "Sure, it's easy now, but keep in mind I know in case of war I just don't stay here on my butt and wait for the wounded. I'll go right along to the front, where-ever it might be."

He was talking to a newly-arrived fellow officer at the bar of the Polo Club, one of his favorite stops after leaving the clinic. He told the man, "Seriously, if you wanted to meet the elite, as the saying goes, the Polo Club's where the elite meet for lunch. Here's the place. 'Course, if you get lucky and meet one of the lovely young ladies who frequent the club, you could always return for a late dinner."

It was at the Polo Club he met a correspondent for the United Press, an important member of the news wire organizations which spanned the globe. From this fellow, Ron Huntzinger, the doctor learned more of Medford, Oregon. That's where the correspondent had gone to school and had first worked in the newspaper business. Robinson's interest was piqued because his late wife's family was from nearby Ashland, only 11 miles or so South of Medford.

"You spend as much time here as you can, Robby," Huntzinger emphasized, looking around the Club, "and you won't miss out on much if you do."

And he was right. Robinson soon discovered that.

Not many days later he received further, emphatic proof of Huntzinger's statement. This time it was a fabulous looking young woman who walked through the club as the pair was seated at the bar. She was indeed striking, with long black hair which accentuated her slightly tanned complexion. And she was shapely too. Robinson determined that through the eyes of Robinson the man as well as Robinson the physician.

He noted she was greeted by several people who were already seated in the lounge, and when she reached their place at the bar she exchanged warm greetings with Huntzinger.

"Hello Ron. How are you doing? So nice to see you again."

This was offered with a more sincere ring than the usual offhand greeting delivered routinely with forced enthusiasm. At least that's what Robinson thought, noting the voice was intriguingly lilting and seemed to end on an upbeat.

Huntzinger stood and responded, "I'm great as usual. How are you doing, Lenora?" and without waiting for an answer, asked, "Have you a moment? I'd like you to meet a friend of mine."

He turned to Robby as he said, "Robby, this is Lenora Compos. She's a reporter with the Manila Herald. Lenora, please meet Wally Robinson, or Robby, as he's more commonly known. Robby's a doctor with the U.S. Army here."

Robby had already jumped to his feet and managed to find his voice with only a minimum of difficulty. Lenora was pretty beyond words. Small wonder he was rendered nearly mute as he actually stared at her. It seemed an eternity before he recovered his poise, asked her to join them and ordered drinks.

He soon learned Lenora and Huntzinger had known each other since the time she'd returned from the United States where she'd journeyed to continue her education in journalism at University of Oregon.

Naturally, Robinson was surprised at her choice of schools, saying, "That's a coincidence. I'm from Oregon. Graduate of the Oregon Medical School. How'd you happen to pick Oregon?"

"My father has had several business associates in Oregon for many years. I'd visited Oregon with him when I was much younger."

"Several times I visited your state. Somehow, I always thought it would be fun to go to college there."

"Were you right?"

"Oh yes," Lenora responded, "it was great fun."

So they went on at their first meeting. Huntzinger was left on the outside of their constant chattering but he seemed more than content to enjoy his drinks as well as the flourishing friendship between his two friends.

And flourish it did. The couple returned that evening to have dinner and spend a few hours on the dance floor. Robinson, emboldened by a few cocktails and truly bowled over by this woman, was frank with her.

"I think I should tell you I am a widow. My wife died just before I was ordered to Manila. Hasn't been all that long.

"You can believe what I'm going to say or not. That's up to you. But since her death I've been absolutely disinterested in the opposite sex. There's been such a gap left in my life. Something one must experience to understand. And even then I'm not sure if there's truly comprehension after experiencing it. If all that makes sense," he finished somewhat faintly.

But he continued, "I must tell you this. And I'm not doing my wife any injustice when I say you are unquestionably the most interesting young woman I've ever met. Sounds terrible, I know, but I firmly believe my wife would agree," he earnestly told the dark-eyed Filipino girl.

He wanted to say more but as he danced with this beautiful woman, he debated. When is too far, much too far? Or not enough?

He came right on.

Words such as this were not new to Lenora. She'd heard much the same adoration voiced in different languages from many different men. Somehow, she sensed Robby's statements came from the heart and were sincere. Not just another of the many babblings of vacuous words she and other women have heard from males on the make. Echoes of such dialogues, or rather, monologues, sounded even more vacuous as she heard Robby talk.

Somehow, she knew this young doctor and she were on the brink of a relationship far beyond that of a casual drink, dinner and dance. She was right.

They spent the night at her apartment. Neither of them ever offered any words of explanation for the speedy consummation of their friendship. Neither of them ever had any regrets. It was a bonding which only the ruthless animals of Nippon could destroy as they laid waste to the Philippines and then magnified these horrors throughout the Far East. Their bonding was destroyed as this terrible treatment of mankind, the most heartless in the history of the world, spread to the Philippines.

That terrible moment was at hand.

The people of the Philippines weren't surprised. They'd fully expected the Japanese. Timing was the only factor in doubt.

They knew they were next.

That's because the citizens of the Philippines knew only too well the philosophy of the Nipponese. It was a philosophy which stated unequivocally they were superior to all others. No other culture was equal to the Japanese. The Japanese had infiltrated the Philippines so sufficiently that the Filipinos detested the people of Nippon. They had personally experienced the cruelty and absolutely inhumane treatment of others by the Japanese.

The Filipinos were not strangers to harsh treatment of enemies either. But unlike the Japanese they didn't consider the entire world outside their country the enemy.

There were many examples of the Japanese extermination of humanity throughout the Far East. Particularly in China. In the provinces of Heilongjiang, which translated means Black Dragon River and in Jilin and Liaoning, which is near the city of Chonghun, a total of five million Chinese were killed by the Japs between 1937 and 1945.

They were killed by forced labor, beheadings, torture, chemicals, through injection and starvation and rank cruelty.

The stories of wholesale killings in Nanking were rampant and well chronicled. A total of 350,000 people were killed in one week. The Tokyo papers regularly listed the killings in a manner reminiscent of newspapers' sports pages in America. They wrote of these deeds against helpless civilians as if they were events of national pride. Indeed, in the culture fostered by Emperor Hirohito, they were.

The Filipinos were uneasy and had every right to fear for the safety of their country and its citizens.

Because the hell that had been China's since the hostilities were begun by the Japanese in the 30s, soon expanded to the Philippines. When the attack on Pearl Harbor shocked much of the world, this expansion of aggression by the Japanese was quickly followed by an attack on the Philippines.

Robinson was with his lovely Lenora the night of December 5, 1941. "I don't know what's likely to happen now but we've been on red alert and there've been reports of Japanese aircraft over Luzon twice this week.

"It's certain the Japanese have the Philippines in their sights. What will you do?" he asked Lenora.

She was surprisingly calm. "It doesn't surprise me. The Japanese have long coveted our country." Her dark eyes flashed with resistance as she looked closely at Robinson and he could imagine Lenora's Spanish mother displaying the same determined tendencies. She shook her head and her long, black hair whirled as it sometimes did when they were enjoying one of their more active dances. "We will not run away from them. We will fight them. They may win but they will know we can fight."

Robby reached out for her and they embraced for a long time, in total silence. It was the last time they ever held each other.

Pearl Harbor was subjected to the unwarranted attack on the seventh and Manila alerted to the threat immediately. At Nichols Field and at Neilson field, there were the P-40s, P-35s and the P-26s of the 17th Pursuit Squadron.

Certainly General Douglas MacArthur, commanding officer of the American forces in the Philippines, anticipated the attack. He and his staff flew out almost immediately.

But Robinson was a doctor. First and always. He had little knowledge of the military. Didn't particularly want to acquire any additional. He just wanted to tend to the needs of the soldiers. He found plenty of need.

When his battalion was told to defend against paratrooper attack, he turned to newly-met American Floyd Bertoni for clarification.

Robinson knew there were some B-17s of the 19th Bombardment Group at Clark Field. How many he didn't know. "Lissen to this," Bertoni said. "Two hours ago, they hit Clark. The commander of the battalion told all the top dogs. Damned few 17s got out. Mostly shot up on the ground. Same with the fighter planes."

Bertoni also told him of the rumored departure of MacArthur on one of those planes that made it out. "We got nuthin' left. The Far Eastern Air Force is shot outta here."

The battalion commander had continued, according to Bertoni's report, and made it clear the battalion was in the field for good. "Oh yah," Bertoni added, "He told us if we got any bizness in Manila, git there and git out 'fore the Japs git there."

That's exactly what they did.

Robinson found his apartment and advised the houseboy of the situation. He told him to take off with his family. "Just get out of the city. Take your wife and head for the hills. Take anything you want but leave the city."

Then he pondered the question. Should he endeavor to contact Lenora, his almost constant companion? The growing confusion rendered the telephones unreliable and answered his question. He wasn't able to catch up with her.

"I hope to hell she's able to stay away from those Japs when they get here. It'll be worse on the women than anyone and based on everything we've learned of the Japs' treatment of the defenseless that's gotta be bad."

Bertoni was at the wheel of the car as they prepared to leave Manila, and the usually garrulous Brooklynite just nodded his head silently.

By the dawn of December 9, Nichols Field was under heavy attack and all personnel, doctors, officers and enlisted men alike, were digging fox holes. They survived. But Nichols, the last remaining airfield, was completely destroyed.

"Now what," Robby asked Bertoni, knowing that he was completely in the dark too.

"Hell, they got where they're goin' in two days. The only thing they don't have is the Navy. Most of 'em got outta here. Headed for Australia. Now we go back to Manila to guard against paratroopers."

It was a short stay. Soon the battalion was ordered to the Bataan Peninsula. The War Department had determined that's where a defense was sadly lacking. Sadly too, the troops from North and South Luzon were forced back by the attacking forces of the Japs.

"Where do we go from here," thought Robby. "This is it."

And it was.

The surrender took place on April 9, 1942. Those in command soon learned the Japanese considered a surrender the worst sin possible. The captors converted life on Bataan into hell as the Filipinos, Americans, Brits and others were caught and marched out.

Bertoni had lived a life of hard knocks in his native Brooklyn but told Robinson, "We're cooked meat. The Japs figger anyone's a traitor if they surrender. They don't have a white flag. Our name's might's well be shit from now on. We're dead meat." Bertoni had been in the service and out in the South Pacific a lot longer than Robinson and he knew.

On the forced march Robinson quickly learned. It was Robby's first contact with the Japanese code of conduct. He couldn't believe it. As the tired, hungry, weak and injured men marched along they were jabbed in the butts, legs or body with bayonets. If they faltered they were beheaded. If some of the many weakened troops fell to the side of the group, Japanese operators of tanks and other military vehicles entertained themselves by running over them.

As they slogged along the rough terrain, Bertoni suddenly grabbed Robinson's elbow.

"Sonofabitch. Wotta they doin' to that old couple over there?" Bertoni asked. He looked off to the side where the Jap soldiers had grabbed the couple, apparently because they were trying to slip some food to the starving soldiers.

"Oh no, they're not going to..." and Robby's voice trailed to nothing. Jap soldiers carefully tied the Filipino man and his wife to a stake. As their leader gave instructions, they finished soaking the couple in gasoline. On order, they set them afire. And the rest of the guards cheered wildly.

Robby knew General Homma was in charge of moving these helpless people along in a March to Death but he mentally set aside one name. And told Bertoni to remember. It was the name of the soldier who tossed the match on the gas-soaked couple.

The volatile Bertoni needed no urging.

"He's the same bastard, sure's hell, that tossed that grenade at those guys. Right in the middleuh those guys tryin' to keep up with the group. Musta killed eight of 'em. I'll git that bastard," snarled Bertoni.

"Got his name too. Azami. Ryoichi Azami. I'll catch 'im.

"Hey, c'mon," said Robby. "You'll be lucky if we get outta this crap. Then we can think about catchin' up with these pieces of shit."

That frightening scene would never leave their minds. And Azami's name never left the mind of Bertoni.

Bertoni's dark eyes were still flashing back toward the burning stake and then toward some of the laughing and joking guards. Robinson again cautioned his hot-headed companion. "Can't do anything now. Wait 'til later."

Robinson, watching him closely for signs of the man attempting to charge the guard, noticed his black hair showed a few flecks of gray. He thought the man's hair will be white before this is all over.

Even as they marched along, trying to avoid the bayonet jabs of the Japs, Robinson's mind kept wandering. First to Lenora, wondering what had happened to her. Was she safe?

He knew there was nothing he could do but despite the continuing horrors they faced on this death march, he kept thinking of her.

Then he thought of his earlier life in Portland, Oregon.

Of his home life with a devoted wife. Of his days at Medical School. As he looked along the desolate trail they were following, his mind contrasted this piece of hell with the scene at the Med school and the life there. He wondered if he'd ever see it again.

In between his efforts to escape the cruel Japs as they took every opportunity to inflict cuts on all of them, and to provide as much help as he could to the injured men, Robby's thoughts returned to Lenora, pondering her fate.

His mind wandered to earlier times. To his life on Pill Hill. Looking at the ugly scene surrounding him here, the beautiful sight back in Oregon was like a crystal clear picture in his mind. And what a magnificent picture it was.

But that was there and he was here.

PORTLAND, OREGON -- 2003

So even though he forced himself to clear his mind of Lenora, it then wandered back to the faroff United States, and clearly that ideal setting for the Med school. His recollection was perhaps enhanced when contrasted with this rough-cut trail in the Philippines where they were herded by these insane barbarians.

The school was high atop the hills of the West Side of Portland. Who chose the locale, Robinson didn't know but it was obvious the person loved the sight of Mount Hood's snowcapped peak, with an excellent view of Hood on a direct sightline from the school.

In addition to the university's properties, the Veterans Administration utilized the area for its extensive hospital buildings.

High on the hills above Portland, it was easy for some newspaper columnist to dub the area Pill Hill. The term stuck. It was used as a reference name by all.

Pill Hill had developed beyond anyone's dreams. It was literally covered with buildings dedicated to the care and healing of humans. Now, in the year 2009, the Pill had just about outgrown the Hill.

One of the problems requiring a solution was getting additional space. Just where to get it was the problem. One plan involved a cable car arrangement stretching all the way from the Hill down to a spacious area near the Willamette River. This cable car plan received more opposition than backing from the populace of Portland. But that was a problem for the politicians.

Within the school itself there was still work proceeding on the 'research projects' ordered by the Emperor of Japan in the 1930s. No, not any of the so-called experiments. But scientists at one of the centers of the school endeavored to determine whether they, or any of their predecessors, had missed any shred of evidence as they endeavored to document the activities of two Japanese doctors. It was the two doctors who had been given orders by then-Emperor Hirohito to develop what they called 'research projects', during World War II.

These so-called studies were conducted in Manchuria and the experiments were performed on humans, while the subjects were still alive, conforming to the precise wording of the Emperor's order to establish his 'research centers'.

It was hard to believe these so-called experiments had been conducted more than 70 years ago. This was after the Japanese had saturated various sections of China with troops who slaughtered millions of civilians. The Emperor had ordered his troops far afield to establish Japanese supremacy everywhere. Present-day medical scientists were able to review what Japanese doctors had done to the helpless victims of the experiments. They looked for any evidence suggesting a reason these doctors had not been treated as war criminals. It was apparent from the evidence at hand, stories in newspapers and statements of officials, that the failure to punish the Japanese, who killed hundreds of thousands in the name of medical research, was inconceivable. Even casual observers of the so-called war crimes trial were enraged by this horrendous oversight.

The present-day investigations revealed no results for the common good which might have been a basis for not bringing these doctors to trial for war crimes.

Of course, when the Japanese were crushed and forced to surrender, precious few of their leaders were brought to face justice for their many uncivilized sins against humanity.

The murdering researchers were not among those who faced the court, nor was the Emperor, who had ordered construction of the killing plant. He was granted amnesty from that and the entire multitude of war crimes committed under his rule.

What amounted to wholesale murder of defenseless Chinese and other civilians was excused.

Essentially, none of the personnel on Pill Hill knew much of the era preceding and during World War II. They knew little of the Emperor's killing field. It was begun in 1937. Some were aware of the much publicized work of Dr. Mengele, the German doctor who copied these Japanese doctors and fled Germany many years later.

Incidentally, the fleeing Dr. Mengele was tracked down in South America and brought to trial.

The coverage of the sins of the members of the Nazi party, notably by the Gestapo and SS, was intense and continuous. But the newspapers rarely took up the cause of those enslaved, tortured, beheaded, raped, starved to death or otherwise mutilated or murdered by followers of the Emperor, whose evil actions were cloaked by a God-like image to his followers.

Coverage accorded the Gestapo and SS and their action against the Jews of Germany and Poland, on orders of Emperor Hirohito's colleague in murder, Adolph Hitler and the time or space devoted to the never-ending slaughters of the Japanese, was alarmingly one-sided.

And few of the residents of the Hill ever had exposure to any stories concerning Russia's heartless ruler, Josef Stalin, who ordered more than 20 million of the intelligentsia killed, most of whom were Jews. Rarely was a word written on the Russians or the Japs and their wholesale killings of millions of all nationalities and faiths.

However, regarding the experiments, the Med school lobby did include an encased display of some material from that era, but that's the only place the students might view any material concerning the experiments. A graduate of the school, a Dr. Wallace Robinson, operated a rehab center in Manila immediately after the long and vicious warfare and civilian slaughter had ceased. That brought the war home to some of the young students.

A couple of them engaged in a long conversation one night after they were finished up and they spoke mostly of those days in Manchuria. The days of those weird experiments.

Both were Portlanders, having attended Lincoln high together.

"Harry, why is it we have never heard anything about these experiments? Using live subjects?" a puzzled young medic posed to his beer tavern companion, fellow medic Harry Bockman. "I'll bet that Robinson could fill us in on some of that."

"Yeah, could be" agreed his friend, "although he was in the Philippines. That's a long haul from Manchuria. And from a more practical standpoint, he's probably not alive."

They were interrupted by the tavern owner, a garrulous fellow who knew quite well the professions and hopes of the students who comprised the bulk of his clientele. He'd seen almost all of them make their way to and through medical school. That's because most of them also made their way to his little place of business, just down the hill from the medical installations. He called them all Doc. "Hey Doc, you want two more?" and off he trudged to the beer tap.

Bockman continued, "It just doesn't make sense. There's all sorts of documentation on these experiments. Freezing these poor devils. Cutting them open alive to see what the reaction is on certain organs. Yet we don't hear a damned thing about it until we're up here actively looking into it."

"No, you're right. It doesn't make any sense. Not at all. Hell, look at the words on that bastard Mengele in Germany. You'd think he started this whole thing. Hell, he was just going to school on these guys," Mickles asserted.

"You got it George. They started this back in the '30s. You and I weren't even around then. Now why in hell wouldn't they study some of the background of that war in the Pacific with the same intensity they've studied the subject in Europe?" he questioned.

The two of them puzzled over the obvious imbalance in the coverage of these outrages by the Japanese in the Pacific by the newspapers as well as the schools, which ignored that phase of history as if hadn't happened.

Mickles took a gulp of his beer and said, "I can remember at school, high school, I mean, in some class or another, one of the guys asking about the Bataan Death March. You ever heard about that?"

"No, not in school. I remember one of my dad's friends talking to him about it once. Was in the Philippines, I think and his father'd been captured there. But in school? Not a thing."

"Well, a lot of Americans, and even more Filipinos, were captured and they had to march many miles. Just where I don't know. But no food and no treatment for wounds or illness. But keerist, it was flat out horrible. Now how can this take place, and we're not taught something about it? You'd almost think the war over there didn't even take place. That it was all in Germany. And the crazy part of it is, the war in the Pacific was started by the Japs. Against us. We joined in the other one. I'm not saying we shouldn't have joined. I think we should have. But the fact is, the Germans didn't attack us. The Japs attacked us."

Both of them sucked up some beer without comment for a moment as they considered this strange inequity in history which had been offered them as a course of study.

Soon they left the subject for one far more appealing than a war, no matter its locale. Two hot subjects, smartly attired, had seated themselves in a booth opposite them. The Docs had seen them before and actually had a beer or two with them.

They exchanged brief greetings and the young Docs ceased their talk and stepped across to join the young women. That was most acceptable.

They too hadn't come to Jerry's Bar just to drink beer.

"Hey Mickles, ready to check out those experiments of the Japanese yet?" was Bockman's greeting to his friend following their extended evening.

"Hell no. I just got through with some experiments of my own not too long ago," Mickles responded.

"Sure, sure but I've got news for you. Those experiments have been made for many, many years and they've been proved in many tests. Anyway, let's get back to Manchuria."

The two were the exceptions in their obvious curiosity regarding those events of so many years ago.

It's doubtful if any others at the med school gave them much thought. But this pair was different in the respect each was driven by a strong sense of the curious. Neither one was content with the surface reports on any project. They had to dig deeper.

Mickles was the product of a well-to-do family and he'd really never had any financial problems, either in high school or later in pre-med at University of Oregon.

Bockman, his buddy since high school and earlier, was the only son of an extremely wealthy investment house principal. His only concern was whether he'd have a new car when he finished his internship. His new car when he entered med school was assured by his delighted mother, who was deliriously happy that her darling son was on his way to becoming a doctor.

Despite his exposure since birth to the heights of Portland, both in physical residence on the hills high above the city and socially, the beach home of the family, plus a residence away from home at "the desert", the local name for pricey Palm Springs, California, Bockman was just one of the guys.

At least he was around Mickles. Their friendship wouldn't have lasted otherwise.

After an initial and cursory review of the previous evening, they subsequently returned to the matter of the experimental projects by the Japanese in Manchuria.

Their research turned up scant documented evidence of this terrible plunge into and beyond the horrors of medieval human treatment. Each of the fledglings in the profession was puzzled by the fact that practically nothing was ever written in the newspapers concerning this monumental testament to the methodical cruelty of the Japanese.

The pair learned a directive from Emperor Hirohito had started it all. He had assigned Col. Shiro Kimura to this project. His assistant was Dr. Ryoichi Naito. Documented evidence stated the appointed pair began and directed the entire operation with approximately 2000 Japanese serving under them.

The camp for this operation was located near the villages of Sadun, Sidun and Wudun and the directors of this death camp funneled thousands of helpless Chinese through the system. It was 100 per cent death for all who entered. It was instant or lingering. The 'researchers' didn't care.

This was in 1936 and the locale was three square kilometers of land, approximately 40 miles South of Harbin. Quite remote. So remote it was accessible only by using the South Manchurian Railway at Pingfan Station.

Bockman and Mickles, once they had satisfied themselves of the origin and purpose of this center, were curious to know how the war crimes trials disposed of the people running a butcher shop such as this. It was inconceivable to them that these murderers weren't even held for trial.

"Can you tell me why both of these people weren't held and tried as war criminals?" The question was rhetorical. Bockman really didn't expect an answer. He received an answer in the form of a question. "How about the Emperor? He ordered all of it to start and he lived. No punishment?"

Mickles insisted Doug MacArthur, the publicity-conscious commander of the military in the South Pacific, was responsible for the doctors and their Emperor-boss escaping execution.

And he had proof.

"Look at this. Tells it all. Our guy MacArthur, who was sent to Tokyo to take care of the so-called unconditional surrender, made a deal with the two doctors who put the whole damned camp together," Mickles said, holding out a stapled pamphlet of plain, white papers.

"Deal? How in hell can you deal with a couple of twisted minds like that?" asked an astonished Bockman.

"Easy when you consider MacArthur. Just look at the record.

"He didn't even consider punishment for the Emperor. He accepted the BS that Hirohito had nothing to do with the war effort. Hell, he was behind all of it, along with his paid military henchmen.

"Anyway, back to the good doctors. MacArthur made a deal with them. He agreed not to try them as war criminals in exchange for the medical data they had acquired during the years they ran this place called Unit 731. With two thousand men they ran this station. They killed hundreds of thousands of helpless people. And MacArthur lets them all off. Including the guy who ordered it all, the Emperor," Mickles rattled on as he lost his composure completely.

"All right. All right," Bockman jumped in. "So what happened to the deal? Did it go through? They were never punished for all these murders?"

"Never. Not one bit. Hundreds of thousands died and MacArthur lets the murderers go free. But what the hell? He did the same thing with that damned Emperor and he was just as guilty and more so as any of the war criminals at Nuremberg," snarled Mickles.

"Well, I don't know about that but it's certainly amazing they got away with these medical murders. Amazing MacArthur was able to get away with it."

Then Bockman thought for a moment and continued. "On the other hand, the sane people, and from what I read of MacArthur his only sane moments were when he was getting ready to have his picture taken, probably were so happy the blamed war was over they were ready to listen to any proposition and get on with the peace. Don't you suppose?"

Mickles finally answered, speaking slowly. "But we won the damned war. Didn't we? Or was the war in Europe the only war we ever won?"

Both of them lapsed into silence. Both of them, training to save life, to help humanity, were overwhelmed by this disregard for humanity and life, by two doctors — Kimura and Naito.

They were repulsed by the mere thought of linking their names with the title of doctor.

When they finally broke for coffee, they managed to leave, momentarily, the medical atrocities of Japan. Only one subject could interrupt their discussion of the so-called experiments.

That was a return to events of the previous evening and the chance encounter at Jerry's.

"So tell me. How was your night?" Bockman asked.

"Great for me," said Mickles, "but I don't know how great it was for her." He laughed and added, "I'll find out tonight when I call her."

"How about you?"

Bockman was considerably less excited about it.

"Well," he said slowly, "I'm gonna call tonight too but I can assure you it won't be for a progress report. My chart is still at the starting position."

"But back to what we've been talking about earlier. Maybe you've noticed this too. Down in the entry to this building, you know, in the reception center, where they have sort of a history of the Med school?" Seeing a nod, he continued, "Well, there's some material in the case there about a special rehabilitation hospital in Manila that had something to do with people who'd been imprisoned by the Japanese during that war, what?, World War II, right? Let's run down there. It might have something there about these two fine fellows who did so much for humanity by scientific killing."

He laughed an extremely hollow laugh as he suggested,

"Scientific killing? Is that where your death hurts the same but you leave a mark on medical science? In addition to a death certificate?"

"Hell, I don't know," answered Bockman. "But that's a good idea. Let's go take a look."

The pair sauntered up to the huge, glass-enclosed display against the wall of the entrance to the school.

They looked at much material but little of it held any pertinent information on these hard-to-believe experiments by the Japanese. It was a subject they'd stumbled into but they quickly found it also closely involved a graduate of the school. Not as a participant but as a man, a doctor, who had much intimate information on the sordid matter in Manchuria so many years ago. This was a man who'd concluded his studies at the Med school back in 1939.

But his experiences certainly were contemporary with the era which interested them.

"Hey, this is right on. This man graduated here and then went into the Army as a medic and damned if he wasn't stationed in Manila," Mickles called out triumphantly.

"Read some more of that. It might tell us whether he was really in Manila during the war or so long afterwards there'd be no way he'd be involved or know of this project," cautioned Bockman.

"Look for yourself. Here it is. Wallace Robinson was in Manila in the Army. After the Japanese over-ran the Philippines, he was captured, was on the Bataan Death March, escaped and then captured again. He was a prisoner for the rest of the war. Worked on soldiers and mostly on prisoners who'd been mistreated or starved, and it sounds like both happened to Japanese prisoners. Then, after the war's over, he stayed in Manila after opening a hospital to accept returning prisoners who needed help. A lot of it was just taking time to adjust to a life of freedom. Not sure. It's pretty vague.

"Well, it probably varied. Some trivial but a lot of serious physical problems which needed treatment. But does it sound like he did this pretty much on his own?" asked Bockman.

"Sounds like it," said Mickles, his eyes pressed as close to the glass as he could get with his own glasses on. "Another thing, sounds here as if he opened a clinic down in Southern Oregon, in Medford, after he got back home."

"Wonder if he's still down there. It'd be great to talk to him about some of the people he'd worked with."

"With the war all behind them, you know. I think that'd be an interesting session."

Bockman nodded. "Of course. No doubt it would. But I question whether he's still around. Hell, he'd be pushing ninety or a hundred by now. Or more,

"However, I'd be amazed if he doesn't have some personal records on that. Let's call someone in Medford and find out. We can do it later this afternoon. Okay?" and they headed back to their offices as Mickles nodded agreement.

Manila -- 1946

Had the pair followed through, at that time and called Medford to talk to the principal featured in the lobby display, they would have, with a little persistence, found the featured doctor. They'd have found their estimate of "pushing 100" not far from the truth but the man would have answered. He was there and had been there since 1947.

And their questions wouldn't be new to him. People who knew he'd been on the Bataan Death March and survived, only to enter captivity in Bilibad Prison in Manila also knew he was one of the lucky ones who survived the systematic torture prevalent there. But they also wondered why he chose to take charge of a rehabilitation center in Manila after the war came to a close, instead of taking the first boat home.

He'd answered them all, "It's simple enough. I saw so many hundreds and hundreds of people, both military and non-military, men, women and children, who'd been terribly mistreated by the Japanese. I knew they needed help. It's hard to believe what the Japs did to the citizens of the Philippines. It's difficult even for me and I saw more of it than I want to remember."

To questioners, Robinson didn't mention his personal stake in it. He didn't mention Lenora, the young Filipino woman he'd met and fallen in love with in Manila.

His beautiful love, Lenora, had been fortunate through her early life in Jap-held Manila. She had survived. When she heard Robinson was held captive at Bilibad she was a daily visitor to the barriers surrounding this prison. That was her downfall. She always carried food with her, hoping to smuggle bits of food to him.

Her efforts on his behalf were of infinite importance to him. They stated graphically, without words, the love which she held for him. A love which he reciprocated.

The few who were aware of this and of her ultimate fate, believed that was the prime reason for his longer stay in Manila than the military required of him.

Lenora was a well-educated woman who actually had gone to University in Oregon. Robby had met her early in his assignment to Manila and they had a close relationship. Once Lenora's presence near Bilibad was detected, the Japs didn't question why. Her days were numbered. Yoshio Morobita, in charge of Bilibad, killed her. Now the war grief hit Robinson more personally and thus with greater impact than any previously.

That's because most of his patients had experienced the incredible, worse than animal-like atrocities of the Japanese; experienced it and still managed to survive. And it was his duty and desire as a doctor to heal them. But Lenora was far more than a patient to him and he found it impossible to accept her fate.

But when the shooting war was over and he began working with veterans at the rehabilitation center the wide variety of patients offered some surprises.

None was a more welcome surprise than the arrival of Bertoni at his rehab center. It was Floyd Bertoni, the buck private he'd met when they were thrown together on the Bataan Death March.

Bertoni grabbed him in a tight bearlike squeeze, released him, stepped back and said, "Doc, you're lookin' great. Heard you'd put some rehab deal together here," his visitor tossed out quickly, "and I hadda come by to see yus. Thinkin' I'm needin' some serious rehabbin'."

As he attempted to decode Bertoni's Brooklynese, an amazed Robby shook his hand and then took a longer look at the man who had been on the Death March with him.

Bertoni's Brooklyn-dominated speech, which Robby had first heard on the March, had held up. More important, he didn't appear to have many ailments. Physically, he looked fine. Perhaps a bit leaner. Certainly not the skeletal appearance presented by so many pitiful prisoners of the Japanese who Robby had seen.

Bertoni was from Sheepshead Bay, Brooklyn. "Yeah. Right near Manhattan Beach. Only a stop from Coney on the train. Great place. Lotsa commercial fishin." Robinson could remember him talking like a Chamber of Commerce man when he'd first met him. "Yus oughta visit sometime Doc. Yuh'd love it." He'd heard it many times. It was meaningless to him but Bertoni's pleasure in telling him was so apparent, Robby listened to more of Bertoni's life in Brooklyn than he really needed to know.

Such as his attendance at PS 206, Reynolds school and Shellbank school. Also high school — fairly close to PS 206 on 22nd Street. Robby had received all this information from a man the doctor knew wanted to tell someone about himself. That's why Robby never stopped Bertoni from talking.

"If I stopped him," he said, laughing as he told a friend later, "I'd never have known he lived on 11th Street and Gilmore Court, close to Sheepshead Bay Station. Trust me though, I found it difficult to understand him sometimes.

"But talking all aside, I'd never want for a better partner in stress time, such as trying to survive the Death March. He was the greatest. And you know, his accent wasn't the worst, trust me. He's a good man. A good soldier and a good friend."

In view of this and Bertoni's resilience, Robinson wasn't really amazed when Bertoni showed up at his boarding house, his jocular name for the rehab center.

"When they took you away from Bilibad, I figured that was the end. Really never expected to see you again. It's great you made it through, Floyd. You're one of the survivors for sure," Robby enthusiastically told his welcome newcomer.

"Well Doc, they couldn't kill us on the March and dammit, I swore to myself I'd get out of Bilibad alive and cut off the balls on that bastard. Yoshio Morobita. He was the real Wolf.

"Or that pitiful chunka crap boinin' up that couple. Remembuh? I'd love to run into that Ryoichi Azami. See, I know da guy's name. You remembuh?"

"Sure, sure, I know him. We'll take care of that. But first, how are you? Any hangover from the camp or anything?"

"Nah. I don't think so. I think I was kept alive by thinkin' 'bout what I'd do to those guys after this got over. Never did think I wouldn't make it. Always knew I would. What about you?"

"Same as you Floyd. Spent most of my time right here in Manila. A lot of my work was at Bilibad. Of course, at the time I didn't even know you were there. Would have been nice to know we had made it alive so far. Now listen, we'll probably see some more of the people we've been with come through here. You'll be here long enough to get a complete checkout and then we'll go over our plans together.

"As far as reprisals go," his voice softened for emphasis, "Don't do anything rash right now. There might be something special for those guys. And their balls," he concluded with a laugh.

Chance meetings such as the surprise reunion with Bertoni brightened Robinson's otherwise sad days.

Because his hours in post-war Manila weren't the pleasant, fun-filled hours he'd spent there before the attack by Japan. Neither in the hospital nor during the scant time he was able to spend away from the rehab center.

Within the clinic he met with survivors of the onslaught by the Emperor's killers. They were virtual shells of humanity. Not all of them had confused minds but all presented physical and mental challenges of some type.

Robinson found himself dealing as much with mental disruption and completely disjointed thought processes as with any physical problems. At times he was wishing he'd just find a nice, simple case of a person standing too close to an exploding grenade.

At least he could see what needed fixing. But it was one sad tragedy after the other.

In his time away from the clinic he wandered through some of the old haunts, not seeking diversion in the way of drinks and companionship but desperately looking for clues of Lenora. He had to know with absolute certainty that his loved one was dead.

It had driven him wild since he had last seen her through the walls at Bilibad. He was aware of the risks she took as she'd come by to bring him food. All for the love of him. And her murder by Morabito. He stubbornly rejected that, hoping the stories were wrong.

He kept these thoughts submerged as if to avoid, or at least delay, confronting the truth. Secretly, he was convinced Lenora was dead. But he had to know for sure. So he looked on and on.

Robinson's available time for personal projects soon dwindled away to nothing because every day another pitiful delivery of men more dead than alive was brought to the overloaded clinic. Robinson was kept busy, with many of the cases conclusive, one way or the other.

They either needed immediate medical attention followed by regular sustenance to build back their bodies or they were almost too far gone physically for any mortal assistance. Those who could think rationally volunteered stories of cruelty that challenged the minds of the listeners.

One young man who was brought to Robinson was more interesting than most.

He was Chinese and Robinson figured about 16 or 17 years old. Maybe younger but not any older. He'd made his way to Manila by way of a Merchant Marine ship out of China, courtesy of a softhearted skipper who was able to make sense of his mangled English and horrendous story of the destruction of his own family. The skipper had also heard of Robby's clinic and knew he had the perfect fit in this young man.

That's how Dr. Robinson met Chiang Luang.

One of Robby's aides brought the young boy in. He was a pitiful sight, his sallow face narrowed to frightening proportions, even though sparsely covered by a growth of frail facial hair.

"Robby, this is Chiang Luang. He's from Manchuria. Wants to give you some information on the experiments there. Speaks a little English."

As his aide left Robby looked intently at Luang. Despite his condition, he noted a brightness in the eyes which told him here was a human who would be difficult, even for the Japanese, to kill. His eyes reflected a fierce determination.

Robinson shook his hand and showed him to one of the rickety chairs in the examining area he had installed.

Luang had already had a preliminary examination so Robinson knew he wasn't suffering physically. No fever. No ailments that time and proper sustenance wouldn't dissipate. Now he wanted to know what Luang had to say of the notorious medical experimenting ordered by the thus-far unprosecuted Emperor of these people.

"Tell me of your home, Chiang," Robby offered in his most solicitous tones, the words mouthed carefully.

Almost as if by automation, Luang turned his head each direction, a habit of caution he had developed during his years of hiding from the Japanese although existing in the middle of them. Then he directed his gaze on Robinson.

With no expression either on his face or reflected by any voice intonations, he told a shocking story that even shook Robinson, who thought he'd heard it all.

"My family all killed. Japanese kill many years ago. When I was child."

He looked intently and directly at Robinson as he spoke and the doctor had to control himself to avoid smiling at his new patient's appraisal of himself as a child, back then, when he was hardly more than a child right now. At least chronologically. His experiences obviously had aged him many times faster.

Luang continued. "My mother dragged away. Raped by soldiers. Killed. My father dragged away too. He taken away to work. No food. He finally try escape. Japs cut off his head. Make my mother and sister watch. From far away I see it too. Can do nothing to stop it.

"My mother was taken away for the Japanese soldiers. They rape her all time. Day night. I hear screaming. Her and other women used. Even my sister. Only so young. They not care. They do anyway."

Luang forced his words out as Robinson patiently listened to his every utterance.

Robinson could not believe this young man could maintain his composure as he told of his family shredded beyond civilized belief before his eyes. It was incredible. Robinson forced himself to break in and ask a question.

"Could you see any certain soldier do these things? Was there one soldier who killed them? One person you remember?"

Robinson repeated the question in different ways to make certain he understood. He understood all right.

"No, no. Many soldiers."

Robinson was trying to establish whether it would be possible to bring those responsible to court as war criminals. He had the uneasy feeling some Americans in charge had entered into an unholy agreement with these people. If so, there'd be no way to make these heathen pay for these specific crimes in that area of Manchuria. There were hundreds of thousands of equally heinous crimes, and worse, as yet unpunished. He knew the offenders would never be punished by the authorities.

He took a moment or two to ponder the direction he wanted to take with this youth. But Luang continued.

"I help to get most. They sleep at night. Many guards stay where we once live. I put fuel at the building. Light it. Poof," and Luang, motionless to this point in their session, threw both arms in the air, saying, "They all die."

It was simple enough to figure out. He burned all of them to death. Vengeance and then some, Robinson thought.

What then, could this man/child be seeking? That's what puzzled Robinson now. What an incredible young person. To gain his revenge on those people at a time when most children his age would be absolutely helpless to do anything.

Robinson was overwhelmed by a combination of approval, downright admiration and absolute incredulity as Luang finished his story. Then he asked, "Do you feel all right now? You are weak, maybe. But otherwise, you feel okay?"

Somehow he thought Luang would understand 'okay'. And he did.

"Oh yes. I okay. Okay. But you know the man who kill all the people. The doctor. Same you."

He hastened to add, "Not same you. He run place where freeze people. Cut them up. You know?"

Robinson knew only too well who the young man meant. It was the man appointed by Emperor Hirohito to direct the experiments at what was known as Unit 731. Experiments on helpless, live humans.

Col. Shiro Kimura. He's the man. He nodded to his latest visitor. "Yes, I know. You don't mean the Emperor," his mouth twisted with distaste as he even uttered the word.

"No. No. The doctor."

"All right. Yes, I know, I think he's in Tokyo. All right?

Luang slowly nodded his head. It was obvious he was considering his next move. How to get to Tokyo.

Robinson made the next move.

"First of all, stay with me. Have good food and get strong. Then we talk more about all this. Okay?"

A faint smile threatened the expressionless stronghold which was his thin face.

"Okay," he said.

Luang left with one of Robinson's volunteers, a Filipino only too happy, as were all of them, to help the good Doctor in his work with the returning soldiers of all nationalities.

Robinson thought of that mix of soldiers. "Those Japs stamped their own inhumane treatment on practically every country in this part of the world, it seems like," checking himself as he remembered the numbers of Americans and English who certainly didn't hail from this area. He had seen plenty of both. The Japanese had brought unbridled cruelty to them, either in Pearl, Manila or Singapore. Not to forget Borneo, Burma and New Zealand.

As he reflected on his meeting with Luang, Robby knew why he wanted to find the experimental doctor, though he didn't state precisely why.

The bad doctor represented the end of Luang's family.

It was the bad doctor who created the House of Death where the Emperor-decreed medical experiments on the live and readily available Chinese victims were performed. Certainly this young Chinese, a mere youth who had managed to escape the slaughter, recognized it for slaughter, no matter how cleverly the Japanese cloaked the killings as part of their medical research. And he obviously wouldn't forget the murders of his sister and parents.

There were hundreds of thousands of sins by the Japanese against mankind, but these seemed more despicable because of the nature of these so-called medical experiments. Living persons subjected to weird, cruel methods of inducing death. By men dedicated to the preservation and betterment of life.

Robinson choked when he even thought of the phrase, 'medical experiments'. What made it even more insane was the fact the place was established on the orders of the Emperor. To the populace of Japan, there was nothing more sacred than the Emperor.

Dr. Kimura and his assistant, Dr. Naito, followed the orders. They used their knowledge to run this camp. Not to save life but to extract it in some of the most horrible and cruel manners possibly imaginable.

Meantime, work at the rehab center went on. Ever-increasing numbers of survivors came to his relatively tiny rehab center. These demonstrated clearly the scope of the Japanese horrors which extended far beyond any individual's own, personal experience or concept. Far beyond the horizons of any civilized person's imagination.

After Robinson took a break from his labors one night, he said to Bertoni, "It seems as if we're in a group, telling stories and each person's trying to top the other. Make his story more bizarre than his buddy's. The hell of it is, as the stories come by, they all corroborate the other stories we've heard. It's scary. Downright frightening. And I thought I'd heard it all.

"Take today for example. We get two Englishmen through the center. One's from Sheffield. The other from a small town just outside of London. Cheshunt. Let me tell you about them."

And he did. Bertoni listened as the good doctor told of the two Englishmen, his most recent arrivals seeking rehabilitation.

"Everytime I get one of these men in here it makes me more determined than ever to stay here and help them. First of all, there was this Hartley fellow. A George Hartley from Sheffield. Up in Yorkshire. He'd been captured and was taken to work on the Burma railroad. Same as a death sentence. But he's tough.

"Anyway, Sheffield's in Yorkshire and those people truly speak a language of their own. But one of Hartley's relatives was a mere boy of 14 when he lied his way into the British Army in World War I. He received only the relatively surface training they were able to take time for in those days and off to France he went.

"He got to the front lines in a hurry and was just another body to throw at the entrenched Germans. He was killed as he, a member of the Yorkshire Pals, went over the top on the first day of the Battle of the Somme. That was on July 1, 1916, if my memory serves me correctly.

"Know how I know that?" he asked an uncredulous Bertoni, who shook his head in total disbelief.

"Hartley told me all that in the few minutes I was talking to him, or rather listening to him. Goes a mile a minute but I'll wager he'd be a good one to have on your side in a fight. He'd heard all about World War I and he had no reluctance in 'jining along' as he put it, in this one. You'll have to meet this man."

He wandered from relating his story and his thought as he contemplated a scenario in which the Yorkshireman and the Brooklynite Bertoni tried to communicate.

"You'd have a great time with this Hartley. They speak a different language in Yorkshire. And you with your Brooklynese. That'd be worth the price of admission just to listen to you.

"But anyway, he was brought here after escaping a work camp in Burma. He'd been on that damned railroad for years. How he lived through it I'll never know. Not many did. He was in brutal shape but the guy made it. The stories he told me," Robinson's voice actually quavered as he mentally shook himself away from the memories of those stories.

"Listen to this one. Do you remember the name of Monditake? He was actually in charge of all the camps here in the Philippines."

Bertoni was silent and Robinson went on. "That's all this Hartley could talk about. Monditake. And he described what he saw the man do to a prisoner one day. He crucified him. Nailed him to a cross. Hartley saw it. Hundreds of other prisoners did too. Then this animal sliced out his entrails."

He shook his head sadly as he thought of the years of punishment wreaked on millions of helpless people. He continued.

"Towards the end, Hartley got himself together, mustered what strength he had, and made a break for it. Can you believe it? The sheer guts it took to hide out for the rest of the war. And he finally made it here. He's going to get along in good shape. But he has one thing in mind. Those people who committed all these crimes against helpless humans. He can't get those bastards out of his mind. I don't blame him. I couldn't either."

Bertoni knew full well what Hartley had in his mind. He didn't know the man but he still knew what the Brit was thinking. Revenge. Against one person or many for the crimes they'd committed. Funny. That's what Bertoni was thinking too.

He suddenly realized Robinson had launched another subject. Actually the same subject; just a different man.

This was the other Englishman. "Now this man Greene, an Ian Greene," said Robinson, "was a bit different. Quite a bit.

"For one thing, you could understand him. Didn't have to wade through that Yorkshire accent of Hartley's. That was too much.

"Greene's home's only a short distance North of London. A place called Cheshunt. He was working at a big company near London before the war. He quit and volunteered. Honestly, it was welcome talking to him. Probably because it was such a contrast with Hartley.

"Anyway, back to reality. Out here, they had him at one of our favorite places, Floyd. Cabanatuan," he added, and Bertoni's head snapped upright at the mention of one of the more notorious work camps in the Philippines.

"Of course, we've heard it all before. Beheadings. Bayoneting. Burning alive. We're almost casual about our acceptance of it. The Japanese people should live in burning hell for the rest of eternity for all the sins of these ancestors. It'll be interesting to see if they do."

"Oh yah, with MacArthur stickin' his mug in everthin. Lookin' for the nearest camera. Up to him, I think they'd all walk." blurted Bertoni. "The Emperor already has."

"But listen," Robinson urged, knowing Bertoni was right, "You haven't heard all of it."

Robinson held up his hands as he asked, "You might remember me mentioning the name of Ahirou. He was in charge of one of the ships used to take prisoners from camps here in the Philippines to Tokyo where the Japs needed more slave labor. Remember the name?"

Bertoni appeared puzzled and Robinson went on. "Greene does. Ahirou. Greene's mind was full of it. He saw the man bring up these prisoners from the hold one day. He beheaded five of them. Made them kneel down and just went along and whacked their heads off. Greene saw it happen. Hundreds of other prisoners did too. Then this animal had his guards use the bodies for bayonet practice. Finally they dumped what was left overboard."

Robinson was spent by the horrible memory of something he hadn't seen but which had been related to him so vividly by a man who had viewed it, that he had the sensation of having viewed it personally.

Again Robinson paused.

He wondered if he'd ever be busy enough to put all this out of his mind. Simply forget it. At first he thought that's what he'd like to do. Then he caught himself. That's a sin that shouldn't be committed. He picked up his monologue.

"Ahirou. Greene went on about him constantly. That name.

"Time after time. In or out of sequence he'd mention Ahirou. It's obviously a name he'll carry with him for a lifetime."

As he reflected many years later, Robinson concluded it was probably Greene's story and his quiet but deepseated determination to meet with Ahirou that helped him form his own personal diagnosis or appraisal of the problems which would beset all survivors. As unwilling observers and fortunate survivors, they were sentenced to carry the clear images of the Japanese beasts and their victims for the rest of their lives.

When another day dawned and Robinson greeted two natives of the Philippines, Sergi Merrando and Ramon Cangleonn, his mind was clear. He'd known them as friends of Lenora, having met them only briefly before the war. No matter, it was another tie to his happy life with Lenora and his continuing love of her, even in death. His reunion with them solidified his conclusions regarding disposition of any problems in Manila, in particular dealing with Lenora and whoever it was who'd killed her.

But his immediate concern was Merrando and Cangleonn. Merrando had been captured when Corregidor fell and he had been on slave labor, worked nearly to death out of the Philippines' ugly Jap camp, Cabanatuan. But he managed to survive the ordeal. Despite that ordeal, he looked fit and powerful. Slightly thinner than when Robinson had met him, which was just prior to the outbreak of the war.

He remembered Merrando conversing with Lenora in rapid-fire Tagalog, the Filipino language. Robby had no idea what they were saying but Lenora told him later that Merrando was voicing his approval of Robinson to her. Robinson accepted Lenora's explanation. It was totally unintelligible to him.

But Merrando longed to join the Army to be able to satisfy more completely his hatred of the Japanese. This was a longing he shared with his friend Cangleonn and the hatred which was common to every Filipino known to mankind. The credo of the Japanese, superior to all, was well-known in the Philippines.

Therefore it was not the receptive harbor that Hawaii and America provided for the Japanese. Japs were not permitted to own land in the Philippines. Only a Filipino or American could own land. The Japs circumvented that with dummy corporations with American and Hawaiian-born Japanese heading them.

As the Filipinos were aware, the Japanese Fifth Column was everywhere. It was not the private property of Germany's military, as some seemed to think.

Robinson had heard nothing of Merrando until he wearily came to the rehab center one day.

"They tell me you are here, Doc. Happy to see you." English was a challenge for Merrando and his emotional overfill contributed to his halting speech.

Merrando wasn't halting in his thought process as he slowly formed the name Maori Mori. "A bad person. He still alive. Shouldn't live." And that's all Robinson could get out of him.

Merrando's fellow Filipino, Cangleonn, also had similarly frightening and indicting stories to tell of Mori even though his stay at Cabanatuan had been brief. He'd suffered along with thousands of others on a troop ship carrying more slave workers to Japan's homeland. The Nitti Maru was one of many ships carrying these prisoners to Japan. There they were slammed into the vast slave labor force on the home island of the invaders.

Aboard the Nitti, Cangleonn saw the handiwork of one Tomika Saitoi. This Japanese officer was in command of the prisoners and on a daily basis held beheading shows. As many prisoners as could be crammed on deck from the crowded holds were forced to watch fellow prisoners have their heads chopped off. The Japanese guards cheered every swing of the sword.

Cangleonn unemotionally described the sight, speaking slowly and without any great emphasis.

He was thankful for life. Only one thing had saved him. The Japanese had changed the markings of the ship from that of a hospital ship which granted it some immunity from attack. As a result a destroyer attacked and sank the Nitti. Those who had survived the strafings and bombings frantically struggled to stay afloat in these days near the end of the war.

"American ship send out boat to help. I was one of those. But Saitoi live too. He had lifeboat from Nitti and made it. Last I heard Saitoi in Tokyo," Cangleonn related with difficulty.

But it was obvious to Robinson the murderous Saitoi had engineered the deaths of thousands of prisoners. His directions for mass executions at Cabanatuan alone accounted for deaths well into the thousands according to Robinson's quick calculations.

The Doctor was more meditative when he met briefly with Bertoni that evening for drinks. His thoughts consistently left Bertoni's chain of talk behind him as he remembered Lenora. His encounter with the two Filipinos had regenerated his thoughts.

He usually had the guilts when he permitted himself too many thoughts of Lenora. Did he place too much importance on it, considering the tragic death of his wife? Somehow that guilt burden seemed lighter now. Perhaps because of the multitude of deaths he'd witnessed and the many more he'd heard described.

Certainly the death of Lenora put all the deaths of personal nature to him in better perspective. Undoubtedly Lenora was dead because she was a Filipino and also a beautiful woman. Hard to say what had happened to her before she fought back and was killed. It hurt that she'd been spotted when she was attempting to help him. Bringing him food at Bilibad.

No matter what conclusions he reached, they were always sad. There were few thoughts of her that weren't sad. He knew nothing could bring her back, no more than his beloved wife could be reincarnated. But now anger rose to the surface through the sadness with greater strength than ever before. Viewing the reactions of others, who had seen friends killed by the Japanese, roused in him a new ferocity. Certainly new to him.

"Why should those bastards live after wasting the lives of so many hundreds of thousands of innocent people the way they did?" His quiet question burst a momentary silence between the two. Before a surprised Bertoni could answer Robinson said, "Some of those people had never carried arms. Some were children. Others were innocent women." Now his thoughts definitely centered on Lenora.

"And MacArthur unbelievably makes deals with some of them to permit them to live out their terrible lives without punishment. Without ever coming to trial. When most of them didn't even deserve a trial. They deserved nothing more than an execution, based on the evidence that abounds. Evidence from the fortunate few who survived."

It was at that moment Robinson cast his lot for the future. And retaliation. It would be with the men he'd been working with in rehab. And with his partner at hand, Floyd Bertoni.

Now it was Robinson's turn to place a name in a safe place. He placed it in a secure area; an area of certain recall. The name was Yoshio Morobita.

It wasn't likely he'd ever forget the name of Yoshio Morobita. That was the man who'd swung the sword that killed Lenora.

Without saying a word, he offered his glass to Bertoni who, though puzzled, touched glasses as he toasted a commitment Robinson had just made.

A commitment to justice.

Actually every day at his Manila rehab was a visit to a particular hell created by a specific Jap or a band of them. His very next day was no exception. That's the day Ian Greene, originally of Cheshunt, England, came in. That's the man Robinson had been talking about. The man truly was a near-skeleton. He had been returned to Cabanatuan after escaping near death in the hellship, Oryoko Maru. He managed to survive death despite the torture, starvation and interminably long work days on the Burma-Siam Railway which killed hundreds of thousands. That's where he had been sent.

Robby couldn't believe the sound spirit Greene manifested, belying the horrors he'd lived each day for years.

His memory was good too. There were thousands of names.

Persecutors and Japanese all. But as he made clear to Robby, Greene remembered one. Sabroa Ahirou. "Just relax, Ian" said Robby. "All will be fine."

Such were the days at Robinson's rehab. The hours were packed together. The days ran up against each other. There was no cessation.

Robinson tried to steal a moment after one day's typical frenzied and seemingly never-ending action as he attempted to review the particularly intriguing victims he'd had an opportunity thus far to meet and attempt to return to normalcy.

First of all, there was Chiang Luang, the young Chinese boy. Robinson had reflected on the boy's life at length and concluded Chiang Luang's life had been turned into a scenario of horror that even fiction couldn't exceed. Luang attributed all his misery to Dr. Kimura, whose actions were authorized by Hirohito and carried out according to his plan. Kimura's mission had resulted in the deaths of hundreds of thousands. Maybe millions. No one was keeping score. To Chiang Luang the name signified Death. Death to Luang's family.

Not in any order, the others fell into place. Bertoni of course. Floyd was with him on the Death March and had experienced the same life horrors. That included the sight of two innocent civilians burned to death by a man named Ryoichi Azami. Robinson would never forget that. Bertoni certainly wouldn't.

But for Robinson, and away from the rehab victims, the death of Lenora was paramount. Robinson had heard all the names of the animals who had led the Japs in their vicious onslaught against humanity, but one name dominated. Just as Kimura did for Luang. It was Yoshio Morobita. That's the name which dripped the blood of Lenora in Robinson's mind.

It wouldn't go away.

Ian Greene, the Britisher, had seen the viciousness of Sabroa Ahirou and lived with the memory of the deeds of horror by this creature.

The same strong memory was stored with his fellow Brit, George Hartley, from Sheffield. Hartley had seen many horrors within the hell in which the Japs had placed him and millions of others, but Mosarina Moditake was the Jap remembered by Hartley. He had committed the cruelest premeditated act of depravity of any Robinson had heard or witnessed. He shuddered as he recalled the story of the crucifixion. Mosarino Moditake. That was the name.

Then there was Sergi Merrando. And his fellow Filipino, Ramon Cangleonn. Both of them had known for years of the cruel nature of the Japanese against any who came from a different culture. This was the attitude of a nation into which youngsters were born and it was a culture in which they were indoctrinated throughout life. These Filipinos knew that.

Knowing that, Robinson shouldn't have been surprised at the particularly vicious memory of Tomika Saitoi which Cangleonn carried with him. Nor at the memory of Maori Mori which burned within the mind of Merrando.

For a variety of reasons, these men and their stories rarely left Robinson's thought process, no matter how busy or how long his schedule at the clinic might run.

His thoughts of each of them, which assailed him constantly, probably was a sickness itself. And it was a sickness Robinson admitted couldn't be healed with any of the so-called wonder drugs or present medical research. They, and Robinson included himself in that general grouping, would have to heal themselves. He could help. But it was necessary each person do what they must to heal these deep wounds. Each must become his own therapist to return to a healthy state of mind.

That's the message Robinson sought to give to all the damaged returnees.

One might compare Robinson's status to that of a coach who was accustomed to winning and one who wasn't likely to coddle or baby a whiner. When Robinson worked with some of these people, so seriously damaged physically as well as psychologically, he kept those problems ever prominent in his plans. Not that he had a preponderance of time to analyze. It wasn't a matter of "Come back next week and we'll talk about that." They had to do most of it themselves. Robinson wasn't aloof to any of them. He didn't turn away when they wanted to tell him their story. Their 'shot down' story as he sometimes called it, recalling a friend of his who was a pilot and constantly listening to a fellow pilot tell him what he termed 'his shot down' story.

There was a fine line between firmness and a kindly, friendly ear. Robinson thought, "Ye Gods, that's not just a fine line to walk. That's no line at all." But he had to listen.

He was constantly in touch with his mind himself so thought he had some basis for telling his injured comrades to buck up and be tough. Tough in mind was bound to help.

ASHLAND, OREGON -- 2009

Robinson's descendants would never know him well enough to decipher some of the messages his mind sent him constantly. Perhaps it was better they didn't get to know him more intimately than they did.

Certainly he was a complex man. He'd experienced enough trauma in only a few scant years, all on foreign soil, that a weaker man would have succumbed to the tremendous pressures long before.

His ability to make decisions, no matter what the situation might be, was astounding. His experiences on the Bataan Death March, for example. He'd made a daring escape which succeeded, but his personal responsibility to heal and to help his fellow marchers was so strong he was impelled to return. The man was different.

His grandson, Robinson the Third, didn't know him that well. But he'd heard enough stories of him and his experiences that he felt as if he knew him well. His mind was full of those memories of him as he began the drive from Lake Oswego, near Portland, to Ashland. His son, like any kid, was excited and impatient.

He was ready for arrival as soon as he climbed into his dad's four wheel drive unit. Impatiently he sweated out the drive to Southern Oregon.

For his father it was a chance to attempt to understand his grandfather's troubled but yet, surprisingly enough, orderly life. Time and miles moved along rapidly as the events of the years gone by crept through his consciousness.

Finally they were there and Robby Four straightened up to peer over the backs of the front seats.

His father came along the entry way to Ashland from the North, leaving the freeway and driving along what he knew was once the highway which made its way through Ashland.

When he came to Sheridan Street he turned right. And up. Up the street. Seemingly straight up. Into the sky. The rig shifted down automatically as it challenged the long, steep rise into the sky. At the absolute end of the street the house itself stood. As it had for so many years.

Except for repainting to preserve the wood but retaining its individuality from the numerous new houses, which had been built down below in what once were cherry and peach orchards on the hillside, the house hadn't changed much.

Robinson the Third didn't think he would see the barn still standing. Or the building holding the incubator he'd spent so much time watching. And he didn't. It was all gone now. He thought it miraculous the house was still standing and in such good repair.

One thing hadn't changed. Time couldn't erode the fabulous view. It deserved the descriptive but overworked term — breathtaking. A vista which swept one's vision down to the floor of the valley and then up the other side to Grizzly Peak, overlooking the entire valley. But they were there to work.

Robby Robinson, nearly-arrived at teenage status at 12, had the distasteful assignment of cleaning up the attic of his great-grandfather's house. His father was taking care of the remainder of the work on a house that had long since lacked any care. Although the first Robby had lived here most of the time since the war, he obviously gave it the care one would expect of an elderly widower. Little.

Robby IV had never really known his great-grandfather. All he knew of him was the smattering of knowledge he'd picked up overhearing conversations of his parents and grandparents. They didn't visit Southern Oregon. His great-grandfather, always a disciplined man no matter his age, loved his solitude.

Of course, Robby IV knew the man was a doctor and that he'd been practicing in Medford, Oregon, a few miles north of Ashland, since World War II. This is where the doctor had established his post-World War II practice. He'd lived in the Rogue River Valley since he'd returned from Manila after the war ended and the need for his rehab clinic there had disappeared.

But that was in 1947. Now it was 2009. There was a gaping hole in the history of the young boy's great-grandfather's life and it would be difficult to fill it.

The youngest Wally Robinson did know his great-grandfather was an Army doctor, was in the Philippines at the time of the Japanese strike against America and was smack in the middle of the terrible conflict. When the Japs occupied the Philippines, Dr. Robinson was captured. From his parents the boy learned of some of the horrors the doctor faced as a prisoner of the Japs. His ties to the Philippines had been strong.

Regarding World War II and Japan's part in the Axis battle against the Allies, Robby had rarely been offered any information in schools to this point.

He was frightened by what he had heard of the medieval cruelty of the Japs. His television had repeatedly told him in great detail of the frightful sins of the German SS and Gestapo and their genocidal treatment of the Jews. But little was offered regarding the Japanese and their sins against millions of helpless humans, regardless of their nationalities or religions.

He began sorting through the mass of material in the attic of the old home. He wasn't prepared for it. No one could be. His emotions received a constant pounding as he read records of unbelievably inhumane treatment accorded millions by the Japanese.

Much of the material was scattered on shelves and the floor. His job was to sort through it and place the material in the several boxes supplied by his father so the papers could be moved downstairs and be readied for disposition. Those were his father's directions. Once into the project, he eagerly followed the directions.

Because he'd discovered some newspaper clippings, yellowed with age, and these shrieked for his attention. Some were bundled together and placed in clear plastic containers or envelopes. Others were in individual plastic containers. He couldn't resist reading some of them.

Once he started, he was captivated. The episodes reported in the clippings gripped him securely. The facts of the Japanese assault against humanity had him spellbound. Stories he'd never heard in his seven years of schooling. A frightening part of history which he and his contemporaries had never heard from their teachers.

He learned of Emperor Hirohito's orders for all the attacks and also the Imperial Forces' dutiful responses to any bidding of the

Emperor, regardless of the deathly consequences throughout the Far East. They crushed any opposition by means too horrible for the civilized people of the world to imagine. These facts were all detailed in the clippings.

This boy's cleanup task had suddenly been given a new dimension. Now it was a learning journey. One which took him into the world of his great-grandfather to accord him a vision of what might have been his world had not his great-grandfather and others of his era been successful in repelling these ruthless invaders.

It was the defense by millions of armed forces personnel from a number of different countries, all fighting for their lives, and the future, which permitted Americans then and now, the right to live a civilized life.

Even the 12 year old Robby was able to comprehend that.

And he couldn't get enough of these clippings. As frightening as they were, he was thoroughly intrigued by what he read. He needed no urging from his father once he realized what he had in these tired old boxes full of newspaper clippings.

He eagerly clutched for more.

No longer was his task a drudge job. Now it was a game. Better than any TV game on the market. It created an adventure for him, simultaneously providing him with a look at history which his schooling had chosen to ignore. This lesson was one which swept him back half a century to the killings, the torturing and endless suffering imposed on millions of people by the ruthless Japanese. With stimulated interest he rustled through the collection of papers in the old man's trunk, tenderly picking up the tiny bits of newspapers, carefully placed in cellophane. All were stories of World War II in the South Pacific. Many of the clippings had notes jotted on the side, scrawled there by his great-grandfather.

One of the clippings had suffered more than most. He found only the start of a story from an English newspaper. It told of the discovery of the body of a Japanese officer, in Tokyo.

The man's identification papers stated he had been in charge of Japanese prisoner of war camps at Cabanatuan and Bilibad in the Philippines. Little else remained of the clipping.

Time had eradicated both the printing and the paper as well.

Disappointed, he was still eager as he reached for another clipping but discovered to his dismay that it too had suffered from the ravages of time. Despite its plastic covering, the major portion of this clipping had also disappeared.

Determined, he gleaned a few words from it. He was able to determine most of it concerned the shipment of prisoners from Bilibad Prison in Manila to Japan, aboard what was identified as a Hellship. He read:

> The first PWs to leave Camp Cabanatuan came to Bilibad where they were kept for a few days,

prior to boarding the Nitti Maru on December 13, 1944.

They embarked after dark from Pier #17, Manila, for Corregidor. During that first night the identifying marks on the smoke stack were exchanged with one of the two accommpanying Jap troop ships.

The article's print faded beyond comprehension at that point in the story but picked up later with the following sentence, which mentioned the 'tentative identification' of the dead man:

... if it was a man named Tomika Saitoi, as the tentative identification suggests, he was one of the officers in charge of the Hellships. Evidence suggests the more than 1600 prisoners jammed into the holds of the Hellship Nitti faced horrors far more inhumane than the Death March.

When the Nitti entered the China Sea, American dive bombers had attacked, as the ship now displayed the smoke stack identification mark of a Jap troop ship.

The bombs of the attacking planes nearly demolished the ship which was beached. Hundreds of the prisoners were killed and the remainder swam ashore within markers established by Saitoi. Those who floated outside these markers were machine-gunned. A witness on board stated:

"Wounded prisoners aboard ship and unable to swim ashore were slaughtered on the ship.

"After three days of suffering in the blistering sun, those left alive were ordered to walk to two new ships, the Brazil Maru and the Enoura Maru.

"Those unable to walk were shot or beheaded."

Young Robby now realized vividly what his great-grandfather had faced during those days when America's fate was in doubt. When the clipping finally deteriorated to an indecipherable blur, he was almost relieved.

But as he read on, the question which recurred in his mind: why his great-grandfather saved these specific clippings wasn't answered. There must have been millions of words written about the war and the atrocities committed by the cruel Japanese from the

1930s in China all through their bloodthirsty rampages against innocent and defenseless civilians during World War II.

So why save these specific ones? Such as the one he had in his hands. To this one his great-grandfather had clipped one of his notes: Ramon Cangleonn sent this Manila Herald clipping to me.

Young Robby read that. He noted the name of Cangleonn, "He must have been one of his buddies. From Manila. I've seen that name in earlier notes Grandfather made. Wonder what that's all about."

As he wondered about that name, his mind again wandered back to a thought which had bugged him right from the start of this intriguing search:

Why had his great-grandfather been so selective?

He wondered about that, as he continued to shovel through the mass of material. Why these particular clippings? The question for young Robby didn't disappear. And the horrors of the war, documented on paper yellowed by age but not bloodied by the marauding Japanese, continued for him in printed form.

Just as young Robby found it difficult to comprehend the horrors described in these stories of long ago, so too would the writers of those missives have found it interesting to hear his fearful intonations as he read them.

Such as "Like awesome," he breathed. "These dudes're too much. Like too much."

"My God, this is awesome," the young boy repeated, his words barely a mere whisper.

He was now delving into an extensive review of the Japanese activities over an extended period of years as they opened and conducted a medical experimentation center using live subjects.

With some difficulty he forced himself to continue reading the clipping. Finally he placed it down on the floor where he sat crosslegged as he studied these words from the past, gazing away as his innocent mind absorbed the horrors of it all.

Many times he had listened as his parents discussed the horrors of the Japanese in the pursuit of dominance during World War II. But he couldn't recall them ever discussing this particular aspect of cruelty which the Japanese had inflicted on helpless humanity.

After a second or so he brought his eyes back to the papers again, wondering as he did so, just what his great-grandfather could have told him of this terrible treatment of humans.

Once again he spoke aloud, again in hushed tones, asking himself, "How could these dudes do it?"

It was a question he'd asked himself several times as he read these frightening stories. Frightening and made worse because they were true.

Now he read of the death of another Japanese soldier. More than the death of a soldier really. This man had been a general, if indeed, the tentative identification was accurate. Furthermore, and this fact really grabbed Robby, the body had been found right here in Ashland. At least, just outside of Ashland. The story was from the Portland Oregon Journal, and the clipping well preserved. In fact, young Robby thought the paper felt relatively recent.

Ashland, OR — City and state officials have requested an identity confirmation by the Federal government of the remains of a dead man found in a tiny structure at Emigrant Lake, South of the community.

It apparently had been placed in a tightly sealed wooden box inside the tiny pump controls hut on the floor of the Lake. Much of the year the floor is covered with water.

Authorities' tentative identification states the dead man is Shiro Kimura, a doctor. He directed the medical experiment station in Manchuria where live Chinese were killed in the name of science. Gen. Douglas MacArthur, in charge of negotiating the peace treaty with the beaten Japanese, traded those lives for the scientific data Kimura and his associate had accumulated at the Japanese killing plant.

A graduate of Kyoto Imperial University, Kimura was sent to 1st Army Hospital in Tokyo.

According to the war records library this was in 1922 and he stayed there only briefly, returning to Kyoto to continue his studies as a post-graduate.

He specialized in bacteriology, serology, preventive medicine and pathology.

He argued the formal prohibition of "bacteriological methods" reached at Geneva in 1925 implied that it was in such methods, that the greatest weapon potential existed.

His extensive studies prompted his orders from Emperor Hirohito to open Unit 731, the infamous research station located on three square miles of land near the villages of Sadun, Sidun and Wudun in Manchuria. This was approximately 40 miles South of Harbin.

The South Manchurian Railway's nearest station was Pingfan Station.

It was at Unit 731 that Kimura was in direct charge of the pioneering research which utilized live humans as subjects in almost unimaginably cruel experiments, these experiments resulting in the deaths of hundreds of thousands of defenseless humans.

But Kimura and his staff referred to these hapless victims as "monkeys" or "logs" and their inventory of "logs" included PWs as well as any Chinese civilians. All were considered expendable by the Japanese.

This pioneering in the use of humans as guinea pigs was accepted by Japan's medical community, prompting no outrage or protest.

Humans were frozen to death and studied. Organs were removed from these prisoners so the results could be studied. Every means of "research" on living humans was utilized.

These experiments included infection with diseases such as cholera, typhoid, anthrax, plague and syphilis. Others were cut up alive just to witness what happened in the successive stages of hemorrhagic fever. Others had their blood siphoned off and replaced with horse blood. Others were shot, burned with flamethrowers, blown up with shrapnel and left to develop gas gangrene, bombarded with lethal doses of X rays, whirled to death in giant centrifuges, subjected to high pressure in sealed chambers until their eyes popped from their sockets, electrocuted, dehydrated, frozen and boiled alive.

Little has been written of Pingfan and the victims there of painful deaths at the hands of Japanese doctors. There's little doubt that Dr. Mengele, the doctor in Germany who later experimented in some of the same ways, followed the script as set forth by Kimura and his medical murderers.

Stories of Mengele and his atrocities have received constant coverage. Conversely, Kimura, the original sinner, and a murderer of much greater magnitude, has been ignored. He originated these experiments and continued them for the duration of the war.

After the war Kimura disappeared from Tokyo. Just how the dead man came to America is not known at this time. It is recorded that he turned over responsibility for a chain-of-command accounting to his colleague, Dr. Ryoichi Naito.

When the war ended, a Lt. Colonel Sanders, a biological warfare specialist on the U.S. Scientific Intelligence Survey, was contacted by Naito. In turn, Sanders recommended to MacArthur that the Japanese "researchers" be granted immunity from prosecution for war crimes in exchange for their data.

It developed Sanders wasn't the only one to share this view. Other U.S. scientists ignored all moral and ethical considerations to agree immunity should be granted.

It is known that MacArthur, in command of the punishment of Japanese war criminals, which fell far short of complete justice to these criminals, sent a top-secret cable to the U.S. War Department.

This cable stated: Experiments on humans were known ... confirmed by Kimura ... if guaranteed immunity from war crimes he can describe program in detail.

MacArthur accepted Kimura's blackmail but the General apparently couldn't prevent Kimura's death. His body's discovery in Ashland, Oregon, thousands of miles from his home and scene of his crimes is mystifying.

Authorities have been unable to explain how or why the body was delivered to Ashland. Investigators have concluded his death occurred elsewhere and the body shipped here.

Medical officers are examining the remains in an effort to determine cause of death.

The investigation continues.

Now Robby found himself looking for a followup story dealing with the bizarre discovery. They'd found the body of a doctor from Tokyo, Japan, right here, only a few miles from where he was seated. Although he was by now almost in a daze as he attempted to absorb these old paper clippings, he shuffled through them quickly, hoping for more on that body discovery. But no such luck.

Of course, the prime reason he was so mystified was simply how the devil a person last seen in Tokyo, was next found, dead, in Ashland, Oregon. There were no explanatory stories. There was mention of the local county sheriff explaining he was as much in the dark as anyone else.

"It's up to the military now. It's out of our hands. Everything we recovered out at Emigrant has been turned over to them."

And that was the end of it. If there'd been an investigation trying to answer the obvious question, how'd the body/skeleton get to Ashland from Tokyo, it failed. A strange mystery with no solution.

However, there were plenty of other clippings to satisfy his almost feverish appetite for more of these horrible and astonishing stories.

He was enriching his education with every story.

The next one had a note from his great-grandfather affixed to it. It said:

"This was taken from the Manchester Guardian and forwarded to me. Thanks to George Hartley."

> Manila, July 24, 1946 — (Overseas Press) The body of Mosarina Moditake was discovered here today. The dead man apparently died of natural causes. He was a veteran of many years of military duty with the Imperial forces of Emperor Hirohito.

His body was found by police on a routine patrol of a shabby area of the city. The authorities offered no explanation for his death. They stated no further investigation was planned.

The police report stated no visible evidence of mistreatment or foul play was found.

Moditake's war record with Hirohito's forces was examined by the allies after Japan had surrendered. The investigation, under the direction of General Douglas MacArthur, revealed nothing to indicate he should be held for trial on war crime charges.

He had served, among other assignments, as an officer in a prisoner of war camp at Sandakan, in the northeastern area of Borneo Island.

This slave work camp was essential to the Imperial war program in the area.

By bringing prisoners to this camp, the Imperial forces kept a constant supply of slave labor to construct an airfield at Sandakan. This air field was essential as a re-fueling point for the Japanese aircraft flying from Singapore to the Philippines.

One of the survivors of the camp at Sandakan had related a story involving Moditake and an exceptionally cruel murder of one of the helpless prisoners by this Japanese officer.

George Hartley, of Sheffield, England, had initially related the story to officials after he had been freed from the camp. His story had been substantiated by a number of other prisoners at the camp.

The story stated Moditake had nailed a live prisoner to a cross in the middle of the camp. When he told the story Hartley was obviously still suffering extreme emotional upset from the grisly scene but he forced himself to tell the story.

He said Moditake first nailed the prisoner's left hand to the crossbar and then had his men force his right hand to the opposite end of the crossbar, where he nailed that hand tightly to the wood.

Thereupon, stated Hartley, Moditake nailed both of the prisoner's feet to the vertical board on which he was standing.

Moditake had his Japanese soldiers stuff clothing in the prisoner's mouth in an effort to stifle his agonized screams of pain as this gruesome act was taking place. It was in vain. His shrieks could be heard throughout the camp, according to Hartley.

Moditake continued. Now he methodically sliced portions of flesh from the helpless prisoner. The Sheffield man said Moditake first cut a strip of flesh from the left side of the prisoner's stomach and then sliced a piece from the right side.

He carefully laid these pieces of flesh on the vertical board at the prisoner's feet.

As the prisoner, obviously suffering unbelievable pain, continued screaming, Moditake calmly placed a rubber glove on his right hand, inserted his hand into the body cavity and pulled out the intestines of the prisoner, which he placed on the board. Then he continued to slice out pieces of flesh from the arms, neck and both thighs of the prisoner, by now mercifully unconscious.

Moditake ordered the board and cross, with its display of his disgusting, medieval torture, placed on the camp parade ground. It was left there, with its rotting, lifeless corpse nailed to the cross, until Moditake and his staff departed for Ranau.

This and other atrocities at Sandakan were investigated by MacArthur and though Moditake was obviously a prime perpetrator of war crimes, MacArthur ignored the evidence. Strangely, the actions of Moditake were rejected as war crimes.

Therefore, he was not held after the war and never punished as a war criminal.

Police here have no clues suggesting his death was a crime of revenge but admit that any Japanese who chose to live in Manila after the many acts of viciousness to the Filipino people, could certainly be the objects of vengeance.

Now the young boy, reading this material, was so emotionally upset by the words that he was completely exhausted. First of all, in his schooling, he'd been led to believe the Japanese were an honorable people who had almost been forced into this war by a few hostile military people among them.

Everything he'd learned from the history of the times in school, was sharply contradicted by the harsh facts as related by eye witnesses and survivors of these horrible days. Why hadn't they been taught this, he wondered.

In fact, now he could easily see the cruelty toward all mankind, except fellow Japanese, began with the revered Emperor. He had ordered all these cruelties. He had fostered the ancient Japanese philosophy that the Japanese were superior to all mankind. That all others were hardly more than insects, waiting for the Japanese to crush them.

This relegation of the rest of the world's inhabitants to the dumping ground of the universe, was an integral part of the Japanese society, beginning at the palace of the Emperor and extending to the lowest ranking soldier or the lowliest citizen.

It was a basic of the Japanese philosophy. The Japanese were superior to all, they were taught. And they believed. Young Robby continued to ponder the question: Why didn't the schools teach these truths? Why hadn't the Japanese people admitted these atrocities? Why hadn't the Japanese been punished for these atrocious murders?

Now he had more questions for his teacher.

But he had a large pile of musty papers to read before he ever got back to Lake Oswego at the other end of the state and thus back into his classroom. His mind pondered the major question for his teacher. Why don't we learn of these things?

In school?

So the pile of reading confronting him was just one big stack of pleasure for Robby. By now he was captivated by the subject and could barely restrain himself.

He certainly had greatly underestimated his thirst for this project as well as the literal thirst his excitement with this material and the dust which covered the paper had developed.

He had long since exhausted his supply of cola.

Down the steep attic ladder he carefully made his way and from the second floor on down to the main floor where his father was moving furniture. He was concerned also with organizing personal papers stuffed in an ancient desk, back in a room which apparently served as the doctor's office at home as well as a library.

This old rolltop desk had family pictures on the top as well as many memoirs of his time spent in the Philippines. It was easy to see the doctor's thoughts frequently turned to that important part of his life.

"How're ya' up there Robby? Stayin' ahead of it?," his father asked, looking at his well-dusted son. "Good thing we wore some old stuff in here, right?"

"Right, dad. This is clean. Up there it's all dust. Where's the drinks and the bathroom too?"

"There's a toilet-only right here. Through that door," his father said, pointing toward the backside of the room. "All the drinks we brought are out in the kitchen."

Before he went back to his attic duties, young Robby asked his father, or rather, made a statement with a questioning conclusion to it as he said, "Boy, it's sure a good thing for us we won that war with Japan. It'd been awesome for us if they'd come over here. Like killing everyone and all that. We were pretty lucky, huh?"

His father had never heard his son express any interest in a war that took place and was concluded more than 50 years before he was born. He put aside the material he was sorting to look at him. He could see his son was serious. Probably because, for the first time in his young life, his son had picked up enough knowledge of the war years, that he realized there would have been frightening consequences for all of them, had the Japanese not been repelled in their methodical destruction of all humanity in their path.

"Well Robby, I agree with you. We were pretty lucky. Pretty lucky we had a lot of people holding them off before they got too far. 'Course, they went far enough as it is," he added quickly as he noticed his son suddenly ready to challenge the 'too far' part of his statement.

He closed lamely, "You're right. We were pretty lucky."

His son was gratified to hear his father's agreement with his assessment.

But young Robby wasn't downstairs to chat with his father. After he peed and stocked up with a new supply of drink he headed back up the stairs. The fun was there. Who knows what would come out of the next box he checked?

He was finding how scary the truth really was about the Japanese and their passionate, ruthless desire to conquer and dominate everyone. The cruelty of the Japanese returned civilization to barbaric days. Aside from that, he also enjoyed the rare thrill any young person feels when a parent has essentially stamped approval on a conclusion the child reached individually.

But he still had the misgivings which had been instilled in him when he first began reading some of this material. The first question; why was the education on these facts of history so lacking? Why was it all glossed over? More than just glossing over. He firmly believed his school teachers had deliberately ignored history and the facts when his group studied those years. But how could they, he wondered?

They'd taught him and his classmates just the opposite.

Robby kept wondering. His wonderment usually was aloud and repetitive. "Why don't we learn any of this stuff in school? It's all about Hitler and the holocaust. That's all we hear about."

He determined to find out from his teacher when he got back in the classroom.

A brilliant idea came to him. Maybe his father would let him make copies of some of these stories and take them to school. So the teacher would know he wasn't just making them up. That these things had really happened. That there really was a hospital or some such thing where real doctors used live people for their experiments. And the crucifixion and everything else.

"I'll ask him if I can keep these and make copies of them."

That much determined, he now shrugged his shoulders and returned to the task at hand.

Not much variety. It was just one clipping after another. Each one told a horrible story of what his great-grandfather and the men he knew had had to suffer back in those years. The same suffering which millions more in other countries in Asia experienced.

To this youthful novice in the field of almost supernatural cruelty of one human to another, it was his worst movie come to life. He wasn't cowed by it. He eagerly looked for more.

In that respect, he had no worries. Although the section of the attic he'd been cleaning was exhausted of a supply of boxes, there were plenty of other boxes waiting for him, dust and all.

He reached up high over his head in the closet to grasp his next source of history.

That was on a weathered piece of thin planking which served as a shelf in the dust-filled closet and Robby corraled another batch of dust-laden papers.

As he brought the flimsy container to the floor for closer inspection another cloud of dust quickly covered him but he was oblivious to such matters by now. He never imagined there could be so much dust in one building. But he knew most definitely there simply wasn't enough dust in this world to keep him away from the most intriguing material he'd ever read.

A few curious spiders, wondering what or who had dared invade their retreat, hastily flitted across the floor after their refuge had been disturbed. Young Robby let them go.

He wasn't interested. He wondered what else these boxes held for him.

There were no disappointments. This time the deluge was not of dust alone. It included dust-covered papers. Many were old sheets taken from newspapers. Efforts again had been taken to preserve them. The efforts were partially successful.

Some of the deteriorated clippings held names he'd seen in earlier ones. There were definitely some familiar names. There was no name shortage on this reading expedition he was taking.

Another yellowed scrap of newspaper dropped to the floor as the young man, with each second of reading generating more excitement, sought more of his great-grandfather's treasures.

He hurriedly sorted through the material but stopped to look at the piece which had fallen, noting his great-grandfather's scrawled notation on an attached piece of paper:

This was sent to me by my good friend Ramon Cangleonn, from Manila, where it appeared in the Manila Herald.

Manila (Worldwide Press) — Police found the body of a former Bilibad prison guard yesterday at the city dump.

They reported the dead man was identified as Yoshio Morobita, who was actually commander of the guard force at Bilibad Prison when the Japanese occupied all of the Philippines during World War II.

No cause of death was reported, with no apparent violence but it was also reported some body mutilation had been inflicted.

Morobita dominated Manila's war-time life of horrible terror inflicted by the Japanese forces on the populace. Morobita turned over most of the operations of Bilibad to his staff but his cruel policies were followed precisely.

It was his policy that had established death as the punishment for everything at Bilibad. No intermediate punishment.

Each time a man attempted to escape the guards would arbitrarily select three or four or more other prisoners and behead them. Of course, the prisoner who attempted the escape would die too.

These executions were well-known to the citizens of Manila as Morobita took special care to spread the news of the beheadings through the city.

Morobita returned to Bilibad frequently. He rarely missed one of the reprisal beheadings and occasionally would wield a beheading sword himself to begin the slaughter.

Regarding the discovery of the body, the police didn't state when they expected to conclude their investigation. Issuance of their final report on the matter concerning the death of the infamous commander of the prison is expected soon.

Bilibad was built in 1898 and housed the worst Filipino civilian criminals.

During the long and atrocity-filled occupation of the Philippines it was also the 'dumping ground' for the remnants of humanity which the Japs would bring back to Manila from the Batangas work details. All of the prisoners taken on these details returned with little life left in their bodies. They'd been beaten and worked to the point of death.

These details involved workdays of 12 to 14 hours or more with meager if any rations. At least one or two deaths occurred daily.

The work force of American prisoners of war sent on the Batangas work detail to the southwest of Manila numbered 125. Fewer than 30 survived the rigors of the three months in hell.

Survivors of Batangas told PWs at Bilibad the clubbing of prisoners was unmerciful and went on for hours. No water was supplied and prisoners were always tied up and tortured by the Japs.

One guard was called The Wolf by the few survivors. No one controlled him as he deliberately tried to destroy prisoners with daily beatings. These beatings frequently mutilated a man beyond recognition. There were no interruptions by his superiors.

What was left of this Batangas work force, consisted only of remnants of the total. These men, mere scraps of human beings, were shipped back and dumped into Bilibad.

His great-grandfather had clipped a notation to this piece:
'It doesn't sound as if the authorities will spend too many hours seeking the cause of death, welcome as it is.'

'It certainly wouldn't take long for the reporter, or anyone else, to determine the man had been self-strangled, you might say. I suppose that's what it would be when one's genitalia are removed and placed in one's mouth and the mouth is then taped until relief, in the form of the man's death, arrives.'

'And no evidence of restraint.'

At this point young Robby shook his head as he wondered how his great-grandfather could know of such a thing, finally assuming the man in Manila, that Cangleonn, had mentioned it to him. How else would he know?

He started to call downstairs to his father thinking he might help him. Then he thought better and whispered to himself, "This stuff's too cool. Dad might make me come down there and do some grunt stuff. This is too awesome. I'll ask him later."

As he continued to read these reports from newspapers, actually clippings from now ancient papers, he finally realized his frequent use of "awesome" simply didn't describe the material he was viewing.

These ancient papers, clippings from newspapers and bits of notebook paper, continued to rise from the dead in the box he'd discovered on the high shelf.

It was now he learned a man named Ian Greene had been taken to work on the Burma-Siam railway, a sentence to death for hundreds of thousands of prisoners of the Japanese forces, crawling all over the surface of Asia.

This native of Cheshunt, England had been imprisoned in Sandakan, on the northern-most tip of Borneo. He initially worked on construction of the airport the Japanese needed so desperately.

Later he joined the hundreds of thousands of slave workers the Japanese brought to work on the Burma-Siam Railway. It was here the slaves essentially were worked until they died. If unable to work they were beheaded.

His great-grandfather supplied this information in an abbreviated note, along with another clipping.

This one was taken from the London Telegraph and forwarded to the doctor from Greene, in Cheshunt, England. The note, scribbled in his great-grandfather's unmistakable writing across the top of the clipping, made that clear. Just when young Robby thought he'd been frightened as much as possible, he saw this one. It dipped to a new and incredibly lower level of humanity.

Robby was getting a documented lesson portraying the Japs at war and their treatment of the helpless, civilian or military. He was particularly impressed with the statements by the Englishman, as printed in the London Telegraph report, telling of the horrible scene Greene had witnessed.

He read it again.

> Tokyo, February 14 (Reuters) — Tentative identification of a body of a former Japanese soldier who had been living on the outskirts of Tokyo was made here today.
>
> The authorities said they were reasonably certain it was Sabroa Ahirou. He was a man whose war responsibility included transport of Allied prisoners aboard ships from outposts to the home island where they were committed to a brief life consisting of round-the-clock work for the Emperor's war effort. Scanty rations and rampant disease with no care contributed to brief lifetimes.
>
> There was no evidence of foul play but preliminary examination failed to reveal the cause of death.
>
> Records at the overseas press office provided additional information regarding the dead man, and permitted positive identity. His name was announced as Sabroa Ahirou.
>
> Further, the report stated he was placed in charge of a large group of men taken aboard the Oryoko Maru bound for Japan and slave camps there. These were Americans captured on Wake Island, and other Allied prisoners of war from a variety of locations.
>
> Relative to this report, the Telegraph was able to speak with Ian Greene, of Cheshunt, a man who had been on the Oryoko Maru and under Ahirou's command.
>
> "We were early in the trip from the Philippines to Japan, all packed in the hold of the ship. This bastard Ahirou brought five men, randomly picked from the hold, up on deck.
>
> "He told them, 'You have killed many Japanese soldiers in battle. For what you have done, you are now going to be killed — for revenge.'
>
> "He told them each had been identified as Americans and they were now representatives of all

American soldiers. Then he quite matter-of-factly said, 'You will be killed. You can now pray to be happy in the next world. In heaven.'

"Then he had the five men blindfolded and in turn, one by one, the men had their heads chopped off.

"A different guard stepped up to perform each of these murderous acts. One by one they forced the prisoner to his knees, stepped back, and swung the long sword.

"Those damned long blades swished through the air and when it struck the neck it made a noise like a damp towel snapping in a locker room. Oh yes, if it didn't bite into the neck deeply enough to sever the head on the first swing, the swordsman took another chop at the helpless victim. Or another.

"All of the Japanese soldiers and sailors were watching every swing. They all applauded wildly at every swing. Regardless how many swings at the poor devils the bastards had to take."

Greene said that when all five heads had been severed, the other men took the swords so they could join in this Japanese sport.

In this event, the other Japs tried to sever the headless bodies in two with a single stroke of the big swords.

Because they weren't skilled swordsmen they hacked away in a welter of blood, flailing away at the limp corpses trying to slice them in half.

Finally, when the arm-weary Japs had had enough, Ahirou ordered a halt. Now he had the bodies propped up against a sake barrel.

Once so placed he had his guards stick them to sharpen their skills with the bayonets. When these men had satisfied their lust for bayoneting the dead men, Ahirou ordered a cessation.

Then the carcasses and the chopped-off heads were thrown overboard to celebrate the entire bloody and cowardly occasion.

The rest of the clipping had been torn off and apparently discarded. Young Robby wasn't upset by the missing portion. He sat back, emotionally drained for the moment.

If some of Robby's buddies back in Lake Oswego could have seen him sitting crosslegged in a dirty attic, avidly reading yellowed newspaper clippings from a world far removed from theirs, they simply would have walked away.

No way that's possible. Not unless his parents were right there, looking over his shoulder.

Why not dump all the papers in the boxes, take them downstairs and out to the recycling plant? There must be a recycling plant there, even in the small town of Ashland.

But for the young man reading all this material, such disposal wasn't even considered. He was so intrigued he hadn't even considered what the final disposition of the material might be.

It didn't occur to him but later his parents, specifically his father, wondered why he hadn't begged off the project after a half hour or so. In fact, his father kept expecting him to come downstairs with some story or another, but with the one, single objective — getting the hell out of the attic.

But there were no sounds from above.

Robby the Third even considered the possibility his son had fallen asleep. He shouted upstairs to him.

"Robby, how are you coming along? Any progress?"

At first there was no answer. Then the father heard some steps as his son walked quickly to the little opening up to the attic. He shouted down, "It's all cool. Doin' great. It's cool."

"All right. Let me know if you want to get out of here and get something to eat."

"Okay, I will," Robby IV automatically answered. At the moment, much stronger inducements than food would be necessary to drag him away from some of the material he'd been reading.

For example, he'd read some notes of his great-grandfather's regarding the "lucky break" they'd received as the thing called the Death March was finishing. That's because the Death March was supposed to finish at Camp O'Donnell.

He saw these notes: "Camp O'Donnell was the terminus of the March. We heard that more than 500 prisoners died each day at O'Donnell. So we were damned happy when we discovered we were being sent to Bilibad instead of O'Donnell.

"Bilibad was no bargain. Sure, it would have the same heartless creatures guarding us but at least the prison was livable. That seemed like a better deal than what the reports from O'Donnell indicated. We didn't have any choice anyway."

Robby looked out the tiny little window in one side of the attic to rest his eyes from the strain of reading these old papers. It was the side of the house that looked to the south and he'd learned enough to know that's the direction of Emigrant Lake, where they'd found that body of a Japanese doctor. He knew he wanted to go out there and look around.

It seemed to him it would form a link between the past and the present. These stories, as staggering and hypnotic as they were, almost seemed like supernatural stories. As if they hadn't happened. As if they couldn't have happened. Then or now.

Here Robby had proof from all over the world. Proof that these horrible deeds had happened. And furthermore, precious little punishment had been dealt to those responsible for all of these atrocities and the millions of needless deaths.

Once again, Robby wondered why in the world they hadn't learned more of the facts regarding this war and the treatment of the prisoners. Here he was only a year or so before high school and he'd had his first education regarding the Japanese and their inhumane actions right here in this musty, dusty old attic in Ashland.

His great-grandfather's musings, as put in various notes he discovered, gave him a chance to learn more of someone he'd never had a chance to meet. Even if the clippings had been less graphic he'd have been riveted to this look at his great-grandfather. It was a vivid link to the past he hadn't lived.

He was particularly interested in his great-grandfather's almost anonymous notes on these terrible happenings. As if he hadn't been one of the victims at all, but merely one who was observing from afar the cruel treatment to which his friends and fellow soldiers and medical men were subjected.

The good doctor had suffered along with the many others and had survived. Robinson had always had an extraordinarily strong and compelling natural compassion for other living beings. Of course, his medical training instilled that. But for him it was an easy lesson to absorb. Despite his many personal problems, never did he permit his personal concern to outweigh that generated by the thousands of suffering men he encountered.

His personal problems always ran a poor second to the needs of others.

Young Robby had no way to know when his great-grandfather could relax at night with a beer or two, that some people could talk to him and learn his deeply-felt concern for others was a motivation carried deeply within him. That was the same source for his constant flow of energy which kept him active, standing his usual upright, flag pole straight self, no matter the number of men waiting or their degree of privation.

His black hair had suffered. It was almost totally gray. Otherwise, even at the height of traffic at the Manila rehab, he looked almost as he had after his internship in Portland.

It didn't take Robby long to realize all of his great-grandfather's notes referred to what the Japs were doing or had done to someone else. It never referred to anything that happened to his great-grandfather.

"It must be 'cuz he's a doctor," he mused, subconsciously referring to him in the present tense, "and all's he's thinking about is the soldiers. He probably just figures he's one of the lucky ones who got out alive from where-ever.

"Hey dude," he said aloud, "If that's lucky I think I'll settle for something else."

He cast aside thoughts of luck as he continued his rummaging through the papers. A new name reference popped up. It was Sergi Merrando.

Sergi Merrando was one of the lucky ones. At least in young Robby's view it was lucky. But as he read more, he reconsidered.

When the Japanese had over-run the Philippines most of his fellow Filipinos fell in the face of the overwhelming forces of the Japanese. Merrando hadn't. What young Robby was slowly learning, survivors suffered cruelty as only the Japanese could devise and deliver to the helpless. So was it lucky?

Merrando suffered first at Cabanatuan and subsequently at Bilibad, where he was dumped, an almost lifeless hulk after the infamous Batangas work detail. But he did manage to survive the war, the imprisonment, and after it was finally over he passed through the Manila rehab setup where Dr. Robinson stood in charge. His memory of the killings and torturing in Cabanatuan and the death-work in the Batangas remained vigorous and strong. It would forever.

Now, these many years later, Dr. Robinson's great-grandson looked over material Merrando had sent along.

Young Robby's rest from reading of the horrors had been brief. He soon was drawn back by the strong magnet represented by the fading type of the newspaper clippings from around the world.

As he shuffled through the collection, another piece from the Manila Herald came to the top. It was dated March 17, 1947 and had the now-expected notation from his great-grandfather, this one crediting Sergi Merrando for sending the clipping from the Philippines.

He read:

Manila, March 17 — Word has been received here of the death of Maori Mori, a onetime Manila businessman who was a captain with the Jap forces in World War II and was in command of the notorious prison camp at Cabanatuan.

Captain Mori was the camp commander and was a Jap reserve officer, although his place of residence was Manila and he owned a bicycle shop here before the war. He was a known spy for the Emperor.

Capt. Mori's death was apparently natural although the police said his medical records indicated he'd had no health problems. They have initiated an investigation.

Capt. Mori's death won't be mourned by any of the five to seven thousand men who were imprisoned at Cabanatuan Prison Camp #1, as it was known. Even though he turned over command of the camp to members of his staff, there was never any indication he wasn't totally in charge of the camp. The suffering prisoners there always held him responsible for the atrocities his guards perpetrated on the helpless inmates. The few who survived his inhumane treatment never forgave the beast. Those who knew of him when he was in Manila said they suspected, without any evidence, that he was working for the Imperial Government of Japan. Authorities confirm his status.

"He was kept under close scrutiny in the years before the war began," one official said, asking his name not be made public. "He was the same as many Japanese here in Manila, with a front of some business or another and actually obtaining information for the Japanese military regarding size of the forces here and places they considered weak points in the perimeter of the defense of the Philippines.

"Where-ever there were Japanese before the war, you can be assured there was an intensive spy ring in operation," the spokesman concluded.

Even young Robby had heard of all the talk in the government concerning Japanese in America, mostly on the West coast where so many citizens of Japanese ancestry lived. Most of this talk was continued in school and he believed the camps to which these citizens were sent were camps of punishment.

Now he wasn't certain. Were some of these people spies for the Emperor's warring followers? He'd also heard of the property stolen from these people when they were absent. But the Federal Government took tax money to compensate each and every person of Japanese descent who had been detained in a camp.

He'd heard this discussed many times by his parents. His father frequently quoted one of his favorite newspaper columnists. From San Francisco. A man named Herb Caen. In particular, young Robby recalled his father talking of an interview note by Caen, in which he asked a man who'd been compensated, a Mr. George Ito, if he thought the compensation was fair.

Mr. Ito said "No".

When asked why he didn't think the compensation was fair he replied, "Because I was a spy."

Perplexed, young Robby asked himself, "Like what do you believe?"

Robby's latest reverie was interrupted by a shout from his father, down on the main floor.

"How ya' doin' up there, Robby?"

Once again Robby's father's strong voice spiraled up the makeshift, fold-down stairway to the attic. "You about ready to get outta here for a while? Get something to eat?"

Young Robby had just found a fresh clipping. There was an ample supply. But this one looked better than any of them.

"Yeah. In a minute Dad. I'm puttin' together some stuff right now. Be right down. Okay?"

"Sure. I'll be down on the front porch. Gotta get outta here for a while. It's a big house but it's closing in."

Young Robby couldn't relate to that statement. He'd have to drag himself away from some of the material he was digesting. Such as the one he'd now picked up.

From the Death March.

It was from the Manila Herald and related a story concerning the death of a guard on the Death March. Ryoichi Azami was the name. Robby's greatgrandfather quite obviously valued this clipping more than others. Had it glued to a heavier backing whereas the others had pretty much survived on their own.

"Wonder why he's got this one glued to the cardboard, or whatever?" mused Robby. "Kinda like the one about that one who lost his balls. That one was on a heavier piece of paper too."

First of all he had to read the preface. Same as all the others, the good Doctor had penned a note of reminder to himself.

This one read, 'My good friend Floyd Bertoni sent this to me from Brooklyn. Haven't the slightest idea how he came by it. I doubt if they have home delivery of the Manila Herald in Brooklyn. Bertoni's a good man.'

Manila, March 28 — Police discovered the badly burned body of a man under a huge pile of garbage at the rear of the huge garbage dump at its Southeast Manila site yesterday.

Initially, they were unable to make an identification. Ultimately, they determined the dead man's name was Ryoichi Azami.

They reached this conclusion by examination of Bilibad prison records. These matched his ID tags, somehow sheltered from the burning. He had been a guard at the prison during the years of occupation by the Japanese. His previous service with the Emperor of Japan's forces included guard duty on the Bataan Death March.

Following that assignment he was transferred to fulltime duty at Bilibad.

After the Japs surrendered he was imprisoned at Bilibad.

The director of the prison, Yoshio Morobita, was found dead earlier this year, but the police haven't linked the two deaths, although admitting it was a possibility.

"It would be logical to assume his death was the work of someone trying to gain vengeance for the many prisoners he killed during the war years," the police spokesman readily admitted. "There won't be any mourners in Manila," he added.

Any records which might identify members of the Death March who are living in the Manila area are non-existent. Police have closed the case. They have stated they have no intention to pursue any further investigation into the death.

Once again Young Robby leaned back and rested for a moment, wondering how and why this man, so heavily involved with the Japanese peddlers of pain and death during the years of occupation, had come to his burning death so many years later. According to the clipping this happened in 1947.

The man was an active member of the Japanese occupation forces in 1942 and 1943. Robby wondered, as he tried to get his 12 year old mind to concentrate on this and other material he'd read, why the man would be a target four or five years later?

Many questions arose from the collection of clippings he had depleted. Robby couldn't readily see any other clippings. He was thankful. He'd had enough of them for one day.

He made his way down the stairway, knowing he'd done mighty little cleaning up although he'd had a great day of entertainment so far. Electronic games or television couldn't touch the stuff he'd been reading.

As he told his father a short time later, it was all real.

"It'd hafta be real wouldn't it? They wouldn't have all those stories in the papers if they hadn't been really happening."

He wasn't really interested in an answer. He was already convinced. His father could see that.

"Okay Robby, what do you want to do? Get something to eat? Whatever." His son's answer surprised him.

"I'm not really hungry right now. I'd like to go see Emigrant Lake. You know where that is?"

Robby the Third glanced at him as if to make certain he was hearing correctly. Then he tried to figure out where it was. He wasn't about to attempt to understand why his son suddenly wanted to go see it. Much less how he even knew about it. "It's not exactly a crucial subject of concern for teachers I wouldn't think," he quickly concluded under his breath.

To young Robby he said, "Well, it's a few miles south of town. Actually it's a manmade lake. It's a containment for irrigation water. Stores it up in the winter and then the farmers and orchardists use it as they need it in the summer. Usually all dried out in the summer. Emigrant Dam holds up the water flow.

"At least that's the way it used to be. No tellin' what it's like out there now. Tell me. How'd you hear about it? Why would you want to go out there?"

"That's where they found the body. In a little shack at Emigrant Lake."

"Wait a minute," his astounded father said, unable to mask his amazement. "Wait just a blamed minute. What body are we talking about? What shack? What's this all about?"

"Well dad, in the newspaper clippings I was reading up in the attic, they were talking about finding this body out at Emigrant Lake. Some Japanese doctor. He'd done some experiments in China a long time ago. Even before the war great-grandpa was in.

Anyway, a long time ago, they found the body of this Japanese doctor out there and I'd just kinda like to go out there and see it. See what it looks like out there. That's all," his explanation dwinded away.

"That's all?" echoed his father. "That's all. I guess that'd be all. That'd be enough. I tell you Robby, I'm still not too sure what this is all about but let's take a run out there anyway. Maybe we can grab a sandwich or something along the way or maybe on the way back."

He suddenly felt the need for some fresh air. Maybe a view of Emigrant Lake from the high walls of the bowl where it was located would go pretty good right now.

So out to Emigrant Lake they went.

It was the time of year when the Lake itself was nothing more than some shallow water lying in large puddles over the bottom of the lake. As a result the little shack which had always been in the center of the lake was above water and quite visible.

That was good enough for young Robby.

"That's it. That's it. There's the shack where the body was found. Just like the story said."

"What story?" asked his perplexed father. "What are you talking about?"

"Like I was telling you, great-grandpa had this story cut out of a newspaper which he'd saved. It was there in the papers I was trying to get straightened out. It told about the body of a man they found out here in that little shack, or least a little shack like that out in the middle of Emigrant Lake," he began as his father broke in with, "Who found it? Body of who?"

"So wait. That's what I'm telling you. The police found the body. They figured out it was a Japanese doctor who'd been involved in some terrible stuff over in China years and years ago. How that body got down here nobody seemed to know. But that's where they found it."

Seeing the disbelief on his father's face Young Robby said, "I'll show you the clipping when we go back to the house. It's right there."

"Oh I believe you, all right," reassured his father, thinking to himself that even his imaginative son would have trouble dreaming up such a scenario.

They drove back to the house more or less in silence, almost forgetting completely about any food. Almost but not completely.

They stopped at a drive-in for a couple of hamburgers. Young Robby devoured his but his mind was still back in the attic. He had a few clippings to go. They seemed to get more interesting as his day went along.

He scampered up the stairs as soon as they reached the house.

He discovered quite a hefty pile of material on his next dip into the past of his great-grandfather. It concerned a person young Robby could relate to from a standpoint of age, if not experiences.

It was the story of a young Chinese boy who was caught up in the horrors of the Jap-inflicted terror in Manchuria, the young boy's home. Chiang Luang was his name and some of the facts young Robby learned from this material made him acutely aware of the soft, easy day-to-day life he enjoyed.

His great-grandfather had made numerous notes concerning Luang, who was about the same age as young Robby.

But when Chiang Luang was a little younger than Robby the Fourth, life wasn't the breeze it had been for young Robinson.

It was 1936 and Luang was growing up in Manchuria.

The Japanese had taken over Manchuria the same way ravaging locusts sweep over a lush field of greenery. When the locusts leave nothing is left behind. That's what the Japanese did. They left nothing behind.

Luang, and his age was still in single digits when the Japs first swept into Harbin, Manchuria, managed to hide from the Jap soldiers. Not so his poor father. Chiang saw his father taken prisoner. But he wasn't a prisoner for long. He was taken into an open enclosure, forced to his knees and his hands were bound securely to his legs so he was tied in a kneeling position.

Then one of the Emperor's finest took a wide and vicious swing with his sword, chopping off Luang senior's head.

Chiang watched as his father's body contorted in the throes of violent death. He watched, still helpless to do anything except weep silently and dazedly. He watched his father's body used for bayonet practice by the Jap soldiers.

Miraculously, Chiang fled Harbin undetected. Not before he'd seen both his younger sister and his mother raped, and along with all of the other females of the community, converted into sexual toys and playthings for the Jap thugs in uniform of the Emperor.

Again, all Chiang could hope for was an early death for both his sister and his mother. It came but only after many months of terrible torture.

Chiang matured quickly. He had witnessed the unbelievably horrid deaths of his family and now had an excellent observer's perch to watch the infamous medical experimental station at work.

It was the new depth in depravity ordered by Emperor Hirohito himself under the guise of medical experiments.

But each day was a challenge to Chiang. A challenge to escape detection which he knew would lead to his inclusion in what later was called Unit 731. At the time it was operated by the Japanese under the name of Water Supply and Prophylaxis Administration of the Kwangtung Army and the Kimura Detachment. Its name wasn't changed until 1941.

To Chiang the name meant nothing. To him and all the Chinese who huddled in fear it was the House of Death. The thousands of subjects captured by the Japs were called Marutas, meaning logs of wood. They were taken to Unit 731 and never emerged alive.

He knew it meant no difference to the Japs whether the logs of wood were military prisoners or civilians. Just Marutas to them. Just logs. Or monkeys.

Fiercely-cold temperatures formed an enemy he couldn't hide from that first winter he was on the loose. Occasionally, he'd find shelter in the houses of Chinese he knew. He was never at ease in those homes because the Japs could strike at any moment and take all of them off into the killing place. Or perhaps some soldiers of the Emperor's might stop by for some 'fun' and they'd all be dead.

Most of the time he found refuge in caves, scrounging for food either in daylight or at night. It was from his various vantage points he was able to observe the Japanese and their experiments. When the weather was subzero he watched them place their Marutas out in the open, waiting until they froze to death.

Then they would gather their Marutas, or logs, or monkeys, bring them into Unit 731 where they operated on them, cutting them up to observe the effects of the cold weather on the human body.

Effects other than the obvious one of death.

But he did survive. And he grew strong as he learned. He learned the names of the prime guilty in this wide-spread scene of murder and scientific killing. He particularly wanted the names of the men who were in charge of these killings.

That was easy. Everyone knew the name of the doctor who was in charge of the entire operation. It had been in the papers because Emperor Hirohito had personally appointed Shiro Kimura to the director's post with Dr. Ryoichi Naito named as his assistant. This was in all the records. Chiang, who had quickly acquired a passable knowledge of Japanese writing and dialogue, was able to pick up that and much other information as he managed to avoid capture.

But his memories of what the Japs had done to his parents and his sister would never leave his mind, no matter what else he witnessed and heard in Unit 731's living experiments.

He knew the name of Kimura. His desire to meet this man and extract from him the payment due for his family's death permitted him to survive all of the rigors of hiding from the Japs for many years in Manchuria.

Later on, Luang was able to relate to others needed information because he heard the guards talking. Information regarding a plan for germ warfare which Dr. Kimura was developing. It had reached a point of perfection. San Diego, in America, was the target for the first attack. The plan was simple. A submarine would carry millions of bubonic plague-infected fleas to the United States coast. These disease laden fleas would go aloft over San Diego on small collapsible aircraft from the now-surfaced subs. When the aircraft reached its target, the heart of San Diego, it would collapse, crashing and releasing millions of the disease-carrying fleas on an unsuspecting city and naval base.

The plan was perfected. The date was set. September 22, 1945.

Only the Air Force's bombing of Japan and the surrender saved San Diego from this frightening and fatal fate. When the Enola Gay and Bock's Car struck the homeland, it put an end to the war.

But until America brought the war to the Japs, as it had with its bombings from the air over Germany, young Luang was forced to hide.

Regardless of his suffering, the name of Kimura never left Luang's mind.

As the war drew to a close, and peace was negotiated, Luang was mystified by what he heard of the peace treaty.

"The Emperor not held as a criminal. A war criminal," he exclaimed in his native tongue to a friend as they looked at a news report.

"How can that be? Everything we have tells us he put this all together. His generals and admirals just did what he said.

"Germany needed to have this General MacArthur at their trials when the war was over. Not so many would have been executed."

The usually placid Luang was incensed with the soft treatment.

"Here they establish a hospital for killings. Germany later copies it to build its own. And the two men who started it and operated it, killing all these people, and the Emperor, who ordered it started, receive no punishment."

And he was right.

Kimura and Naito were both granted amnesty by MacArthur. He exchanged their lives for the information they had gleaned by taking the lives of thousands of innocents during the operation of the Emperor's House of Horrors in Manchuria.

When Luang read of this full pardon, he was livid with rage. "Some day, Dr. Kimura, we will meet. I not forget you."

Now the new year of 1946 was nearing and Luang was in good hands in Manila, under the remote but still watchful eye of Dr. Robinson. Luang wasn't quartered at the rehab center but a good friend of Robinson's arranged lodging and watched over the Chinese youngster.

Luang had one objective. That was to get to Tokyo and find Dr. Kimura.

Again, the good doctor urged patience. He did understand the boy's urgent need to reach Tokyo. That was apparent. He quietly said, "It will come with time. I'll help you get there."

Robinson was thinking of some plan by which the young boy could pursue the bad doctor. Rumors of the gross activities at Unit 731 had been heard by Robinson. Until young Luang came along he had no eyewitness account. He had long since given up listening to reports from the peace conferences. For whatever reason, the Americans had definitely assumed the role of the losing side in the peace treaty negotiations on this side of the ocean.

Perhaps fortunately for Robinson's peace of mind, he had other matters far more pressing.

One of them concerned his friend Floyd Bertoni, the loquacious Brooklynite. He had come to him earlier in the week, almost speechless, a condition which would never completely corral Bertoni.

"I spotted the bastard, Doc. Bigger'n hell. Right here in Manila. It's heaven-sent. Right here."

Robinson, mystified as usual when trying to decode Bertoni's mad rantings, managed to ask, "Who? Who was it you spotted?"

"Dat piece a crap what boined those people. He's here.

"Somebody's doin' good for Bertoni, Doc. Served 'im right up." Finally it dawned on Robinson. He grinned widely, with a serious glint in his eyes which conflicted with the grin. But he knew he'd figured Bertoni's jibberish correctly. After checking his weathered notebook in his desk for some details, he came to the name of the man he was sure Bertoni had located. He tested it. "You found Mr. Ryoichi Azami. The servant of the emperor who burned those two people on the March." He cringed as he said it.

"That's right Doc. I can hardly believe it. He's here and he's all mine."

This is when the doctor in Robinson took over and he counseled Bertoni to take great care and approach this cautiously. "Don't do anything to him right now. Take your time. Watch him. Don't, and I repeat, don't, touch him under any circumstances. Find out where he's living. Try to get his schedule if he has a regular one. But don't do anything to him right now. He won't be leaving and if he does you'll be the first to know because you'll be watching him. Then you can take some action."

Bertoni was subdued only slightly. "Why don't we waste the sonofabitch right now? Why wait?" He pressed Robinson to give him the signal to go.

But it wasn't forthcoming. Bertoni finally calmed down, convinced Robinson wouldn't let him down. Besides, he told himself, how could Robinson louse up the deal. He, Bertoni, would have the guy scoped out all the way. There's no way Robinson could louse it up even if he wanted to.

So he went along with it.

Robinson went back to his more pressing problem. That of getting young Luang to Tokyo. He had already coached Luang in some of the details of his project but he knew the solution to the remaining problem rested with the transportation group. They owed him favors big time and constantly sought ways to repay him.

He'd take care of that easily enough. After that arrangement was made Luang was in good hands for his entire project.

Now he had a moment to think of himself and his thoughts turned to Lenora, her murder and the matter of closing this issue in his own mind. It wasn't a new sensation for Robinson. Whenever he wasn't racing to a new project, her fate and her murderer dominated his thoughts.

Yoshio Morobita, the killer, was still in Manila. Was held in his old prison, Bilibad. He was under heavy guard. Robinson had seen to that. He wanted him where he could locate him in a hurry. It couldn't get much closer than that.

Meantime, he had the two Englishmen to work with. He looked at his notes. Ian Greene didn't appear to harbor any mental problems and both were gaining strength daily. But George Hartley was still having mental convulsions. He still remembered vividly the crucifixion he'd witnessed. Here he'd underlined a notation: <u>Hartley has a hatred, bordering on the insane, for that guard named Moditake</u>. Mosanori Moditake. That was the creature.

Robinson had used a few of his many contacts to establish the fact that Moditake had been returned to Manila from Borneo and somehow Hartley had discovered that fact. Robinson knew Hartley had to locate Moditake but cautioned him,

"George, you've simply got to erase the thoughts of that butt from your mind. When you're able to close with that you'll start feeling better. That's when you'll be able to get square with the world again."

Robinson realized his preachments to Hartley and to some of the others who came to his rehab unit dazed and bewildered and their minds full of the devils who had made them that way, were words that he should be directing to himself.

Until he could come to grips with the dreaded facts of Lenora's death, he'd have a difficult time returning to a normal life.

"Normal life," he choked out after Hartley had left and he was alone. "What the hell's a normal life? Have I ever had one? I wonder."

It was after his meeting with Hartley he came to a full stop in an effort to establish what would constitute full and total closure of any residual thoughts for any of them who'd undergone all this mistreatment by the Japs.

He thought he knew the solution but it was too ugly to consider. He forced it from his mind. It was repugnant even in this society, depraved as it had become during the years the Japanese had been rampaging, unchecked.

He forced himself to consider avenging the unjustified, and who knows how horrible, death of Lenora. No question that vengeance caused him much anguish even to contemplate. But in his heart he knew that in this case, an eye for an eye was the only answer. Call it vengeance or anything else. It was necessary.

Repugnant. That's the word which Robinson used as he mulled the vengeance which was now so strong in his mind. He knew vengeance wasn't the answer. Or did he?

Revenge certainly didn't bother any of the others, non-medical men but men who had come under his care. And Robinson could understand that. All had been mercilessly mistreated by the Japanese when they were on top. They had seen other innocent humans by the millions tortured, starved and murdered. And these were people not in uniform but merely innocent bystanders to the scenes which Emperor Hirohito had created.

And the supreme insult. They had seen their own Allied leaders refuse to send the cause of it all, Hirohito, to his death. None of the people who had been on the receiving end of Hirohito's planning and the atrocities committed by his slavelike followers, accepted or agreed with the delicate, almost deferential treatment of the detestable person, the Emperor.

Particularly, they couldn't rationalize, much less accept, the fact that Allied leaders pressed for the deaths of the people in Germany responsible for the deaths of Jews but were content to let the dominant person in the far greater slaughter of millions more people in the Far East go unpunished.

There was no mistaking the mood in Manila. Or all of the Philippines, for that matter. Robinson knew from his pre-war time in Manila there was intense hatred for the Japanese. The Filipinos would never trust them, knowing most of them were spies for the emperor's devious goals.

When Robinson first arrived in pre-war Manila he had met several Filipinos, and at least two of these were also acquainted with Lenora Campos, and her family.

In his post-war life in Manila, at the rehab clinic, he had become almost immune to any shocks or surprises. But he was a little of each, surprised and shocked, when the two men who had known Lenora came to his center for medical attention.

As they had told him earlier when they first encountered him after each had escaped from the Japanese, the sins of the Japanese were so many that punishment would almost necessitate sinking all of the home islands into the water.

Of course, they had recognized him immediately. One was Sergi Merrando and the other Ramon Cangleonn. They repeated their sorrow at the fate of Lenora.

They also repeated many times their desire to wreak vengeance on any and all Japanese they encountered, now and in the future.

Robinson attempted to dissuade them of this wholesale hatred, reminding them that for the present the dominant and warlike attitude of Japan was held in check. Whether it would be held stifled forever was another matter, Robinson knew, but he was attempting to persuade these two young Filipinos, intent on gaining revenge, that there were wiser courses of action than the almost wholesale attacks they seemed to advocate.

He talked to them at length, attempting to learn of their plans, if any.

They spoke English relatively well and communication with them wasn't nearly as difficult as it was, for example, with Chiang Luang.

"I'm going to stay in the Army," announced Merrando. "I think it will need some men who have seen some of the work of these creatures. Just because the war is over now is no reason to believe the enemies will not still be out there, waiting and planning to rise again."

Robinson shook his head sadly, unable to disagree.

It would take years, decades and perhaps centuries to heal the wounds opened by Hirohito's hordes which swept over the Far East. Maybe it would never happen. If the proper education was offered in all countries regarding the background of this war and full revelation of what had taken place there, he believed persons responsible for all of these atrocities would be punished, starting at the top.

Both Cangleonn and Merrando shook their heads emphatically when the talk turned to any acknowledgment of guilt by the Japanese. Robinson got the picture. The pair didn't believe there'd ever be an admission of guilt by the Japanese. Nor did they believe the Japanese would ever be punished by the western world.

Again, Robinson could only hope they were wrong and attempted to explain to them he agreed with them. Sadly so, but he did agree with them. He asked himself. Those civilians who were worked to death. Would their relatives be paid by the Japanese for those years of forced labor under gruesome conditions and little if any food? And immediate beheading or worse for those who faltered? And he answered his question easily and quickly. "It won't happen."

He tried to explain as he said, "More and more I'm becoming convinced that after all this cruelty toward mankind, the Japanese of the future will never know the truth. Not from their own government and not from my government or your government. Individual action must replace it, so that individual peace can be attained."

That was as close to telling them he believed individual reprisals must take place if some individuals who suffered lasting mental injury will find peace again.

He didn't want to state his position more strongly. He avoided telling them to find a specific Japanese and satisfy their own problems with that individual.

"Don't rely on the government. The peace treaty is laughable," he declared. "And the surrender now seems to be nothing more than MacArthur and Hirohito deciding what works best for each of them and leaving it at that.

"Doesn't anyone remind MacArthur that Hirohito and his predecessors long ago told their people they were superior to all others in the world. That the Japanese were supreme and when they came to fight they must be supreme or they were disloyal and didn't deserve to live.

"As you people know, the Japanese look upon Hirohito, the Emperor as more of a God than a ruler. If he gave an order, it was followed without any question.

"How else would they have developed the certain death plans for the Kamikaze pilots? No, when MacArthur failed to insist that the Emperor must stand trial for his war crimes, the surrender failed. In effect, the entire war effort failed. It amounted to a treacherous conclusion to a war that was thrust upon millions of people. Treachery to millions of people who are dead because they were fighting to suppress the forces of evil which came from the islands of Japan. And from the evil mind of Emperor Hirohito.

The two Filipinos had silently listened to Robinson. They struggled at times to understand what he said, nevertheless comprehended sufficiently. They made it quite clear they agreed with what he was saying.

"Yes, yes," they said almost in unison, nodding their heads as they looked at Robinson. They'd never heard him carry on to such an extent before.

He'd never let himself go in this manner before. He also was surprised at himself. His long speech was quite out of character for him. But he believed every word he'd uttered. Nothing had happened thus far since the war concluded to contradict what he said.

But for now, he wanted to help all of his friends and comrades here, and all of the others who came to him. Then he wanted to see to his own psychological wounds and get on with his own life. He knew his future life was many miles from here and he was getting ready to travel.

His ample supply of unfinished professional business in Manila obscured Dr. Robinson's nagging urge to get back to America. His wife was gone, yes. But his son was still there.

Despite the fine care the boy had received all these years, Robinson believed his father was needed.

Certainly, Dr. Robby had one strong weapon in his struggle to forget the death of his wife and the subsequent death of an adored woman here in Manila at the hands of the Japs. The thousands of deaths he had witnessed, personally, all due to the brutality of Hirohito's followers, created a mental torment of inescapable persistence.

Perhaps more crucial, and perhaps his prime weapon, was his schedule.

It was non-stop. Non-stop caring for victims of the years of torture. Trying to help them find a path to return to mental stability. They needed all the psychological help they could receive, once they'd been nursed past their wounds, disease and malnutrition.

Many of Robby's pilgrims from pain suffered from all three.

There were occasional exceptions such as those who had such mental control they wouldn't submit to the pressures their lives of the last several years had inflicted on their minds and bodies. Of course, Robinson had great empathy for those unable to force themselves above it all. The occasional or infrequent visitor to his rehab center who was able to walk in, state his name strongly and seek Robby's advice was certainly a moment of welcome relief.

George Hartley was a prime example of this antithesis to the usual. Additionally, he was a man whose manner of speaking took brief but frequent visits to the dialect of his home district. Hartley knew that when he spoke rapidly, with the elements of his

Yorkshire background dominating his speech, unless he was with others who'd been raised in that area of England, those listening might just as well be deaf. There was no way they could understand him.

When he became excited it simply was impossible to fathom his speech. During these speech lapses Robinson quickly learned there was no way to understand the man. Usually Robby could anticipate when Hartley was getting wound up and he'd try any diversion to help him calm down. This was a scheme he hadn't had to rely on too much recently. At first it was a devil of a thing because Hartley simply didn't realize when he'd made the transition from English to Yorkshire. And it was a big difference. The patient Robinson worked with him.

"Knock me back when I do that," Hartley said one day after he'd gone into his Yorkshire manner of speaking. The truth was, Robinson rather enjoyed it when Hartley started one of his spiels. Even if he couldn't comprehend all of it. He was aware Hartley tried to know when his audience was being blocked out if he reverted to his more natural jargon.

Robinson knew Hartley had far more mental problems than the average returnee from the wars, and spent considerable time attempting to stabilize him mentally. He wasn't a psychiatrist but had acquired many of the skills needed in that field as he worked with the men heavily scarred by sights of the inhumane activities of the Japs. He knew that Hartley suffered more emotional tearing than any of the other men who had come to his rehab center. Watching a crucifixion and a piece by piece, slice by slice murder. He shivered as he created a mental image of this display.

Robinson couldn't say whether his rudimentary therapy or merely the passage of time was responsible but Hartley had learned to control his emotions somewhat, certainly better than when he first was returned from Burma to Manila. Robinson was now better able to comprehend the man's tale, as he related what had taken place since the fall of Singapore and his shipment, along with thousands of other slave workers, to what soon became known as the Death Railway.

"They had us when Singapore was captured," Hartley had told him remorsefully. "Along with hundreds of thousands of other prisoners throughout Malaya, Java and Sumatra. What better source of manpower? The Japanese military couldn't handle all those prisoners so it was logical to them to grab them all and put them to work on the railway. Until they died.

"That's what they did."

The cruel Japs viewed the prisoners simply as a source of 24 hour a day workers who complied until they died. When the combination of long hours, frequent beatings, disease, injuries and less than starvation rations took its toll, the Japs just sent out for more. When Hartley first arrived for servitude he estimated the Japs had 60,000 prisoners working on the railway.

He also figured by simply rounding up the local natives they had another 300,000 available.

Hartley tried to enlighten Robinson on what life was in the area to help explain why the death toll was so extreme for the poor devils enslaved there. He desperately attempted to describe the viciousness of the elements faced by the prisoners and how that too worked against them.

"Maybe you know what the monsoons in that country can do. In the spring of 1943 the monsoons broke and a lot of what the slave laborers had done before was wiped out. Bridges were gone. Where we'd put in railbeds there were now streams of water. And water was everywhere. In huge pools. All stagnant. Now all this brought on new outbreaks of sickness."

Robby interrupted to ask, "Did you have medical help there? Were there any doctors?"

"Nowk," came back an increasingly tense Hartley, lapsing into his Yorkshire dialect as he thought about it. Seeing Robinson frown as he sought to understand, he returned to a more coherent style. "No bloomin' doctors. No medical help. And the guards? Those blokes were the worst of all. Jab you with the bayonet as look at you. And no food. Sickness. Working more than 16 hours a day in the jungle and the endless marching into the jungle to the building locations. That wiped out thousands of men. It was over one hundred fifty miles into the jungle, you know. That was all on forced march, too.

"On those marches the Japanese guards there were even worse. They flatly said they'd build the bloomin' railway on the bones of the prisoners. That's sure what they did.

"Routine beatings for no reason with whatever tools they had at hand. Pick handles. Chunks of bamboo staves. Swords. Made no difference. The guards didn't care. Prisoners who couldn't move on, or were corpses, were left by the wayside for the prisoners still alive to clean up. We did this after the bastards let us off the work force each day."

Robinson, listening to his story, thought it amazing Hartley was as physically fit as he was. He also marveled at the fact he had as many of his mental facilities functioning as he did. He'd seen many men crumble under far less grueling conditions.

Hartley went on.

"The bloody railway finished late 1943. More'n 100,000 prisoners. Mostly native slaves, had died under the control of those bastardly Japs. Doctor," and he leaned forward to look intensely at Robinson, "they had 400 men's bodies for every 250 miles of railway."

Robinson privately thought, as he listened, that many of the deaths weren't directly caused by the murderous actions of the Japs. Hartley conceded that without prompting or questioning. During his recital he granted all of the deaths weren't caused by the beatings, whippings and bayoneting.

As a result of the living squalor, other factors killed many.

Parasitic diseases, mosquitoes, no food. All of it shared in the death toll of the humans enslaved by the Japanese.

Finally Hartley was getting to the part of the story Robinson really wanted to hear. Not because of the gruesome content of the true relation but simply because he thought it would be of assistance to Hartley to relate it. Just to tell someone of it. To unload.

So Hartley continued, in better control of his emotions and thus easier to understand.

"We'd later been taken to Sandakan and put to work building an airfield for the devils in that area. That's when I saw the most horrible sight I've ever witnessed.

"The bastardly guard crucified this prisoner. A man named Mosanari Moditake did it. I'll never forget his name. Or the sight."

Hartley's voice dropped from its previous high volume to a mere whisper as he described the crucifixion to Robinson.

Listening to him Robinson could more readily appreciate how deeply this scene had hit the man. No doubt this was the cause of Hartley's mental chaos. Hartley had escaped from the area and unbelievably had been able to survive the rest of the war, finally getting to Tokyo after the war and then here to Manila.

Robinson noted his condition when Hartley had first arrived but had simply written it off as a result of, first, his terrible treatment working on the Death Railway and second, the results of his many months of hiding out and trying to survive after his escape.

As he listened, he tried to place himself in Hartley's position.

It was difficult. For himself, he was carrying the wounds of a needless murder of a loved one and the memory was indelible.

Sure, the man who was victimized hadn't any particular relevance for Hartley but still, they were both captives and both had already gone through all the hell that's possible.

But Hartley had seen this terrible act take place.

The doctor thought he had the right therapy for Hartley. But for now he just listened.

His reluctance to say anything even mildly suggestive to Hartley was fed also by his increasing anxiety to get on with his project. He was increasingly anxious to zero in on Lenora's murderer.

The disposition of that murderer, one Yoshio Morobita, still in prison at Bilibad, was prime. In Robinson's mind nothing on earth took precedence over dealing with the murderer of Lenora Campos.

Robinson made frequent visits to Bilibad. The prisoner, Morobita, knew Robinson was a doctor but was unaware of his relationship to this particular woman he'd killed here. There were far too many.

And Robinson planned his daily trip to blend with the delivery of the prisoners' meager luncheon fare. A prisoner such as Morobita was considered too likely to escape to permit much freedom within the prison so he wasn't permitted to leave the confines of his smelly cell. His food was taken to his cell.

The food at mid-day was a daily soup. It was easy for Robinson to drop a medicinal capsule in it each day. The item imparted little if any flavor to the watery soup but perhaps it enhanced the flavor. His input to the soup bowl taken each day to Morobita carried no life-threatening elements. Just relaxed the human body and it became effective through daily use.

He explained to the supervisor at the prison he was concerned with Morobita's health and that he needed to observe him. "It's not something I want to alarm him about but when I saw him enter the prison it seemed to me he manifested some signs of health problems. That's why I want to keep an eye on him. From afar."

That empty explanation seemed to satisfy the supervisor. He was so mystified that any doctor would have concerns regarding this notorious butcher's health that he didn't consider anything else. The supervisor told the guards, "It's all right for the doctor to come in anytime he wants to. He just wants to check on a couple of the prisoners." That's how it came out in English, anyway, according to Robby's interpretation and regardless, it worked. And that's all he wanted accomplished.

His 'treatments' were working too. After several weeks of this Robinson informed the supervisor of the prison that, as he suspected, Morobita's ailment had worsened and it appeared it would be necessary to transfer him to the rehab clinic for some immediate and serious treatment.

"I fear the prisoner's condition has steadily worsened and it will be necessary to keep him under closer supervision," he explained, and continued to ask, "Will it be possible to have a guard posted outside the room I'll have prepared for him at the rehab clinic?"

Again, in his native tongue, the supervisor turned to one of his guards to explain the doctor's requests. Robinson was certain the man elaborated to add, 'Let the dirty rotten dog die. Help him along' but he didn't comprehend Tagalog well enough to know for sure.

Regardless, the transfer request was granted and the move was immediate. Morobita was definitely in a dazed condition and the need for a guard probably was non-existent but Robinson wanted to make certain the prisoner wouldn't be visited by anyone other than himself. And the guard would do that.

"Just visit him each morning and see if he is all right," he explained to the guard as best he could, "and I'll check him later to give him whatever treatment he needs."

Again, the guard nodded, and Robinson thought the man echoed his supervisor's attitude as in, "Let the dog die."

But he had the guard inside the room while he gave the prisoner-patient a quick examination. It was mostly for show. Robinson already knew what Morobita was suffering from and he already knew what the treatment would be. It was diabetes and the treatment was insulin. He had predetermined the ailment and treatment.

Of course, the insulin must be taken by injection only and the patient couldn't self-inject the insulin. There were no nurses in the tiny clinic, so that meant Robinson himself would have to inject the patient.

"I hate like hell to do it but I've got to keep giving him some soup. I don't like to waste this good soup on him but I can't stand the smell of that stuff over at Bilibad so I guess I'll have to let him have it."

He told the guard, and also his replacement guard, to help themselves to a bowl from the soup-pot Robinson maintained in the main entryway to the clinic.

They eagerly accepted his invitation. Their rations at Bilibad at the time weren't that much better than what the prisoners were getting. The Japanese had left the Philippines so depleted and in such a sorry condition that Robinson's soup at the clinic was probably as good as any available in the entire city.

Robinson reviewed the passive punishment and so-called justice meted out to the people who had committed these many dastardly crimes right here in Manila. He was convinced he must personally handle Morobita.

"Maybe I'm only trying to rationalize what I know I have to do," Robinson told himself, "but this man doesn't deserve to live. He should die a horrible death, the same deaths he brought to the hundreds and thousands of people here. And he should get no mercy. He's helpless and that's how Lenora was, helpless. And he murdered her without mercy."

Robinson made ready for the deed that night. Fortified mentally after thinking about the criminal in the clinic, and thinking particularly of his beloved Lenora, who was guilty of nothing, Robinson had no qualms regarding his personal mission.

He gave him an injection for diabetes. Enough insulin to make certain he'd never be bothered by diabetes again. The next morning, when the guard inspected the room, he came immediately to Robinson to report Morobita was acting strangely.

Robinson went with him to the room and the two looked at the murderer together.

He put his hand on the guard's shoulder and said, "You're right. He's acting funny. I think he's close to death."

And speaking to Lenora, and many, many other dead Filipinos he added, "Soon we can all rest."

Then he called the motor pool and asked for the vehicle he kept there for use by the clinic, explaining he needed it for overnight clinic operations.

He hauled the inert body of Morobita out the back door of the clinic and shoved it into the back of the vehicle, a panel delivery rig. With his bag beside him, he drove away.

Drove to the city dump. Southeast of the city of Manila. On the far side he dumped Morobita on the ground. As he lay there, near death and half covered already by flying garbage whipped up by the breeze, Robinson took out his scalpel, and concluded his project with the scumbag Morobita, murderer of Lenora.

Robinson skillfully removed the man's penis and testicles and carefully placed the bloody package in the murderer's mouth. The man's breathing soon ceased.

He didn't permit himself even so much as a second to ponder his actions. A doctor. Dedicated to the saving of humanity. Reduced by the years of vicious actions by these specimens to such reprisal. Minor though the reprisal may be, nevertheless, he knew he'd sleep better that night.

Without a backward glance he walked to the rig, threw his bloody surgical gloves on the ground, and drove away in the darkness.

Robinson drove away from the stage where he had disdained his real-life role of a doctor to appear as a hardened, cold-blooded, cold-hearted avenging lover. But it wasn't an act.

At that moment he was a cold-blooded and cold-hearted avenger. It was his secret but that's what he was. He knew it but no-one else would know it. Not from his lips.

Although Robinson occasionally saw Bertoni at the clinic, he didn't relate to him the misfortune which had befallen their old prison boss, Morobita.

"It's my secret. It had to be done. For Lenora's sake and the sake of hundreds of thousands of others, I'm thankful I was able to do it." That's what he told himself and that's what he meant.

Then life went on. But as Robinson ruefully reminded himself, not for everyone and particularly not for Lenora.

In his meetings with the various patients who came through the clinic, Robinson heard a variety of stories which expressed much of the same vengeance-laden attitude which he had carried within himself for so long. Robinson still refused to discuss specifics with any of them. Except for Bertoni.

Bertoni was a different matter than the others.

"Robby, what'll I do. I got this bastard Azami, or whatever, right in my sights at Bilibad. I gotta do it to him soon. I'll be gittin back home pretty soon."

He was almost pleading with Robinson.

"I don't know what to tell you. Your decision is yours and you'll have to figure it out. Bilibad's not difficult to get into. It's another matter getting out again."

When he saw Bertoni's frown, he added quickly, "Floyd, I'm only kidding you. And I shouldn't because I know how serious this is. And it should be."

They sat quietly in the little bar after work hours. As he lifted his mug to take a gulp of the brew he made a decision.

"Tell you what I can do for you Floyd. Don't know whether it will help but I can give you a note to the head man at Bilibad. It will get you in and give you a chance to see Mr. Azami."

"Yeah, yeah Doc. But what the hell good'll that do. Can't waste him there."

Robinson held up a hand. "Just wait. I can include in this note the request that you be given custody of that piece of dung. I'll tell them to put ankle chains on him and that you're going to deliver him to me.

"I'll explain to them the prisoner needs some attention and that I need to have him here at the clinic for an unspecified period of time. I don't know if he'll ever be back. Now how's that sound?"

Bertoni whacked the table with his right hand and raised it toward Robinson to whack hands together. "Great. Dat's how it sounds, Doc. Great, 'cuz he won't be back. That one ain't —, he started until Robinson held up a warning hand, silencing him.

"Again, and I repeat, I don't want to hear about it. Once you get him out of Bilibad, he's your bag. Where he goes and how is strictly your business. Don't get me wrong. I'm not suggesting to you that whatever you're thinking about is either right or wrong. Because I'm not. I just don't want to know anything about it. And you'd better get at that right away. If I remember correctly, you're taking that slow boat next week for San Fran. Right?"

"Dat's it, Babe. Next week. I'll be ready day after tomorrow for dat bastard. Gotta get a coupla things. This is great. Have another brew."

Then he stopped. "I need, ya know, a rig of some kind. Ya got anything?"

"No problem," Robinson responded. "We've got a rig here at the clinic," and he hurriedly added, "Completely safe" as he saw Bertoni's face change to one of doubt. "No one will connect it with anything or anyone."

Bertoni relaxed and enjoyed his beer. Then he wanted to give Robinson some of the detail. But Robby wouldn't hear of it. "Listen, Floyd. You do your thing. One other way I can help you once you make your contact. In one way or another, get your party to take this capsule I'll give you. Break it up and dissolve the powder in a drink. Anything. That'll put the party out until you get to where-ever you're going. To the dump or any place else around Manila. Lasts for about an hour. Okay?"

"Great. I'll get goin' on it right now. That's great Doc."

Once again Robinson took time to consider his present status. This fine, free year of 1946 was rapidly closing and he couldn't see his way out of Manila for at least another year, and although his son was in good hands with his sister, time was running out on him.

At least that's what he thought as he tried to rest between clinic assignments. Also, he couldn't see his way clear to a departure for at least another six months, and probably more likely another year.

"With Bertoni here to shepherd, and the others still around, who's going to look after them if I take off?" he asked of the blank walls around him at the clinic. He was thinking of Hartley, Greene, Cangleonn and Merrando.

He knew there wasn't anyone they could rely on. He had to guide them through what could be some scary periods in their lives but periods that would be crucial to their future well-being.

Meantime, his sister had arranged a postal box for him in Ashland so he wasn't going to miss any mail. They had placed a Hold order on the mail, just in the event some material might arrive before he made it home.

Thus did Robinson reassure himself, although it was reassurance much in the manner of a youngster of old whistling to buoy the courage as he crossed a cemetery.

He didn't need much assurance regarding the present status of one important matter.

That was perhaps the only aspect of Robinson's life which seemed securely in place at the moment. He had openly and willingly accepted responsibility for young Chiang Luang, the much-abused boy. He realized the young man had no refuge from his life's torment. No relief from his tortured memories.

The timing of his meeting with Robinson was indeed fortunate for him. That's because one of the survivors from Robinson's early days of the Death March had shown up at the clinic just about the time Robinson took over close guidance of Luang.

Sam Nicolet was almost a storybook soldier-of-fortune type but with even more of a twist to his persona than that. The man, now approaching 30, had been in the regular Army as an enlistee before Pearl Harbor in 1941, and had gone through the hell inflicted by the Japs. But he had become infected with the desire to get into the medical profession.

It all started when the pair met on the March and he helped Robinson, more or less fulfilling the role of a nurse, in ministering to the needs of the sick, bleeding and dying. That was the majority of the mistreated prisoners on the Death March.

The two of them had blessed little to work with but Nicolet did whatever Robinson asked of him and spent a lot of his time trying to keep the prisoners on their feet during the intolerable times of the March. Both Robinson and Nicolet knew, even if the other prisoners weren't yet aware, that a stumble was an invitation to a beheading or bayonet thrust. It was a certain death warrant, because in addition to the guards leaping to behead the stragglers, a fallen prisoner was an immediate target for passing tanks or Jap army vehicles whose drivers crushed the helpless ones. The ones who didn't have the strength to pop to their feet or crawl out of the way. The Japs watched for the stragglers and so did Sam. He saved a lot of them, by pulling them to their feet ahead of the swords, bayonets or anything else the ruthless devils could use.

Despite the lack of facilities or supplies, Nicolet learned plenty just watching Robinson as he attempted to keep the suffering at a minimum.

When they each survived the March and met years later at the clinic, Robinson was overjoyed. He needed all the help he could muster. And Nicolet, though lacking in knowledge and with zero training in the field of medicine, had sufficient acquired skills to help Robinson give shots, take blood pressure, draw blood for tests and handle the many time-devouring tasks which Robinson frequently had to perform himself.

"Sam, I don't know whether you're serious about entering the field of medicine but you could certainly qualify, with damned little preparatory study, as a registered nurse."

Nicolet looked up at Robinson, listening as the pair relaxed with a beer on one early evening, after a typical horrendously busy day. He looked at his face, thinking the doctor was kidding.

Robinson continued.

"Seriously, with little study, you'd pass any examination to become a registered nurse. Now maybe that's not what you want to do but you've learned so much since you've been helping me here I really would have no qualms in assigning some relatively difficult jobs to you." He added, "I'm really serious. I mean that."

This confidence instilled in Robinson by Nicolet's work enabled the doctor to make a decision of some import rather easily later on.

He needed someone to shepherd young Chiang Luang around Tokyo when he returned to the capital city of Japan. Robinson knew Nicolet had been in Tokyo and knew his way around. He was also smooth enough he could circumvent some of the barriers installed by the Americans who were essentially running the city.

"Yes," Robinson said to Nicolet, "I think you're the man for the job."

"What job? What are you talking about now? That nursing thing? I'm not at all sure that's what I want to get involved in. I'm happy I'm able to help you out here but I, quite frankly, don't have any interest in any of that after we leave here." When Robinson gave him the highlights of the plan he'd devised for Luang, his eyes narrowed and reflected great intensity as he could imagine himself helping this young man avenge the death of his entire family.

Together they shaped the plans for Dr. Kimura, he of the infamous killing clinic of Manchuria.

"First of all, you'll have the help of Gerry Francis to locate him in Tokyo and zero in on him. So that's easy. I'll have plenty of money for you so you'll have a place to stay. We'll try to get you a hop from the field here at Nichols to Tokyo and that shouldn't be much of a problem. I've got the contacts for that.

"Once you get to Tokyo my friend Gerry, with the so-called occupation army there, can take over. A medical man. He'll get you whatever you need although I think I can give you all you need for the job. Some pills that will render a man barely conscious without any ill effects. By the time he's ready to regain consciousness, Francis will be all through."

He added grimly and with great significance, "And he'll be all through too."

Nicolet learned later Francis was a doctor and far beyond. He was mindful of oldtime movie star Douglas Fairbanks. Or perhaps the later Cary Grant. He packed suave into every pore.

He'd missed all the life of the sentenced in Manila, because he was on the staff of MacArthur. Therefore, when MacArthur flew out of Manila in front of the advancing Japanese, Francis was with him.

Nicolet was accustomed to adjusting to the problem of the moment. That's why he'd been a skilled athlete in his younger days in Southern California. He played baseball for Rod Dedeaux at USC and, take away Pearl Harbor, he might have been in the majors.

Nicolet was also a realist and knew the military was full of 'mightabins' so didn't waste time on the past. He was ready to go right away. Now Robinson had to arrange with his old friend back in Southern Oregon for shipping from Tokyo. It would be by boat from Yokohama to San Francisco and then by truck to Southern Oregon. During one of his frequent telephone calls to America to talk to a son he had never seen, the doctor detoured to talk to Bob Booth. "Bob, it's Robinson." The surprised Booth sputtered a moment or two and then Robby was able to continue, "I think it'll be a few months away now, maybe even a year, but I've got that shipment I mentioned to you quite a while ago on the planning board. Send me whatever information I need at this end, or rather, the Tokyo end, to wrap it up. Okay?"

His friend was more than willing to put it all together.

He was also curious as to when the good doctor planned to return home. "What the hell you gonna do out there, Robby? Take up residency? Got any clue yet when you're heading home?"

"I really haven't been able to put a date on it yet. I'd like to move along and get something started again in Medford but there's so much work that needs attention here. So many people in bad shape. I'd feel guilty turning my back on them, so to speak. And Bob, I really appreciate what you're doing. One of these days I'll clue you in as to what it's all about. Thanks again for your help and say hello to everyone. Assuming there's anyone there I still know."

"Don't worry about anything at this end. I'll get a notice from Transasia when it's on board and then we'll track it from either San Fran or Portland, whichever port they use. Good luck and we'll see you soon."

Robinson bid him goodby and wished silently he'd be able to resolve his homeward journey as easily as that.

Then he returned to duties at hand which included some attention to his friends at the transportation section who were arranging a couple of hops for his use. Actually, for the use of Luang and Nicolet.

First he had to brief Nicolet on precisely what his assignment entailed. At least as close to a precise description as Robinson could offer. That's why he thought Nicolet was perfect for the project. He had the savvy, could improvise and still knew that certain hurdles they'd encounter required some careful attention to protocol. Nicolet had done it all and should be able to handle it. As they sat in Robinson's office the doctor apprised him of the details.

"We'll have to lean on Gerry Francis in Tokyo. As I told you, Francis will take care of most problems. He's an old friend and I also have one other man who can take care of the shipping.

"He's got the container and everything's all set. Has to be driven to Yokohama. These people are all old friends. They'll help you with anything you need.

"When Chiang, that's Luang's first name, you know, gets there, with you, of course, you should first go to this man's office, not to Gerry's office. I'll give you the name and address. The less either of you know, or what you remember, the better. But he'll know what I want him to do. Got that?" asked Robinson of the listening Nicolet.

"Sure Doc, it's easy so far."

"Well, the next part might be tougher. You'll have to contact this man and his name's on the card. You memorize it and when you get to Tokyo, that's the key man for you to find."

Nicolet seemed to rise in his chair, his face reflecting the astonishment he felt that he, or anyone could be expected to ferret out this one individual within the gigantic population of post-surrender Tokyo. Robinson raised his hands.

"No, no. Sounds crazy. But he's a member, or has been a member, of MacArthur's staff. He understands our mission and is in agreement with it. He'll locate the target for us and get him to the doctor, whose card you have."

"Doc," Nicolet couldn't hold himself in check any longer, "You say this guy understands OUR mission. Whadya mean? OUR mission? I don't know the mission myself. So far it's get the kid to Tokyo, meet this doctor friend of yours on MacArthur's staff. So what is our mission?"

"I'll get to that Sam. Try to be patient. This is quite involved."

Nicolet nodded his head vigorously, up and down. "You bet. Involved and then some. So go ahead. I'll listen and talk when you're through. I just don't wanna louse up this thing. Whatever it is."

"You'll do fine, Sam. Hold on here and listen a little longer. I think you'll find it works out nicely. And you're a good fit for the job."

Then he continued.

"So far you've met the doctor. He's the medical advisor on MacArthur's staff. Now he's the key guy because he knows what to do. He knows what our objective is. He also knows the transportation situation."

Nicolet couldn't restrain himself. "Hell, if he even knows who the target is, he's way ahead of me." Then he held up his hands as an apologetic gesture and said, "Go ahead Doc. Sorry."

"No problem. I understand. So, you've made that crucial contact and Gerry will put you with another man, who's in transportation. He'll be on the plane with you and also will have quarters for you in Tokyo. They've already been arranged. Then he'll take you to the dock where special transportation equipment is waiting for you and your target.

"You with me so far, Sam?"

"I think so. Mostly it's a matter of meeting these people and then they guide me to where-ever we're supposed to go. That's about it as I see it."

"Yes, that's about it. If everything goes together as it should, it'll be a piece of cake. But now comes the tricky part of it all."

Nicolet was poised and strained to hear what in hell could be more tricky than what he'd heard. But Robinson was interrupted by an aide.

"Doctor, that Hartley fellow is having some problems. Wants to talk to you right away. Can you break away?"

"Yes, I'll come right away," said Robinson, and turning to Nicolet said, "We can use the break anyway. Let's meet for dinner and I'll finish it up. Hartley's the fellow from England who's had some trouble adjusting. Okay?"

"Sure Doc. I've got plenty to think about anyway. I'll see you a little later."

They left Robinson's office. He went to check out Hartley.

Nicolet went to have a beer and stew over what Robinson had told him thus far.

"Where's all this going?" he exclaimed to himself. "This is weird. Mighty weird. But interesting."

He could hardly wait for the rest of the story.

As Robinson left Nicolet, he was happy he'd encountered the younger and obviously athletic man. He'd be a great help and help was something he could use right now. He wanted to get back to him and fill him in completely. But now he went on to Hartley who, at first glance, didn't appear all that agitated. Robinson quickly could see any upset the man was harboring certainly didn't measure up to his aide's description of the request to see him, which had him bordering on hysteria. He quickly found out the man actually was inquiring on behalf of his British buddy, Ian Greene.

Hartley elaborated, in words Robinson could understand. "Now he's an OK bloke, right? But he's hung up a bit on asking you." And now he got to the point. "He's heard you might be able to get him to Tokyo by plane. He'd like to go."

Robinson was somewhat taken by surprise but had long since learned to conceal such surprises. "Well, under special circumstances I might be able to get him over there," he said slowly, "and I appreciate you talking for him. But I think I should talk to him directly on this. It might work out better. You don't mind do you?" he asked the eager Hartley.

"Oh no. No, no. You go see my man Greene. He'll tell you," Hartley said quickly, apparently quite happy to remove himself from a task he didn't relish in the first place.

Although Hartley didn't manifest any of the alarm suggested by Robinson's aide, it was obvious to the doctor he was pleased Robinson was taking him out of the picture entirely.

Robinson went on down the hallway to see Greene.

"Come on in," urged Greene when he saw it was Robinson tapping lightly at his door. He chuckled and said, "Come in if you can find room, right," realizing his room was like most of them at the clinic, designed for barely one person.

"After all these years, we'll manage, Ian. Yes, We'll manage quite well. Now, what's this I hear about you wanting to get up to Tokyo? I'd think you'd be more concerned about getting on home to good old England."

"Yes, yes. That's true. I do want to get on. But I may never be this way again. I'd like to see Tokyo. If it's at all reasonable. I thought you might know."

Robinson leaned against the door, looking at Greene almost eye-to-eye as the two men were approximately the same size. He watched closely as he asked, "Why is it you're willing to forego a trip home to see the family in favor of visiting a city where you may have an acquaintance or two, that's true, but damned unlikely you'll see anything except Japs who despise anything in our uniforms? Are you looking for someone in particular?"

Robinson wasn't really pushing to find out what he suspected he already knew was the motive for Greene wanting to see Tokyo but he thought he'd give him a chance to answer.

Greene wasn't as bold as say, Bertoni, in disclosing his motivation. "I can get passage from Tokyo to England as easily, perhaps easier, as I can from Manila. So I thought I might go if I can make it without too much trouble."

Robinson could see the man wasn't planning to reveal more than he'd said thus far. But Robinson knew Greene's simmering hatred of the man who slaughtered the helpless attempting to escape the sinking Hellship Oryoko. The doctor knew that man, Sabroa Ahirou, was in Tokyo.

Did Greene also know? Robinson slowly asked, "Are you aware the man Ahirou, who was responsible for the carnage of the survivors of the Oryoko, is now in Tokyo? Have you heard that?"

Robinson thought Greene almost reluctantly nodded his head affirmatively. Greene's eyes seemed to narrow ever so slightly as he said, "Yes, I know he's there. I also know he's not being held as a war criminal. He will not be tried and punished as the killer he is. Yes, I know that."

He said all of that slowly and with intense feeling.

Robinson needed to ask no additional questions.

"Ian, I've already made arrangments for at least two men to go to Tokyo from here. There's no reason why I can't include you. Once you're there and you're finally ready to go home, I can also give you the name of the man who can take you to the British representatives there. They can arrange for your passage home."

Robinson paused as he again looked intently at Greene and then asked, "Are you sure that's what you want to do?"

"Oh yes. Oh yes. That's exactly what I want to do."

He could barely contain himself as he repeated his desire to get to Tokyo.

"Well, I think we can work it out. You probably know the geography. But it's 2000 miles north of here. Almost due north. So it's not just an afternoon cruise. Or if we can find some space on a flight up there we'll go that route. But we'll work it out. You just relax and I'll get back to you."

A grateful Greene straightened up in a typically Brit-military, exaggerated and stiffened attention posture, as he said, "I'm most grateful to you, sir. Grateful for what you've done for me and all of the many others and grateful for what you're trying to do now. I thank you, sir."

"Relax Ian. We're not on parade. You know you would do everything you could to help me. So that's the least I can do for you. I approve of your attitude and your approach to the situation. I heartily approve."

Robinson didn't approach any further towards the mission, thinking Greene realized he, Robinson, was privy to the program and approved.

The pair shook hands and Robinson left the little cubbyhole. The doctor had to return to his medical world and see if anything required his attention in the clinic.

He readily could see things were calm. He told his nurse she was in charge. "I've got to get out of here for a while. But I'll be back early. I'm going to meet Nicolet for a beer or two. Feel like relaxing a little. Are you all right with that?"

"Of course doctor. I know where you'll be if it's for beer with Sam, and if something happens I'll get in touch with you."

Robinson walked out thinking he'd just about filled out the travel list for Tokyo from Manila. There'd be young Luang, Nicolet, Greene and Cangleonn. Had he thought too quickly? Overlooked one or more?

He shrugged and muttered, "We'll make room for 'em. If we can do one we can do 'em all." He left to find Nicolet.

As the doctor scurried about like a travel agent without an office or tickets, arranging planes and passengers, his man at the terminus in Tokyo was ready. While Robinson had been fighting the odds in Manila, trying to restore sanity and health to the broken men who came to his rehabilitation clinic, his old friend from med school days was in Tokyo.

That's where Gerald (Gerry) Francis was now posted. He had been in Manila with Robinson in pre-war days but the luck of the draw permitted him to escape the misery suffered by those left behind when MacArthur slipped away from the Philippines ahead of the invading Japs. Francis had gone to Australia with Gen. Douglas MacArthur, thus had missed all of the horrors of the Philippines as created by the marauders from Japan.

The two soon made contact after the war had ended. Francis visited once, briefly, when MacArthur brought a group from Tokyo to Manila. He frankly didn't know what purpose his presence could serve, with the American government's man-in-charge, MacArthur, there. He was handling all the peace negotiations.

The two enjoyed it, regardless. Robinson told him, "Hell, the man wanted you to check on his property in Manila. Make sure it's safe and being kept up." Then he added, "Actually, he wanted you to work as makeup man before the pre-arranged cameras pop out somewhere along the line.

"The pictorial history of the world proves MacArthur's always available for a photographer."

Francis was the medical advisor to MacArthur, and had been by his side since the hurried departure from the Philippines years before. He knew the man quite well.

"Don't tell me, Robby, I know it's crazy," Francis had said, shaking his head as they talked briefly in their single reunion, "We watch them behead, mutilate, starve, beat, rape and you name it, engage in every horrible physical mistreatment of a human, military or civilian, man or woman, adult or child, and we're over here acting as if they've done nothing. As if they're honorable enemies on an honorable battlefield. What do you suppose it would have been if they'd won the war? Why we haven't treated them like the Germans, and why that damned Emperor isn't headed for an execution I'll never know."

He laughed drily, "The General," and he emphasized the word as he stated it clearly and slowly, "doesn't consult me on a number of matters."

Robinson remembered quite well the conversation touched on the killing camp the Emperor had ordered the good Doctor Kimura to establish in Manchuria.

"I've looked at some of the statistics on that operation and quite honestly, Robby, you wouldn't believe it. These numbers are straight. There's no justification in the world for what the Emperor ordered and what Kimura and Naito did.

"But what's worse, MacArthur entered into that trade-off with those two fiends, giving them their lives, almost with a commendation of appreciation for heroic duty, in exchange for what data they managed to extricate from those medical experiments on living bodies and then murdered people in Manchuria since 1937."

"Did he, MacArthur, ask you about it? What did you say about it? More important, did he even listen?" an amazed Robinson managed to squeeze into his friend's monologue.

"That's a good question. He did ask my opinion. Among those of many other staff members, many of them medical personnel. As far as I know, I was the only one who said they should be treated as the worst of the war criminals, responsible personally for more cruel and unnecessary deaths than any other single individual.

"And yes, you're right. He ignored what I had to say. He'd already made up his mind. It was one of those situations in which he listened only to the opinions which echoed his. That's exactly why those two bastards are alive, or out of a cell, today. Living the good life in Tokyo. Along with that damned Emperor who MacArthur seems to think is some sort of deity."

Francis's voice cracked as he talked of the decision to spare those criminals. It's obvious the decision had shaken him.

Had driven him to a despairing wall of frustration and disbelief.

"Well, what will you do now? Are you staying on with MacArthur, heading up his medical staff of advisors?" asked Robinson.

"The man hasn't asked me to step down, so the answer is yes for now. But I'm waiting until the chance comes up to make a graceful exit from that MacArthur theater. I've had all I can stand. I didn't enter the Army for a career and I think the job's done now. But what about you?"

Robinson thought a moment before answering. Slowly he said, "I must finally put my own family ahead of all of these hundreds and hundreds of suffering people who I've elected to help. So when I get a few loose ends tied together, yes, I'm with you. I'll be getting out of the Army. My wife isn't living and I've been fortunate my sister's been able to provide a fine home for my son in Oregon."

He had told Francis of Lenora. "With Lenora murdered here, there's nothing to keep me here, except the obvious and that's the victims of the Japs who keep coming to the rehab center. I've taken care of one important duty which I accepted as a moral responsibility which I couldn't retreat from. That's been satisfied and now I want to help a couple of more people get their lives straightened out and I'll be joining you. On my way home."

"Well, wait a second here, Robby. I'm not cut loose over here yet. Don't jump the gun. But I'll be going just as soon as I can. In the meantime, if there's anything I can help you with, you know you don't have to keep quiet about it. If you want to come to Tokyo I can arrange that. As you probably know, we have planes back and forth on a regular basis. The General still has a number of interests here in Manila, as you have mentioned."

The pair smiled broadly at the term 'interests' as MacArthur's pre-war investments in Manila had been many and quite real. "Yes, I know. One of the first things I'd heard in Manila was someone saying, 'Oh yeah, that's MacArthur's hotel. Or, MacArthur owns this or that.' so I suppose he does have some people coming down here to check things out."

He sipped at his drink and, looking at his old friend, took some of their precious time together to tell him of the young Chinese boy, Chiang Luang and his personal debt with Dr. Kimura.

"Think there's some way we could get him, and my aide, Sam Nicolet, up there? Maybe with a couple of other people who'd like to find a couple of Japanese who are owed something? If you catch my drift."

"Hell yes, I follow you. That kid, Luang, must be tough as hell to go through all this. Have to admire his guts and the desire to get back to Tokyo for a chance to meet that trashcan Kimura. You bet I can help. What do you have in mind? Anything specific?"

Robinson gave him the general outline of the trip for Luang and they parted. Francis was committed to the program and Robinson was at peace now because he knew Luang would be watched over by Francis. He could have no better guidance.

Cangleonn and Greene wouldn't need that much help but they too, could count on Francis. Both in getting to Tokyo and return and for assistance while there.

Robinson returned to the clinic the next day with his head cleared of many problems which had cluttered his thought process recently.

Francis could accommodate all facets of the project at the Tokyo end. That brought Robinson major relief.

After Francis had left that day, Robinson took a moment to reflect on their past together. Both in school and here in the South Pacific. On the same battlefield briefly and now meeting again after a span of almost five years.

It was difficult to avoid dreaming of what might have been had both of them gone to Australia with MacArthur.

He jerked himself to mental attention, forcing himself to heed the words of Satchel Paige. That's how he avoided the retrospective second guessing of his decisions. Never Look Back; Something Might Be Gaining On You. He had always tried to follow that advice.

Besides he had too damned much to do right here and right now.

Such as specifications for the various equipment Francis had assured him he could provide in Tokyo. He needed a shipping container, and knowing the supplies that funneled between the war zones and America, he was certain that posed no problem. It would require some time to prepare according to his specs and he certainly didn't want to waste any time in getting it together. He knew that when the time came for action everything would happen at once.

Francis had already confirmed the fact that the port-of-call in Japan was Yokohama, in pre-war days, for the ships utilized by his Southern Oregon friend, Bob Booth. Therefore, the first project for Francis to coordinate with Nicolet, Luang, Greene and Cangleonn, was transportation to the airport and then for Francis's drivers on to Yokohama, about 20 miles south.

Francis had assured Robinson he'd have quarters for all of them when they arrived. Also, Francis had told Robinson of the airport which had been taken over by the American military. It was the Tachikawa airport, located East of Tokyo, about 20 miles from the city. Robby was grateful for the presence of Francis. He'd be invaluable to the entire program and crucial to Luang as well as the others.

His medical knowledge was an essential contribution.

That was something Robinson had been concerned with but the presence of Francis, with his knowledge of and familiarity with Kimura and his habits in Tokyo, put to rest almost all of Robby's concerns.

It was now a matter of coordinating all the details. He'd received ample assurance from Francis that he could take care of any of the details necesssary from the Tokyo end. Just a matter of putting all the pieces together, he assured himself.

His first chore was getting the group passage on a military flight from Nichols Field to Tachikawa. There would be Cangleonn, the Filipino, and Greene, the Englishman, in addition to Nicolet and Luang. That could be easily arranged through the many friends Robby had in the military. After all, he'd taken care of the bulk of them at his clinic, although Robby still thought of it as a rehab center rather than a clinic.

But regardless, he had plenty of favors out that he could start pulling in when needed. The need was rapidly approaching.

While he was figuring out these details time passed along quickly. Suddenly he realized Francis had been back in Tokyo for almost a week and hadn't checked in with him.

Almost as if they were in contact telepathically, his telephone rang and it was Francis on the other end.

"Robby," and Francis typically got to the point immediately, "I think I've got the container you wanted for that shipment. It's a firm plastic box, fairly shallow, maybe a foot or so deep, and a little over two or two and half feet wide. It's not much over five feet in length."

Robinson responded enthusiastically. "Sounds great. Certainly the right size, wouldn't you say?"

"Yes. I'd say it's right on. Also," Francis responded, "There's an outer covering which encloses the locks of the container out of sight with the outer covering of thin wood, almost impervious to rips or that sort of shipping damage. When this baby's locked, with the clasps on each end, that's going to take as much punishment as you could expect on a trip like that. Plus, it's all waterproof."

Robinson was astounded. "I'm not even going to ask where in hell you found that. I'll settle for you finding it. But what about the cost? I'll compensate you for that."

"Oh come on now, Robby," scoffed his friend. "You know I've been in this Army long enough to know how requisitions work. Either in daylight or midnight. It's already delivered. I've fixed up a rig for work here and to carry it to the harbor in Yokohama when we're ready. It's all set to travel."

"Gerry, thanks so much. I don't know what I'd have done without your help. Even if I could get away from here, which I can't or least shouldn't for a while, I don't have the know-how there that you have. I really appreciate it and you know damned well how many thousands of others appreciate it too." Robby was visibly affected by his friend's willingness to step up and take care of things. It bolstered Robinson's thinking, too, to know that someone else understood and agreed with his own thought process. Francis didn't think he was too far out of line.

"Listen Robby, try to get up here before you go home. But otherwise, maybe we can get together in Portland or maybe down in San Francisco, assuming we ever get the hell out of here."

A grateful Robinson said, "Absolutely. We'll have to do that. Let's make sure of that. And thanks again."

His next move was to locate Nicolet and apprise him of the work of Francis and to continue plotting out the specific details of their project. Then it was getting together with Cangleonn and Greene.

Slowly, he thought to himself, what originally appeared totally impossible to accomplish was coming together. "It can't happen too soon," he muttered softly.

TOKYO – MANILA -- 1946

With Cangleonn and Greene, Robinson anticipated no problem. They had their own contacts in Tokyo. Robinson accepted the responsibility, willingly, of getting them there and returned to Manila.

Chiang Luang presented more of a problem. That's why he was so happy to have Sam Nicolet available for squiring Luang to Tokyo and from there to Manchuria, back to Manila or where-ever he wanted to go.

But Gerry Francis was the man. Robinson could readily see that without the expertise of Francis this project would present some insurmountable obstacles. All was in readiness, both here in Manila and north in Tokyo.

The curious group of travelers made its way to Nichols Field, with Robinson driving his assigned truck and the others packing only a change of clothes, uniforms in most cases, and a light duffel bag. At the field they met the crew of the C-47 which Robinson's friend had managed to have assigned for this trip, which appeared on the necessary paper-work as 'medical emergency'.

The skeleton crew didn't know what that meant and they really had no concerns about it. They just followed orders.

Robinson bid all of them good luck, went back to his military rig and moved well back off the hardstand where the transport was parked, with props whirling.

He couldn't bring himself to leave without watching the takeoff and he held his hands high in farewell as the aircraft roared down the runway and into the sky. He watched until it became nothing more than a blip on the horizon and then he bounced into the rig, happy that everything seemed in order.

The flight was uneventful. They arrived at Tachikawa without mishap. This old veteran C-47 had no trouble with a routiner such as this one. These workhorse planes had taken more than their share of punishment during the war.

Sure enough, just as Dr. Robinson had assured them, Gerry Francis himself was at the field to greet them. He was accompanied by a pair of his assistants, who were more of a military bent than medical. It was obvious they'd be handling the details.

To the group Francis extended greetings as he shook hands with all of them.

"No problems on the flight, I take it," said Francis, glancing quickly to each of them as they met. Luang nodded, partially bowing and smiling as he repeated, "Okay. Okay."

Nicolet followed up. "It was great, Doctor. Smooth flight and no problems at all. Right, men?" he asked, turning to Greene and Cangleonn.

"Righto" said Greene quickly and Cangleonn, less polished in English than the others merely nodded his head in agreement.

The two men with Francis guided them to the Army van they were driving and without ado they were on their way, about a half hour drive to Tokyo.

Francis let them look around at the scenery as they bombed along the highway and when they arrived at their lodgings, a medium hotel not far from the Imperial Hotel, he dismissed his men. "Now you'll be back here at 6:30 tonight, right? Any problem with that?"

"None at all," said the spokesman for the two. "We'll see you in the lobby at 6:30," and the two of them drove off.

"You're all checked in. Just come along to the rooms. Take those stairs over there," said Francis, pointing to a corner of the extremely small hotel lobby. He followed right along, handing each of them a key as they moved over to the stairway.

Sam Nicolet, who hadn't uttered a word to this point, had to ask. "What's the deal now, Doctor? Do we wait here for you or just what is the plan?"

"I'll fill you in as soon as we get inside one of the rooms. Probably in yours."

Once in Nicolet's room, Francis laid out the evening's program.

Looking at Greene and Cangleonn, Francis said briskly, "If I understood Robby correctly, you two are on your own. Is that right?"

They both nodded.

"So you know where you're going, what you'll be doing and apparently know the city well enough to get to your objective and return here without any trouble. Right?"

Again they nodded.

Looking at Cangleonn, Francis asked, "You know Tokyo well enough to help Greene here with his directions and language?"

"Yes, yes. We make it," said Cangleonn, with conviction if not great clarity.

"Now this is important," and Francis emphasized the word important. "I want you back here by midnight. Sam, Chiang and I," he said, looking at those two as he spoke, "have a dinner we must attend and then we have a duty to perform. But I want all of us back here by midnight. As you know, the plane's pilot and crew are planning for an eight o'clock takeoff in the morning and I don't want to hold them up. Is that workable?"

Greene spoke up. "Right. The evening's put together neatly. I should have no problem. And Cangleonn is in good hands here too, so he'll make it back in just a bit. No problems so you go and keep your engagement. Don't concern yourself with us."

Although he was amazed and somewhat skeptical of Greene's confidence, Francis was quite pleased to hear his assurances.

"Very well, then, we'll be on our way," looking at his pair of fellow travelers. "Why don't you, Sam and you Chiang, go to your rooms and get cleaned up and I'll go ahead to the lobby. I don't want to miss my men and I also want to use the phone in the lobby to confirm my meeting tonight."

The three of them left.

Francis went immediately to the telephone, calling the desk at the Imperial Hotel to confirm his 7:30 reservation in the dining room. That was all set so he next called his two assigned men at their quarters to make certain they were ready.

"My bag's in the van, is it?" he asked one of them.

"Yes sir," briskly responded the man on the phone. "Everything's in the van and ready to go. It's fully gassed up and we should have no problems at all."

"Very good, then," said Francis. "I'll see you here at 6:30. Call me here in the lobby if anything happens."

Waiting was a punishing experience in this project, no matter which island you were perched on.

For Robinson in the Manila Clinic and for Francis in the hotel lobby in Tokyo the wait was maddening, even for men trained in a field requiring the ultimate in patience.

Robinson's suspense would last longer.

Francis was off the hook promptly at 6:30 p.m. when the van pulled up at the little hotel. He popped out the door and after taking a look around the vehicle's interior, settled in the second seat and said, "Okay men. Let's go."

And they were off to the Imperial Hotel, Francis shortly entering a lobby that was far more deserving of the name than the one which he had just departed. As one of the men with him parked the vehicle, Francis asked Nicolet, "Now, do you know where the park, Hibiya Park, is from here?"

Nicolet rather tentatively shook his head but said, "Well it seems to me it's just back on the street we left. Is that right?"

Francis smiled and said, "Your memory's good. That's exactly where it is. Off the Hibiya Dori, which is the street we just left. The reason I ask is to refresh your memory. That's where we'll be going when we leave here in about an hour or so. To finish our project. Okay?"

"You bet. I'm with you. All the way. You call the shots and I'll be there. But I still don't have it straight. Am I going to the dining room with you? Or do you want us," Nicolet indicating the doctor's two aides, "To wait out in the lobby?"

"I think in the lobby is better. Just keep an eye on us as it's always possible I'll need some help getting out of the dining room."

Nicolet thought he understood what Francis meant by that but he wasn't sure. He figured he'd let it play out and act accordingly.

The dining room captain showed Francis to his table where Dr. Kimura awaited him. They went through the usual elaborate greetings. The straight-talking Francis never liked this habit and could barely stomach it with a person who was so revolting.

"You have no idea how pleased I am to meet you," Francis voiced with a sincere ring. As his dinner-mate was having a drink, Francis also ordered one, finishing his as did Kimura. They ordered two more and then Kimura rose, bowed and excused himself to go to the restroom.

Francis didn't hesitate.

He quickly pulled a plastic capsule from his pocket. Deftly, he held the capsule over the death-doctor's drink. The contents of the capsule dissolved quickly, absorbed by the liquor. When Kimura came back they continued their small talk, not yet ordering their dinner.

As they talked, Francis watched Kimura closely. It didn't take long. His additive to the liquor began working immediately. When the doctor actually showed signs of slumping, Francis moved quickly.

"Here, let me help you to the lobby. You need some air," he said, mostly for the benefit of fellow diners. Certainly not for Kimura who was fading rapidly.

Nicolet, keeping a watchful eye on the table from his vantage point in the lobby, signaled the two aides outside as he saw Francis leaving the table with a strong arm around the much smaller Kimura. When the pair reached the lobby, Kimura's legs weren't really functioning.

"Sam, get an arm under his shoulder there. I've got a good hold on him here and we'll sort of drag his feet. That's the stuff," continued Francis as he felt Nicolet's pressure on the other shoulder of the nearly-inert body of Kimura.

"Okay, out the door we go," said Francis, smiling at the concerned doorman and also indicating with his free arm his companion's overindulgence by placing his hand to his mouth several times.

Then they were at the drive-through and the aides helped put Kimura in the rear of the van, pulling the curtain which divided the rear of the van from the first and second passenger seat rows. Francis hopped in the rear portion and the two aides smoothly, quickly but without attention-attracting haste, drove across the Hibiya Dori to the Hibiya park.

Opened in 1803, it's questionable whether the park had ever been utilized for the purpose which ensued shortly.

Even as they were driving, Francis was at work. He stripped Kimura, taking note of several jugs with suction attachments as well as his medical bag and everything else he had requested to complete his mission.

As he prepared his equipment, he mused aloud, "Hell, all I'm missing is Boris Karloff to play the role of the monster. I'm sure I'll handle the mad doctor role easily enough." The entire grisly scenario was mindful of Hollywood's frightening movies of more than a half century ago.

His rationalization for the entire matter came readily enough. He reminded himself, "These bastards killed hundreds of thousands of people in a meaningless project, killing them in a manner almost too cruel to imagine."

No, there were no second thoughts regarding completion of his mission.

He lofted the doctor's feet into a sling across the back of the van, leaving his upper portion down on the floor of the vehicle. He placed a bucket on each side of the man's head. Deftly, he affixed the two hoses, one on each side and each to the carotid artery carrying blood to the head.

After that, and he was talking to himself, "We'll just take a quick, clean slice of the artery, place the saturating materials around the opening, insert the hose and let the blood-letting begin."

Francis made the same quick move with his scalpel to insert the hose on the other side and the project was underway.

"Hmmm, about 10 or 11 pints will do it. In view of all the horribly painful deaths this man created, it's almost a shame his present condition doesn't permit him to be aware of what's happening.

"But the vengeance is the same, awake or asleep," he summarized as the flowing of blood continued.

After all the blood had been drawn from the body, the doctor removed all the equipment and opened the container at the side of the van. The little doctor was, as Francis granted to himself, dead weight but relatively light and posed no problem as he hoisted him carefully into the box and strapped him in.

He then closed the lid and snapped the clasps shut tightly.

Following that he pulled the sections of the outer covering together and snapped shut the clasps along the top and each end of the container.

The fairly short and thin container was ready to go. And the shipping label, supplied by Robinson, read: Bob Booth, Booth Packing Co., Medford, Oregon, USA.

Francis had only one observer to the entire procedure.

Silent though he was, his face showed the relief of a young person who has just had an enormously heavy weight removed.

Francis knew Chiang Luang could find peace at last knowing his beloved family's deaths had been avenged. Chiang Luang had promised Dr. Kimura: "I not forget you."

Now he could.

Luang quickly helped Francis clean the van, which really showed no evidence of his labors. He secured the tops of the two buckets as he placed them in boxes with the hoses and attachments inside. Francis then rapped on the screen, "Sam, I'm all set to go if you people are."

He crawled in beside Nicolet and gave him the high sign, thumb up, and the drivers sent the van on its way.

"Sam, I'd like to stop along the way at any garbage dumping ground. Before they let us off at the hotel and they get started to Yokohama, maybe we can find a big dumpster of some sort to dump this crap in back. Take the caps off the buckets. Empty them on the ground. Burn any ID."

"Sure, that's no problem," Sam said, telling the driver.

When they stopped at a dumpster, Sam got out to help with the disposal. "My God that's clean back here. What the hell juh do? Take it to an auto wash?"

After their stop at the dumpster, the rear of the van was almost empty. Nothing remained except a container, slightly over five feet in length, maybe 10 inches high, and tightly sealed.

The two men dropped Francis, Luang and Nicolet at the hotel.

"You know where it goes in Yokohama, right?" Francis asked. "Yes sir. Got it all right here," came the crisp response.

"Very good, men. Thanks for your help. Have a safe trip."

And the grisly package was on its way to a packing plant in Southern Oregon, after a stop in Yokohama and way points in the Pacific Ocean.

Early the next morning the group at the little hotel rendezvoused early downstairs, and at least three of them were wondering how Cangleonn and Greene had fared the previous day.

"Not to worry old man," pooh-poohed Greene as the two of them greeted the others in the tiny lobby and Nicolet hailed them with, "Glad you made it, men. We wondered if you'd be all right."

"Had a fine leader here," continued Greene, indicating a smiling Cangleonn, "he really knows his way around Tokyo."

Cangleonn concurred, trying his best to communicate his lack of concern for their project. "Tokyo big. I know all of it. No problems. And you? All okay?"

Nicolet laughed and put his hand on Cangleonn's shoulder as he said, "Right. All okay here too. Now we head to the airport."

So the four of them, Luang, Cangleonn, Greene and Nicolet waited out front for the military rig Dr. Francis had arranged for them. Without ceremony, their jobs done, they jumped in the vehicle and they were off to Tachikawa, the air base which was about a 20 minute drive from the city.

The aircraft assigned to fly them back to Manila, another bit of military magic performed by the medical men, waited for their arrival at the airport. They were soon back in the air headed for Manila.

Robinson was at Nichols waiting for them and, anxious to hear if everything went well, listened as he drove back to the clinic in Manila.

Luang, obviously more relaxed now that his family obligation had been satisfied with the help of these men, and certainly the absent Francis, now looked ahead to his future in Manila. There was no home in China anymore. His future was Manila.

His future had been the subject of several discussions initiated by Robinson. He had been impressed with the fortitude of the young Chinaman and more than sympathetic with his problems.

To Bertoni he voiced some of his concerns and possible solutions to his problems.

"Tell me I'm crazy on this one, Floyd. What about me taking Luang in hand? Giving him some prep work in operating on the fringe of medical care. More or less give him some of the knowledge our nurses acquire in a venue more conducive to learning, yes, but perhaps with fewer practical cases than he's bound to encounter right here? What do you think?"

Bertoni snorted affirmatively. "Kid's gonna loin here. Hell yes. He's no dummy. It'll work."

"Thanks for your vote," Robby laughed. "Seriously, I've come to put a lot of faith in your judgments. And I think you can help with Luang, too. I mean, the poor kid's got nothing to go back to Manchuria for. No family. Nothing but terrible memories of what the Japs did to all his family, all his relatives and all his neighbors."

Robinson was reluctant to get any more involved personally with Luang than he was already. Nevertheless, he had developed an affinity toward Luang which overpowered that unwillingness. With Luang his sympathy was strong. He'd experienced that from the first time he'd met the young man and became aware of his experiences. He knew he had to pursue his original thoughts. And somehow, he had positive reactions to the possibility of success for Luang.

"Yeah, this just might be a pretty good beginning of a new way of life for him," Robinson concluded as he found his enthusiasm for the program increasing by the minute.

Then he added, "Just what I need. Another damned project here."

"What's that Doc?" Bertoni asked, turning his head to face him again.

"Oh nothing. Nothing. I'm trying to figure out when the hell I'm getting out of here. You too, as far as that goes. Brooklyn's not getting any closer for you, is it."

"Hell no. It's comin' up. Quick. Gotta use dat rig from the prison this week. Okay? Remembuh, yuh said I could take it for a project? Got that worked in now."

Robinson knew he was speaking of Ryoichi Azami.

"The rig and the man are both available anytime you want them," he assured Bertoni.

Bertoni didn't waste any time at all in getting together with Azami.

When he got the rig he went immediately to his quarters to pick up his material. A curious collection of items. A five inch cotton swab which he had fashioned and fastened to the upper end of a long plastic stick. At the bottom of the stick, a fuselike string dangled. And Bertoni had some gasoline in a can, which prompted the guard at Bilibad to ask him if he was going on a trip. "No. Don't wanna run out. The can's just in case," he laughed.

So when he went inside to pick up his passenger, ostensibly to transfer Azami to the clinic, Bertoni was well prepared.

His paper from Robinson worked without a question. The guards were happy to get rid of this one. They knew his background too well.

Azami's hands were quickly tied behind his back with some twine and Bertoni marched him to the rig, wishing only that he had a bayonet with him to use as a vicious cattle prod. As Azami and his mates did on the March.

He settled for tossing him in back, on the floor. He then proceeded to the city dump, well Southeast of the city of Manila. He had the place well cased and knew exactly where to drive.

Once there, behind a mountain of debris, he hopped out, grabbed his equipment and hurriedly started his project.

First of all, he drove a sizeable stake into the ground.

Then he grabbed Azami by one arm and stood him over by the stake. Getting out some more of the hemp which he'd used to tie his arms, he tied one of his legs to the stake.

Following that he quickly taped the man's mouth and pulled his loose pants off. Then came the part he'd been thinking about for months.

He had the rig well away from the scene of activity. He opened the can of gasoline. As he stuck the swab inside the can, allowing it to soak up the fuel, Azami was terrified, smelling the fuel and not knowing what was going to happen.

Azami's tiny eyes darted back and forth, fearfully watching Bertoni's, thoroughly confused by all of his captor's actions, but fearing the worst.

His fear was justified. Bertoni came over to him, grabbed him by the neck with one of his huge pawlike hands and shoved his head down between his legs. Just as quickly he grabbed the gas-soaked swab-stick and with another quick, powerful motion, shoved the swab, stick and all, up the ass of the writhing Azami, leaving only the wick-like string hanging from his body.

Following this painful insertion into the captive's innards, he stepped back to avoid any spillage on himself as he doused the writhing, helpless Azami with the gasoline. The overflow soaked the ground beneath the staked Azami.

Without ceremony, but with much caution, he placed the can on the ground, and with a long stick with a tiny flame on the end, ignited the string of the swab.

The reaction of Azami was immediate.

He couldn't scream. His contortions were so crazed and violent Bertoni feared he might break his ties to the stake. But they held. Just as his thousands of victims had been helpless before this creature's terrible tortures of death, so too was he helpless before the flames, which ate their way furiously through his lower intestines, to create a level of absolute agony to Azami.

Of course, the fumes from the rest of the gasoline were ignited almost instantaneously and the flames roared on as Bertoni, long since moved to a safe distance, watched.

"Boin you sunuvabitch. A lotta people love it." The burning was quick. Bertoni's task was finished.

As he drove away, he growled aloud, "Hell, dat's just some more garbage boinin' at da dump."

Back at the rehab in Manila the next morning Bertoni stopped by to give Robinson the key to the rig. He matter-of-factly said, "It's out front. Where you always leave it. Okay?"

"Yes. That's fine," said Robinson, not continuing the dialogue or courting any continuance by Bertoni.

And then it seemed only a few hours passed before Bertoni was hauling his duffel bag to the harbor and the ship waiting to haul him on his first step back to the states. "You need me here, I'll stay. I'm outta the Army so I'm free."

"No Floyd, you've been great but you've been away from home long enough. All of us have. I couldn't have accomplished anything without you. You're a good friend and a good soldier."

Bertoni knew that was one of Robinson's favorite expressions. With an expressionless face, he stared intently into Robinson's eyes, shaking hands long and strong. Without looking back, he took long strides toward the truck headed for the harbor.

He waved as he got on the truck.

Quite logically, Robinson figured that was the last he'd see of Bertoni. He was right. The man was headed for his beloved Brooklyn. Robinson could relate to the man's unbridled enthusiasm at the prospect of getting to his home, a home he'd thought many times he'd never see again. Robinson shared the wish for home. He certainly wished he was headed for Oregon. Instead he was due back for more of the almost endless days at the clinic. He hoped things would go as well there without Bertoni as they had when he was on hand to handle all jobs, easy ones or tough ones. With an effort, he cleared his head for the challenges at the clinic.

Once there, he had a caller. It was George Hartley, the Yorkshireman, who was remarkably calm as he exchanged greetings with Robinson.

"Me chum Greene's back. Right? I think we'll be getting along here soon. Just hoping it's before next week. I'd like to get home. It'll take forever. Like snail mail. But we'll get it.

"How about you? You going to stay on forever. Right?"

Robinson grimaced, waiting for Hartley's monologue to cease and then raising his hands as if to ward off such a thought as staying here forever. "No, no, I'm trying to get everything settled so I can leave. With Nicolet here, I can almost see my way clear now. Couple of more things to take care of.

"But you're all finished up and ready to go?"

The Yorkshireman looked at him. Slowly he said, "Almost whacked. A day or two."

His entire demeanor was deliberate and stated clearly his purposeful intent. Robinson had never seen the fast talking Hartley in quite this mood. Not since the time he'd first talked to him and Hartley explained the scene of the infamous crucifixion by one Sabroa Moditake.

He was certain Moditake was on Hartley's mind as he was talking.

Hartley abruptly shook his hand and bowed as he walked out of the office.

Hartley had been watching a certain area of the city for a number of days, actually for several weeks. Since he'd received his expected report of the return to Manila of one Moditake. He'd also discovered Moditake had taken an active role in the Manila undercover activities of the Japs prior to the strike by the Emperor's forces against Pearl Harbor, the Philippines and all of Asia.

Therefore, he zeroed in on the scummy part of the city. It was easy to determine the location of the Manila slum area. It was in the southeastern section of the city, same as the city garbage dump.

That's where Hartley had been spending much of his time. He had now determined where Moditake was living a solitary life, venturing out only at night and then only for essential reasons.

A day after he'd talked to Robinson, Hartley also ventured out one night. The slums of Manila held no fears for the burly Hartley. He slipped along the dark streets until he was standing in an alleyway immediately adjacent to the stairway leading to Moditake's room.

Then he waited. He knew Moditake wouldn't be coming down the steps until almost nine o'clock and it was only a few minutes before the hour. Moditake didn't disappoint him. Hartley could hear his feet creaking the boards of the decrepit stairway as he made his way to the street.

Reliably enough, Moditake looked both ways as he left the stairway, and then turned toward the alleyway.

That's when Hartley's strong arms and huge hands reached out to pin Moditake's neck to the wall. Hartley quickly used all of his strength to apply a sleeper vise to the vulnerable neck of his hated enemy.

Hartley actually thought as he held an unyielding grip on the rapidly sinking Moditake, this action is almost too merciful, in view of the horrendously cruel crucifixion of that helpless prisoner a few years ago. His thoughts almost prompted a heavier application of force but Hartley made himself ease the hold to the pressure he needed. He didn't want any unnecessary marks on the little mass murderer's neck.

It was over almost too quickly. But Hartley was satisfied, as he walked away from the crumpled, lifeless body in the black alley.

An important debt was satisfied.

It dawned on Robinson suddenly. These debts had rapidly been reduced.

And slowly the population of Robinson's clinic in Manila dwindled. The broken men, who had found their way to this rehab center, regained their faculties sufficiently to return to their lives. The good doctor soon realized his departure was imminent.

He voiced this reality to Hartley shortly before the Sheffield man and his partner, Ian Greene, embarked on the long trip back to the United Kingdom.

Later on, as he sat with the two Filipinos, Cangleonn and Merrando, he wondered when they'd be out of here. "Wait a minute," he said, absent-mindedly correcting his mistaken thoughts, "you people live here. This is your home."

He said this in Tagalog, the language of the Filipinos. Robinson had scant command of Tagalog but could speak it well enough for them to have a reasonably intelligible conversation.

The two natives of Manila looked at each other as if they figured Robinson was finally in need of what he'd been offering to others — rehabilitation.

"Of course. This is our home," said Cangleonn, smiling his big, toothy smile. "We're not going any place. At least not for a while, I hope." He was a picture of delight since his return from Tokyo.

His friend Merrando echoed his words. "Not for a long time, I hope. But what about you, Doctor? When are you leaving?"

"I don't know for sure but I think it's soon. Our clinic's just about finished its work. All the seriously ill people have been taken care of. There's not many more straggling in, as you know. There's little to keep me here now. And there's a lot of reasons to get on home."

Of course, he didn't know what was bugging Cangleon's fellow Filipino, Merrando. But he did know he had a motivation factor similar to Cangleonn's. He also concluded the man's objective didn't reside in Tokyo.

In either case, the doctor didn't continue the questions. Cangleonn's smile was the only form of communication. That didn't supply much information. Merrando simply smiled too.

This was no surprise. They just weren't communicative. As far as Cangleonn's trip was concerned, Robinson didn't probe for the details, just as he had resisted discussing the mission to Tokyo with Ian Greene. He knew the pair of Hellship animals, Sabroa Ahirou and Tomika Saitoi skulked in Tokyo, thinking they were safe from any justice. That's all he needed.

Both Saitoi and Ahirou had been placed on Robinson's list after he'd heard the stories of Cangleonn and Greene regarding the pair of Japs aboard the hellships, the Nitti and Oryoko.

Robinson, as he had through all his experiences in the Manila clinic, simply listened and offered only medical advice. And caution. He could see no reason to change this pattern. He was the same with Merrando, who had begun exhibiting what Robinson thought he could detect as signs suggesting impending action. He hadn't been wrong yet. Of course, as Robinson admitted to himself, most of the others had made little or no effort to conceal their intent.

Not so with Merrando. Except for his conversations with his fellow Manila native, Cangleonn, this man formed few friendships and didn't indulge in much casual conversation. Robinson had always received prompt attention to any of his requests and Merrando seemed always available.

His family was among the several hundreds of thousands of Manila residents who had been killed by the Japs when it was declared an 'open city' and then occupied by the Emperor's marauders. Merrando refused Robinson's offer of living facilities at the clinic, preferring instead to take his quarters elsewhere but in the general vicinity of the clinic.

On most nights away from the clinic, Merrando followed a regular routine.

He prowled the streets of Manila. He prowled the streets in Manila South of the city center. It was the seamy part of the city but Merrando knew instinctively the man he was seeking would unquestionably be somewhere in this vicinity.

It was Maori Mori. Before the war Mori was a Manila resident. He was termed a part-time bicycle shop owner but like all adult Japs in Manila, a fulltime Japanese spy for the Emperor's war machine's planning. This had been the base of his spying activities with the bicycle shop a convenient cover. After the war he had returned to Manila, the principal city of the country where his country had inflicted death and suffering on hundreds of millions of people. Merrando knew this.

Merrando needed no introduction to Mori. He'd been imprisoned at the prison camp at Cabanatuan, where this devil had seen to the death of thousands of Merrando's fellow prisoners. Yes, this little Jap spy was in charge and Merrando held him personally responsible for the deaths of those untold thousands. Plus the suffering of untold thousands more.

He wanted to ask Dr. Robinson what this Mori must be thinking. "Why would he come back to Manila? He must know that if I'm still alive he's dead. That if I'm still in Manila then his life is gone." But he couldn't ask. Or at least he didn't think he could.

Instead he checked with his many friends in Manila, many of whom had suffered at the hands of Mori, and learned more than enough of the habits of the creature.

Merrando, unlike his comparatively diminutive friend Cangleonn, was at least six foot tall and a burly, strong six footer. Although his impassive facial appearance imparted no hint to anyone, his mind was zeroed on one objective. To catch Mori. "For a talk. That all. Just talk. No swords like Japs. No bayonets. Just talk."

He finally had a chance to indulge in what he identified in his mind as talk. Vengeful talk, yes. But just talk.

Merrando was certain he'd find his quarry out in the Southeast section from the city center. Because it was the slum area, comings and goings there were overlooked by the authorities.

But the coming and going of a pre-war spy for the Emperor, alive and in one piece in Manila after all of the wholesale killings, certainly would be noted. This one had been noted before.

When he thought the time appropriate at the clinic, things had slowed down and the doctor was taking it easy, Merrando slipped out the door. He made his way to the slum area.

As a youngster, he hadn't lived too far from here and knew the area well. It was Manila's section that had long since been forgotten and not an area where Douglas MacArthur had bought any property. There had been joking references to the well-known habit of the American general's acquisition of prime Manila property. No, this area had never seen the dramatic profile of MacArthur.

This was only Merrando's second postwar, daylight visit to this scummy district. He'd made several nocturnal visits, however. As a result he was quite certain he knew where Mori was housed. He was in the basement of one of the many squalid buildings, apparently anonymous structures of ancient vintage and questionable quality.

As nearly as Merrando was able to ascertain, Mori emerged only at night, leaving his hovel under the kindly cover of darkness, slipping away to some unknown destination and returning in the early hours of morning.

"That is good," Merrando told himself. "For me there is no need for light."

When he returned to the clinic he knew he was ready to make a final trip to the southeast of the city and confront Maori Mori, the devil of Cabanatuan.

First of all, he wanted to talk to Dr. Robinson. By himself. He needed no audience. Probably easier to get a frank, straight-forward answer from Robinson in a one-on-one situation with no onlookers.

At the close of the day he had his opportunity. Only the two of them were in Robinson's little cubicle which he considered his office.

Robinson looked up as Merrando walked to the door, glanced in and silently asked permission to enter and Robinson nodded, pointing to a rickety chair in front of his littered desk.

"Hello Doctor. I have a question. Okay?"

"Of course," Robinson responded, somewhat surprised by what he thought was a reticence on Merrando's part, and he reassured him by adding, "Anything from you is okay, Jorge. You know that. What is it?"

"I must know. If a man is hit here by another man," and he clenched his enormous fist as he brought it to bear on his chest, and in the area where he might believe his heart was located, "will he die?"

His question was a sneaker for Robinson. He didn't know just what he anticipated from Merrando but he certainly didn't expect a consultation on how to conclude a man's life as opposed to extending it. But he concealed his inner thoughts as he tried to answer a question which he could see was serious. There was nothing frivolous in the question. Merrando was indeed serious.

Robinson hedged his answer slightly.

"It depends, Jorge. I would say in general, yes, a severe blow to the heart could be fatal. But specifically, it would depend on the individual.

"As you may know, when a man's heart fails, a sudden blow to the chest sometimes can be helpful in restoring the heart to its normal operation. The same can be true of a blow delivered to a heart which is functioning normally.

"Another consideration is the heart's condition itself. I said if the heart is functioning normally. If, for some reason, the heart has some weakness, some blockage of the blood flow to or from the heart, its operation would be more vulnerable to such a shock."

Robinson was attempting to keep his explanation brief and thus simple in an effort to enable Merrando to understand what he was saying. He concluded by saying, "Yes, a man could die from a strong blow to the heart. It's not certain but it's certainly possible. Okay?"

Merrando rose to his feet. It was obvious he'd heard the words he wanted to hear. He stepped away from his chair, almost bowing slightly from the hips as he thanked Robinson. He was so formal Robinson was almost embarrassed.

He offered his hand to Merrando to shake as they departed. A grateful Merrando grabbed his hand in a strong grip, thanking Robinson profusely. "You are good, Doctor. Thank you. Thank you," he said as he backed his way out through the opening of the cubicle.

Robinson leaned back in his chair to relax. He wondered. "Who's it going to be? There are so many deserving of such a blow. I'll probably never know."

Then he turned to more important matters. Such as his official and imminent departure from the clinic, from the Army, from the Philippines.

He had been cleared to go whenever he deemed the clinic's services were no longer needed. That time had come. He was ready to go. Some goodbyes and minimal packing remained. The plane waited at Nichols. Robinson realized he was ready.

When it came right down to the knuckle-crunching point, Robinson wavered. No doubt he was ready to get on with it to home. But he also wanted to write finis to the missions of vengeance. There was just one of seven left.

When Merrando left Robinson's office he was truly a man of purpose. All he could see in front of him was the sight of the cocky little Mori strutting in front of the battered, bruised, and dying prisoners at Cabanatuan.

He was striding toward the clinic exit when he finally realized his friend Cangleonn was calling to him. By now he was almost shouting. Merrando was so devoured by his thoughts he'd walked right past him.

"Where are you going? You went right past me. Without even looking." Then Cangleonn realized what had happened.

"You're going for the man. Right? Don't answer. I can tell. You want help, say so. If not, I see you tomorrow."

Merrando simply shook his head quickly. Once. Then he raised his hand and said, "Tomorrow. Okay."

Then he was off to his room where his coldly, calculating self took over. As he mentally previewed his plan, he went to his battered mattress, reached inside it, and pulled out an old U.S. Army .45 revolver.

He placed this in his trousers just back of his right hip. "Just in case," he said to himself. Merrando wasn't leaving any opening for his hated target to escape. One way or another, Mori was his.

It was only a short bus ride to the area Merrando was going to cover. Once within the general area he was seeking, he hopped nimbly off the bus and surveyed this specific area. It was typical of this section of the city. So many of them presented the same discouraging picture. Just a few small shops, some operating and some not, surrounded by many empty buildings, all in a state of disrepair. Most of them were beyond repair.

Merrando knew this was where he wanted to concentrate his patient search. He quickly spied a bicycle shop which he was convinced was the one operated by Mori before the attack by the Japs and was his front for his espionage program in Manila.

Happily it was one of those buildings which seemingly would require only a puff of air to send it crashing to the ground in a mass of splintered, aging boards.

Yes, this was the place Merrando wanted to skulk for the rest of the day and on into the darkness of the night.

He slowly made his way toward his objective, knowing full well his leisurely pace would get him to Mori's domicile just after dusk. Mori had been watched closely. Unless something totally unanticipated occurred, that's when he'd be coming up the steps from his basement accommodations.

Merrando would be waiting.

He'd waited several years for this meeting. As he came along the narrow streetway on which Mori's place was located he wondered once again why Mori had chosen to return to Manila. Surely he must have known his reception would be less than civil.

Why wouldn't he have returned to Japan. To Tokyo, or whatever city he once called home.

Merrando didn't know this but the fact was simply that Mori was less acceptable in Tokyo than he was in Manila. Merrando had been advised that Mori had given his chiefs some information regarding military installations and strengths in Manila that had proved faulty.

This misinformation had cost the Japs heavily as they sought to take over the Philippines and then strengthen their defenses to hold their positions. His chiefs hadn't forgotten. That's precisely why the little bicycle peddler, as the Filipinos had termed him, chose to hide in Manila.

His hiding place had been discovered though. As he made preparations to go forth into the night, prowling for whatever he could find, he carefully looked up the few steps to the street level and then cautiously moved up to the walkway. At the walkway, he looked carefully in all directions and then turned to his right. It was only a few feet to the corner.

Merrando knew all of his moves. He could have counted out the number of minutes the entire procedure took. When Mori reached the corner, he was waiting.

In Tagalog, which he knew Mori could understand, Merrando jumped in front of him and with his left arm fastened the smaller man's head virtually in a vise, snarling, "You slimy bastard. We meet again. This gun I have at your head can blow you apart. Don't move."

The trembling Mori couldn't have moved even if he'd had the desire. Merrando was a big man and his arms were huge. The smaller Mori had no strength, without his crew of prison guards and their beheading swords.

He continued to tremble as Merrando pulled him by his head farther on down the almost cavern-like darkness. There was a small inset in the building only 40 or 50 feet or so from the corner and that's where Merrando shoved him. Merrando knew the inset was here. He had carefully planned each of these moves so far.

For a second time he searched him for weapons. His first search had been cursory in nature and Merrando now wanted to make certain. Mori carried no weapons.

Merrando almost carefully placed him up against the wall.

From only a step away he told him, "There are thousands and thousands of men, women and children now dead because of you. There is no way you can be punished sufficiently for these murders of innocent and helpless people. There was no reason for you, even in time of war, to take the actions you did against these people."

The little guy Mori acted as if he was going to say something. Merrando's left hand quickly smothered his mouth, forcing his head back against the building as he said, "You keep mouth shut. I will talk."

Mori again trembled in silence.

"There is no way to punish you for all of this. I wish there was. Just killing you doesn't seem strong enough punishment for you. But what will happen to you is a payment for all of those people at Cabanatuan you had killed. You are to die of natural causes."

Without another word, Merrando pulled back his beefy right hand. It was a doubled-up fist of huge knuckles. He planted it squarely in Mori's chest, precisely where Merrando had learned the heart would be most vulnerable.

Mori crumpled, his collapsing body emitting a soft sound as if it were a suddenly-opened, air-filled bag releasing its contents. Indeed, that's what it was.

Merrando let Mori fall to the filthy ground.

Carefully he checked for a heartbeat. He found none. He found a cloth in his jacket pocket and held it tightly over Mori's mouth and nose.

There had been no movement since the little spy and treacherous prison chief hit the ground. There was no movement after Merrando calmly walked away from the scene of retribution.

Merrando's mission was completed. He didn't look back.

MAINLAND – USA -- 1947

There was really little but memories remaining to hold Manila dear to Robinson. All of his comrades had gone home.
As he stalled going to Nichols and the plane home, he appraised the situation.
Of course, Cangleonn and Merrando were already home. The clinic had slowed to such a degree that subordinates could take care of it. Chiang Luang was adapting nicely to his orderly role.
Robinson could feel his homeland beckoning more strongly each day.
Finally he told the commanding officer of the American forces in Manila he wanted out.
Of course there was no argument. A minimum discussion. Some paper work which would continue his role in the reserve with no responsibilities except those he sought. Robinson laughed at that clause.
"There's only one I'll be seeking. That's to stay at my old house in Ashland, Oregon. That's my responsibility. To the property and then, perhaps, start a general practice clinic there in Southern Oregon. And then try to enjoy what's left of this crazy mixed-up life.
"Does that give you a general idea of what I have in mind?"
"Exactly. Right on," returned the clerk. "We'll have the papers up right away. A day or two at the most. And then we'll get you on the list for a boat out of here."
"Wait a minute," Robinson said quickly. "I think we're going to work out a spot on one of those transports out of Nichols. Either a C-47 or a C-54.
"I get pretty sea-sick," he added.

"All right. I'll put you down as transportation all set, and good luck to you Doc."

Robinson's hands closed tightly on the papers, signing one set for the man to forward to Washington, D. C. As he did so he realized he was still another step closer to home, although he wasn't positive exactly where his home was. He also realized that anywhere on the West coast of America was in the neighborhood of 7000 miles away.

"What the hell. It's a step in the right direction, finally."

As he was going through these routine steps in arranging his departure, he realized how much he was going to leave behind him. Mostly it was Lenora and what they'd meant to each other. The fact they'd had such a brief segment of their lives together, obviously made that segment even more precious.

She was one of those millions whose lives the Japs had ripped away, plundering everything and everyone they could possibly put their cruel hands on.

He shook his head as he contemplated the meager time they'd had. The few happy hours they'd had together. A few hours out of the seemingly eternal hell the Japs had brought to so much of the world.

Robinson returned to the clinic or rehab area for perhaps the final time and suddenly realized he'd be getting on a transport tomorrow and head for the States.

"It's not like an hour or so in the air. Hell, it's over seven thousand miles just to San Francisco. Not counting the stops at Wake and Honolulu for refueling. I'd better not plan on anyone meeting me there." He was saying this aloud, prompting a curious, "You want me?" question from Chiang Luang, walking out of one of the little offices Robinson used.

"No, no, Chiang. Just talking to myself," patting him on the shoulder as he went past. That's one accomplishment Robinson cherished. Giving this young man a chance at a life anew was a project to which Robinson had particularly dedicated himself. Fortunately, he'd been helped in this by Cangleonn, who also had assured Robinson he'd take Luang in charge and stay with him as he became adjusted both to Manila and to the life in the field of medicine and healing.

Robinson was confident he could leave Luang, knowing he was facing a much brighter future than that which was left to him in Manchuria by the murdering invaders.

He collected his medical bag for the last time in the clinic. He looked around carefully, making certain he wasn't leaving behind any memento of any of his compadres. Luang. Cangleonn. Merrando. Hartley. Greene. Bertoni. Any little scrap which would recall one of these men to him years down the road, he wanted in his bag.

One last look around and he was out of there.

Now all that remained was to go to his quarters, in the same building, toss his clothing which he wanted to retain in his duffel bag, and then wait for time to go to Nichols.

He had about an hour to waste. He knew where he wanted to spend it. It took him mere minutes to toss all his belongings in the bag. He hadn't been left much and there'd been little to collect since the so-called unconditional surrender of the Japs.

Once packed, as he laughingly referred to it, he scurried out the front door to catch a ride down to the Polo Club. It was only vaguely reminiscent of the place he remembered as the lovely club in which he first laid eyes on Lenora, had the pleasure of dinner with her and danced with her.

But it was all he had left of her now. He looked longingly at it. Then he returned to the clinic, his eyes turned from Manila forever.

When he hauled himself and his bag aboard the C-47 early the next morning, he figured the plane looked as if it had as many miles on it as he felt he had logged.

Uniform was an extremely kind name for his when he looked at his almost threadbare outfit and attempted to remember the unie on that dapper-looking young captain he was on arrival in Manila in 1940. Most charitably described, his uniform was worn. But it was all he needed. "There's not gonna be many inspections between here and San Francisco. Right?" he grinned and joked with his companion on the floor.

The Master Sergeant, no youngster and as was Robinson, simply happy to be on a plane headed for the West coast, and away from the hell almost all of them had experienced for the past several years, smiled grimly and nodded with deliberate intensity.

There was little frivolous talk on the plus-4500 mile trip to Honolulu. At Wake Island, the scene of some bloody work by the Marines and Army as they set about the almost impossible task of unseating the Japs from their positions of strength in the South Pacific, the pilot landed to load on fuel. The passengers jumped out to hit the head and stretch a little.

Then it was back inside for the next segment of the long journey. This one took them to Hickam Field in Honolulu. For most of the tired travelers the stop at Hickam was for the same two reasons they landed at Wake. Let the passengers check out the plumbing and get the plane serviced for the final leg of the trip to Hamilton Field. This was a base he knew well, just across the Golden Gate bridge to Sausalito and on toward Santa Rosa. Not too far from San Franciso. His excitement grew.

After the Hickam stopover, once again they flopped on the floor of the crowded plane ready for takeoff on the final segment of their long trip. Now Robinson felt the pangs of hunger after watching some of the others chomping away on the sandwiches loaded aboard. He grabbed one along with a bottle of pop. His suppressed excitement had also submerged his hunger for most of this memorable day and the good-tasting GI sandwich made him realize suddenly he was damned hungry.

He also took the time to consider what his next move was. From Hamilton North to Redding, with his sister and her husband, presently enroute to the base. He'd advised them of his travel plans. His thoughts raced in all directions. He wasn't the calm, calculating physician. Finally, he'd get a look at his son, a young man from whom he'd been separated so many years it seemed as if he'd never seen him at all. Now he was old enough that he was probably driving his sister's car down the highway to help pick up his long-missing father. Not quite. But he faced the fact which was, Robby's son was in elementary school and his father was hardly more than a rumor or a fairy tale. Because when Robinson left for Manila, his son hadn't yet been born. He had to shake himself to realize what had gone by the boards since he'd headed for Manila. In retrospect, none of it seemed real.

All these thoughts kept cascading through his head as the plane droned its way toward San Francisco. This was the shortest segment of the three legs of the flight, with something over 2500 miles between Honolulu and Hamilton Field.

Nevertheless, it seemed an eternity as the pair of engines in the Douglas aircraft chugged away to keep those propeller blades biting into the ocean air.

Although Robinson's sister lived in Redding, in Northern California, she had gone to Ashland to see what she and her husband could do to restore the old house there to some livable condition. Her evaluation, as she considered how she'd describe the place to her brother was, "There's only one part of it worth saving. That's the view. Dump the rest."

Of course, she knew he'd never do that. Nor would she seriously suggest it. After all, the house had been in his wife's family for a number of years, since they'd built it in the 20s in that small town. She was certain he'd keep it at all costs.

When the plane finally landed at Hamilton, a grateful Robinson bounced down the steps and across the hardstand to his waiting family.

After an eternity of tearful hugs all around, the foursome made its way to their car, headed for Redding.

"I feel as if I've been moving for three days. Just keep me pointed in the right direction and tell me when I'm there. If you've a deck of cards in this car maybe Robby can keep me awake playing rummy."

He caught himself. "Maybe you don't play rummy. How about hearts?"

At that word his son came to attention. And that's what devoured the time between Hamilton Field and Redding.

The meeting and greeting was to Robinson's satisfaction. Relatively without emotion, which was fine to a man whose emotional tank had been running on empty for a number of years, but still a memorable meeting between father and son which would remain vivid in their minds forever.

Robinson had planned to stay with his sister for a few hours and then rent a car and head on up the highway to Ashland, which was a little over 100 miles north.

When they arrived at his sister's house, he said simply, "I'm going to lie down for a minute or two. To rest my eyes."

He awakened the next day. That's when he began his preparations to drive the rest of the way to Ashland.

While Robinson let his body play catchup, sister Sue and her husband, John Davis, an auto dealer in this Northern California community, shared thoughts concerning her brother and the young boy they'd raised from birth.

"Sue, why don't you just tell him what we think?"

"And just what do we think?" responded his wife. "Do you really think I should tell him that Robby's happy here with us, that all of his friends are here. His pals he goes to school with are here. I know all that. How can I tell a man, my brother though he is, that his son's better off with us than with him. That they're strangers. Don't even know each other.

"Do I tell him his son doesn't want to leave here? As he's told us several times. Just how in the devil can I tell my brother that he's lost a son too, after everything else in his life has been lost too?"

Her troubled mind opened to let her thoughts, her genuine feelings, spill out in random pieces.

She tried to force her mind to put some logic first and sentiment second as she tried to determine what was the best course of action for the boy and the father?

John Davis knew the anguish which this matter had brought to his wife. And to him, to a lesser extent. Busy as he was, he didn't have to face the home schedule each day, as did his wife, so he was somewhat removed. But knowing the turmoil he was certain would accompany Robinson to Southern Oregon, he was firmly of the opinion that the young boy should stay with them.

"Sue, I understand your concern with this. You should be concerned. But I also am convinced you're right on when you say Robby should stay right here. With us and with his friends."

"But what do I do? Tell my brother we want to keep his son?"

"No, no. Just try to relax. After he's awake and sort of caught up mentally with his physical movements from one hemisphere to another, we'll talk to him. Frankly, I'll be amazed if he doesn't see it the same as we do. In the meantime, fix something for him to eat. A good old bacon and eggs breakfast and after that we'll talk to him."

A relieved Sue gave her husband a big hug and made her way to the kitchen, saying over her shoulder, "That's a good idea for a nice big breakfast," laughing as she added, "I suppose you'll just want your cold cereal. You wouldn't want bacon and eggs too, now would you?"

"Since you ask, yes, I'll have some. Probably wouldn't be nice to let your brother eat alone."

Sue would have been happy to fix a breakfast for a regiment, she was so relieved to state her beliefs on her nephew's situation. When her husband so positively echoed her words, her self-confidence soared.

Nevertheless, she didn't look forward to discussing this with her brother.

Finally he awakened. She could hear him in the shower upstairs and when he came down the stairs, he seemed to have regained command of his customary vitality.

"What's that I smell? Bacon? Tell me it didn't come out of a can, Sue. Tell me it's real. And eggs? And not a trace of powder on them. Sue, I've had powdered eggs for so damned long I swear the chickens had sold out to Johnson and Johnson baby powder company."

"Not quite. John said he thought you'd like a breakfast like this so have at it. He'll join you because frankly, he usually fixes his own breakfast and you can be sure it's not bacon and eggs. Here's a couple of slices of toast. Anything else you need?"

"No Sue, just sit down and rest. Have something yourself".

Her husband came along and animated table conversation gave way to animated appetite appeasement.

When the final forkful had been delivered, Robinson leaned back in his chair and sipped on his coffee.

"That was great, Sue. Just great. But you know, I owe you so much already. For Robby I mean. And that's something I want to talk to you about."

Oh, oh, here it comes, thought Sue as she could see her brother's demeanor change from that of a satisfied breakfaster to what she divined was a concerned father.

"I'm just wondering what the best thing is for Robby now. I mean, I'm practically a stranger to him. He's grown up right here with you people and he couldn't have asked for a better home. Furthermore, this is home to him. I'm not stupid. He's in school here and I'm sure he's got some buddies he spends a lot of time with. What I'm getting at is simply this; how would you people like to have him stay on with you? Until maybe I get my clinic open and operating in Medford or maybe until he gets out of high school and headed for college?"

He stopped to look at his sister and at John to determine how his proposal had been received.

Sue and John looked quickly at each other. Their faces were devoid of expression. Almost immediately Sue's serious demeanor had changed to a spontaneous smile, expressing both pleasure and relief. Her less demonstrative husband had the same reaction.

"Oh Robby, I'm so happy you said that. Yes, he's your son but we look on him as our son too. And we agree with your conclusions. That his friends are here. Not somewhere else. Maybe later, sure. But right now, this seems like the best place for him. And if you're asking us, whether he can stay, the answer's yes. As long as he wants to."

She jumped up and went around the table to hug her brother. Robby's tired face brightened in view of the enthusiastic reception. The last thing he wanted to do was 'farm out' his own boy. But just as strongly, he didn't believe his son should suffer another trauma, that of leaving what he now considered home, after having had to accept the reality of a dead mother and an absentee father for so many years.

Another gigantic load had been lifted from Robinson's life. He knew his son's life here was the best thing for him.

Later that day he sat with his son.

"Robby, you've had some tough breaks in your life. And you're still young. The pain of your mother's absence can never be eased. And it shouldn't. Fortunately, you had your aunt and uncle here to help you. I think you've done great living with them. Are you happy here?"

His son responded quickly and enthusiastically. "Uh huhh. I like it here."

Then he endeared himself to his father even more as he said, almost as if he'd been eavesdropping his elders, "I'll do whatever you want me to do. But I'd rather stay here with them and go to school here if that's all right with you."

Robinson, with his arm around his son's shoulder, squeezed and said. "That's more than all right, Robby. It's really all right with me. I'm just so happy you're well, such a fine boy and doing so well. Just keep it up.

"And remember, I'm really not all that far away. Just up in Southern Oregon a hundred miles or so."

"Well, whatta you gonna do now?" his son asked, curious to know what his father's future held. "You're still a doctor, right? But no Army."

"Yes and yes. I'm a doctor and I'm out of the Army. I'm going to open a doctor's office in Medford. That way I can come down here now and again to visit you and of course, I'll be in that big old house in Ashland and there'll be plenty of room for you to visit there if you want to."

That's the way the arrangement was left and Robinson was delighted his sister and brother-in-law were so enthusiastic they had actually suggested it themselves. It couldn't be much better than that.

Now he made ready for the final lap of his trip home.

Later that day his sister, with a mischievous smile on her face, asked, innocently enough, "How do you plan to get to Ashland, Robby? Bus or rental car? What?"

"I suppose rent a car. Sounds like the easiest way."

His brother-in-law spoke up. "Too bad we don't have a second car. We did have one but we had to give it up."

Exchanging a glance with his wife, he continued. "Tell you what. Come on out here to this second garage we've got. You might be able to make this thing work."

With a puzzled look on his face after John's statement, Robinson followed the others to what they called the second garage, separate but adjacent to their regular garage.

John pulled up the garage door, and there inside with its light blue finish gleaming brightly was a magnificent 1939 Ford convertible. It was Robinson's 1939 Ford convertible.

He was speechless. He held up his hands and said, "I'm amazed. This thing. I hadn't even thought about it. You brought it down here. And it runs?" he asked.

"It runs perfectly. We brought it down here a couple of years ago. We run it now and again," said John. "We told Robby not to mention it to you because we wanted to surprise you. I'd say you were slightly surprised. Right?"

"I guess so. Kee-rist. Last thing I expected to see when you opened that door was this car. I love it. That's why you said you used to have a second car but no longer. Right?"

Sue was laughing as she said, "Robby, you should have seen the look on your face when you saw your Ford. It was priceless."

"The feeling was priceless too. It still is. C'mon. Let's take a ride. Make sure I still know how to drive a decent vehicle. With that funny blue paint. Instead of the olive drab vehicles I've seen for years."

And so they did. Just around the block but far enough for Robinson to convince himself he still knew how to drive a civilian's car. Furthermore, he was now a civilian and this was his own car.

"It may sound silly but that was a real thrill. Just driving that thing. Thanks for keeping such good care of it. All I have to do is fill it up and head north."

"When are you planning to leave?" his sister asked. "We'd love to have you stay as long as you want but I suppose you're anxious to get to work on that house. And all the other things you have to do."

Robinson wasn't at all sure. He was divided. He'd like to hang around. Mostly for his son. That's what he said. "I'd like to make myself available to Robby, without inserting myself into his new life. After all, I'm pretty much a stranger and I'd like to go at this slowly. Maybe a couple of days, if that sounds workable with you people. After all, this is your life."

John offered immediately, "Just as long as you can stand us. It must be pretty dull after the life you've led for the past few years but we'd love to have you stick around. It's a pleasure for us. Certainly no trouble."

"We've planned for you to stay on as long as you want," Sue chimed in. "We have room and there's no problem."

Robinson nodded to show his appreciation, raising his hands a little to emphasize his point, "I know that and I want you to know I appreciate your help and your thoughts. But I'm sure you must realize I'm really antsy. I really must keep moving because there's so much work to do in Ashland. And over in Medford if that's where I begin my practice. And I do want to get that started as soon as possible."

That's the way they left it. A couple of days later, Robinson was on his way north. Headed up U.S. Highway 99 toward Oregon.

The last town of consequence in California was Yreka, where he stopped to get some gasoline, and then, unless you count the tiny hamlet named Hornbrook, there were no more towns on the highway to Oregon. He was familiar with Hornbrook because that's where the old railroad 'helper' engines and crew laid over after helping to pull the long freight trains up the steep slopes of the Siskiyou Mountain Range. He saw it all as an intrigued youngster. At Hornbrook, the 'helper' engines would turn around on a rare bit of railroad machinery called a turntable, and head back to Ashland, after spending the night. That was in the days when the main railroad line came through Ashland and then up over the Siskiyou Mountains.

When the railroad was diverted east of the Cascade Range and into California via the friendlier grades of the Central Oregon region, Hornbrook became a ghost town and whatever was left of the business section, maybe a gas station and a food store, moved up alongside Highway 99 and then to I-5.

These are just some of the meaningless thoughts which paraded through Robinson's mind as he drove north. Finally, atop the summit of the Siskiyou Mountain Range, he started down the twisting roadway, occasionally taking his eyes off the narrow highway to steal a cautious look at the fabulous view of the valley far below.

Soon he was in Ashland, driving along the Boulevard and down the hill past the open-air theatre where the Shakespearean Festival plays were held each year, and then continuing in the northeast direction until he found Sheridan Street. It turned to the left and up. Mostly up. It seemed as if the end would never be reached. He had forgotten how high this street stretched before the old house was reached at the absolute end of the street. By this time he had given the low gear in his Ford a good testing. The street seemed straight up.

He parked on the dirt driveway which led to the steps to the house, fumbling in his pockets for the keys which sister Sue had given him in Redding. His first task was to open all the screened windows and doors. The musty smell was nothing more than he'd expect of a closed up house but it was overpowering.

He checked one of the bedrooms and found it more than satisfactory. He wryly thought this was like the Ritz or Savoy in London compared to some of his beds in recent years.

A quick look-around was all he needed. Everything seemed to be in working order. Water. Electricity. Heat.

First of all, he drove downtown to locate the telephone office. He wanted to place an order for a hookup immediately. After that he wound up his gleaming Ford again to drive to Medford. He wanted to make contact with his old friend, Bob Booth.

They had some important shipping business to attend to.

SOUTHERN OREGON -- 1947-2009

He cautiously headed down the extremely steep Sheridan Street to the highway and a sudden impulse prompted him to turn right, to the highway's southwesterly direction.

He immediately realized he should have turned left, the direction which would take him to Medford.

But his impulse had directed him to take the route which would take him to the locale he'd tentatively selected for the baggage coming to Booth's Packing Plant from Yokohama. It was Emigrant Lake. He knew the area and was aware the water level should have dropped well down with the advent of summer.

Still, he wanted to take a look at it. "Better check and see if my memory of that place is as accurate as I think it is."

When he got there he wasn't disappointed.

Viewed from afar, it revealed only a shallow covering of water in the center of the lake. The lake itself was created by Emigrant Dam and the water level would soon diminish more. Down to the zero level, as the numerous orchardists and farmers began their annual syphoning of water to nourish their respective crops which would soon be thirsting in the typical warm summers of Southern Oregon. Satisfaction of these water needs came from irrigation ditches on each side of the valley. Of course, these ditches received much of their supply right from here, at Emigrant Lake.

Even now, early in the irrigating season though it was, most of the tiny shack out in the center of the lake was visible. In his younger years, Robinson had been venturesome enough to trek out to the shack. As far as he knew, there was nothing kept in the shack. There could be some recording instruments, of which he was ignorant, but there was little evidence of that.

Satisfied things were normal as in the past, Robinson wheeled his car around and picked up the highway to retrace his path through Ashland on into Medford, only a dozen or so miles away.

When he entered Medford, he simply drove along until he came to Main Street, where he turned left for only a few blocks, taking a left turn just after crossing the railroad tracks. Booth's operation occupied a sizeable portion of the next block.

This is where the company packed the select pears for special sales worldwide. Needless to say they also handled the bulk pears which went to the canneries. The packing plant handled the entire crop, from the bottom to the individually wrapped quality pears which were the elite and thus on top of the crop.

As usual, there was plenty of activity both in and outside the packing plant.

Robinson's friend spotted him as he pulled into the parking strip in front of the office portion of the plant. Booth bounced out onto the steps leading up to the office shouting, "Welcome home Doc Robby, where-ever the hell home is."

Robinson shouted just as loud, "You'll never know how pleasant the sound of your voice is. And I never thought I'd say that either."

Then the two were silent as they embraced, two old friends meeting after each had almost given up all hope of ever seeing each other again.

"Come on in. Fill me in on what you've got planned and whatever else. For openers, the shipping notice arrived. It's underway. But you probably know it's fifty or sixty days before we'll sight it here."

Robinson reassured him. "Time's not important. When it gets here, that'll work out just right. I'm gonna set up living in the old house in Ashland and presently I'll be opening offices here in Medford. That's my program. So we'll be seeing each other. Whether you want to or not."

"Want to?" said Booth. "Hell, I'm so happy to see you. You'll never know the number of times we'd written you off. Those bastards don't exactly have a reputation for treating prisoners with kid gloves."

Robinson laughed. "And their reputation's deserved. They're bastards is right. You used the right word. Or think of a stronger one. Lots of men, women and children had it much tougher than I did. I knew hundreds of them. But that's behind me now."

Robinson stiffened as he said that and, turning to Booth to face him, said, "There's one thing we can't let happen. We can't let ourselves forget what millions and millions of people paid for with their lives. I don't mean soldiers, either. Women and children. People too young or too old to carry weapons. The animals, and that's an insult to most animals, literally chopped them up or starved and worked them to death. The women? Well, you know what they did with the women. Terrible people. And they believe the teachings of their fathers that they are superior to all others and others don't deserve life."

He shook himself and forced out, "Let's not get too involved emotionally in that. I know I'll never forget what they did. Let's just hope that damned MacArthur doesn't fuck up the peace which so many people helped get at the cost of their lives."

Booth quietly said, "Amen. I think you're late. It looks to me like that's exactly what he's done and is doing. But you're right. Let's get on with your life.

"What about young Robby? Is he here with you?"

Seeing Robinson shake his head he asked, "Where is he? Still with Sue in Redding?"

"Right Bob, and tell me I'm doing the right thing on this. He's got to look at me like a stranger. And he's going to school down there. All his school friends and buddies are there. I just thought it wouldn't be fair to him to bring him here, away from all of his friends."

Booth digested those words and said, "Hmm. I didn't even think of that. Just figured he'd come right along. But hell, you're right. You're a stranger to him. He's got to kinda get acquainted with you. But leaving his friends down there. Now that's another matter. That'll be tough no matter how well you guys hit it off."

Booth's observations provided welcome support to the difficult decision Robinson had almost settled on. To leave Robby where he is for the moment. Not even consider moving him. If he says or indicates in any way he wants to, great. Otherwise he stays put.

And Robinson went on about his business in Medford. That consisted of a long session with Booth and then some serious thinking about locating his clinic.

When it came to the matter of deciding what section of town he wanted to check out for a clinic location, he didn't have a clue. From Booth he learned the old hospital was on the east side of the town of Medford. But he also learned another hospital building was on the drawing board.

Fortunately, it also was on the east side.

Further in the future an ambitious project was planned for a self-contained retirement home, with more independent living offered in luxurious but not grandiose houses encircling the retirement home.

In itself this wasn't of particular interest to Robinson but within the retirement home itself was planned a cared-living arrangement which offered some of the services of a hospital.

As Booth said, "The clincher is the big new hospital that's planned out in the same area but a little south of town. That's gonna happen. No doubt about it. When is another matter. But that's something you might nose around with some folks in town and get the dope on. I'd never thought about that much but I'll see if I can't find out some more definite dope on it too."

They had retired to the golf club, also up on the hill in the east section of the town, to have some lunch. It gave Robinson a chance to get some thoughts Booth might have on Robinson's first decision, that of location.

"Let me ask you a question. I know the old hospital's on this side of town. The east side. And from what everything you tell me is in the wind, the new hospital and clinics are going in this area too. Right?"

"Nearly as I know, that's the way it looks. There's really never been any suggestion by anyone to build any hospitals on the other side of town. But as you know there's no telling which way it might go in the future."

Bob leaned back in his chair and asked, "What are you thinking of? Maybe locating on the west side?"

"Well, nearly as I can tell, the population's fairly evenly split on either side of town. But if I read things correctly, there's probably more people living on the west side. Does that sound right to you?"

Booth shrugged and said, "I suppose that's true. Not much difference though, I don't think."

"Here's another angle. Again, this is from memory of only a brief time here but I seem to recall the wealthier folks lived here on the east side. Not that there were nothing but paupers on the other side but isn't that right? Didn't most of the so-called rich people live out here?"

"Well, as I say, I suppose that's true," conceded Booth. "But what's the point?"

Robinson paused and then said, "I just think I'm going to take a long look at putting in my offices on the west side. See how that works out. What do you think about that?"

"Why not? I mean, we're not talking about Portland or LA. This isn't a big town. People make it from one side to the other pretty easy." Noting Robinson poised to suggest the transportation question, he hurried on to say, "We've even got a bus service now that can get people from one section to another. Not real fast but fast enough. Sure, I think you'd be in good shape locating on the west side."

And then he added, "I know you mentioned you had some work to do in Ashland. On the house. While you're over there checking that out, and doing whatever other catchup work you have to do, I'll look around here. See if there's some property, either just the dirt, with no buildings, or maybe even a building that would be suitable. How's that sound?"

Robinson grinned. "That sounds just great. I appreciate any help you can give me. Getting that started is a high priority but you're right, I do want to get back to Ashland. There's plenty to do there. I'll get back over in a day or two."

"Do it. Maybe we can have dinner. I can buzz over there too. I'm really not too busy right now. You've got my number so just give me a call if you need anything. And I'll keep you posted on the shipping news."

"Don't worry about that. When it gets here fine. There's no hurry."

The pair finished their lunch and headed back to Booth's packing plant.

Without any additional delay, Robinson made his way back to the highway and guided his convertible back to Ashland. With the weather on the sunny side it was inevitable the top must come down. He felt like a kid wheeling that baby along the two lane roadway leading back to Ashland.

When he wheeled his car up Sheridan Street his thoughts turned to the old barn out in back. The driveway of sorts which led to it wasn't too badly overgrown and he was able to park in front of the big doors.

He felt as if he should cross his fingers before opening the doors but found to his surprise and delight, the spacious area wasn't as jammed to the walls as he suspected it might be. With some moving around of the 'stuff', he thought his car could be slid in there and kept out of the elements.

His use of the term 'stuff' was the only way the material inside the barn could be identified.

It ranged from old pieces of furniture to an incubator dating back to the days when his wife's grandfather, or was it her father, he puzzled, hatched chicks in the barn. He looked past this material, figuring he'd get a start first on the house and then transfer his energies to the barn-cleaning.

It didn't take him long to attend to such essentials as the hookup order to the telephone company and also calls to both the Ashland and Medford newspapers to begin daily deliveries. The other utilities were activated, courtesy of his sister, and he was in business in the house in a matter of minutes.

The housekeeper his sister had employed had kept the interior spotless. The beds were freshly made, awaiting his arrival, and Robinson found himself in the unusual role of someone who had nothing urgent awaiting his attention.

Then he nudged himself. "There's the little thing of getting my clinic open and ready to go in Medford. Then I can sit back and relax."

As relaxed as he would be for the rest of his life. He called a Realtor in Medford and made plans to go to the office and look at some properties.

"Hey Robby, I just had a thought here you might want to kick around a little." It was Bob Booth's excited voice on the telephone from Medford, just catching Robinson as he was getting ready to leave the house to do some basic shopping.

"What is it? Did that container arrive already?" Robinson returned. "You're really wound up."

"Well, maybe I'm a little too excited about this but it seemed to me it just might be your answer to some location problems here. And no, the container didn't get here. This has nothing to do with it."

"All right Bob, what is it?"

"Okay, I was at the Elks Club having lunch and a bunch of us were talking about you coming to town and looking around for a spot. Someone mentioned the fact that old Doc Hayes was thinking about bringing in someone in his clinic because he wants to plan seriously about retiring. He's no kid you know. You do know who I'm talking about, don't you?"

He paused for a moment in his rapid-fire delivery, but not long enough for Robinson to slip in a response to his question.

"Anyway, you might want to give him a call or just drop by his place. It's right here on East Main. Whadya think of that?"

Robinson finally was given the clear channel to say something. "Bob, that's sounds real interesting. It would certainly give me a leg up and beat the hell out of starting from scratch. Hayes, Hayes, that name's familiar but I can't quite make it click. Been there a long time, right?"

"That's right, Robby. Been in the valley long's I can remember. Do you want me to set up a meeting with him? I can do it real easy. Or would you rather handle it yourself?"

Robinson thought for just a second. Probably better if he initiated the contact with the man but also probably advisable for Booth to call and tell Hayes of Robinson's presence and his desire to talk.

That's what he suggested to Booth.

"I'll do it. I'll call him right now and simply tell him of your plans. Then I'll just leave it at that. That you'll be calling him in a day or two. Okay?"

"That's great, Bob," said a grateful Robinson. "Saves me a lot of trouble if it works. If it doesn't work out, the good doctor probably can give me a lot of tips that could help me out no matter which way I go. With him or on my own."

Booth was delighted. "I'll get in touch with him right away. Today. I'll let you know what he says and you guys can take it from there. Talk to you later."

"Right Bob. Let me know," and they hung up.

Robinson went to his car to go downtown and shop for food with a feeling of confidence that one of his major problems had been solved.

After a brief stop at the first grocery store he came to, he went on to the post office. He definitely wanted to check on the box he'd ordered there. Also, to pick up any mail which might have filtered in.

He sifted through the small stack of mail quickly, disposing of the non-personal junk addressed to the box only and saving three or four letters addressed to him.

One of the letters he latched onto quickly. It was from Japan and was quite bulky. From Gerry Francis.

He went to a nearby cafe with outside tables, grabbed a cup of coffee and quickly opened the letter.

Dr. Francis got right to the point:

"Dear Robby,

"I assume you're home by now and I also assume you might be interested, as a fellow physician, in a story which I've been following in the local English language newspaper here in Tokyo. I don't know whether it's been picked up in the States yet or not but it's obviously a big story here. And I suppose in China, too.

"It concerns the mysterious disappearance of one Dr. Shiro Kimura. To refresh your memory, if need be, he was the director of the infamous living medical experiment station in Manchuria as ordered by the Emperor. My little joke.

"The clippings which I've taken from the papers here follow the story quite closely. Their interest was piqued particularly because he had been absolved of any war criminal responsibility by General MacArthur. Our leader had negotiated an unholy arrangement with Kimura exchanging his life for the data he'd acquired in the wholesale cruel killings which he disguised as 'medical research'. Robby, it still hurts to write those words."

But good news. Take a look at these clippings.

> Tokyo (Worldwide Press) — Authorities here have reported the disappearance of Dr. Shiro Kimura.
>
> Kimura was in charge of the infamous medical experimental station ordered by Emperor Hirohito in 1937 in Manchuria. Kimura and his assistant, Dr. Ryoicho Naito, used living specimens as the objects of their experiments which continued until Japan was brought to the table for surrender.
>
> Neither of these two, like Hirohito, was ever punished for these war crimes.
>
> Police here are mystified regarding the whereabouts of Kimura. He has been close to General Douglas MacArthur's headquarters here but failed to appear at his offices two days ago. A concentrated search for him has failed to find him.
>
> Officials are mystified.
>
> Colonel Gerald Francis, the doctor who is Gen. MacArthur's aide, said he last saw him on the day before his failure to appear at the office.
>
> "He appeared in good health, spoke of no problems and left with no suggestion that he might not return to the office the next day," Dr. Francis stated.
>
> The search for Dr. Kimura will continue.

Robinson leaned back, letting the clipping rest on his knees as he rejoiced in this printed proof of justice having finally been served in the case of Chiang Luang.

"They'll never be able to even the score those two murdering devils ran up there at Unit 731. Or the Emperor's soldiers killing helpless women and children for the sport of it while the so-called doctors 'experimented' on the victims which they hauled in.

"They can't even the score for Chiang or any of the millions the Emperor's soldiers killed, starved to death or worked to death. The beheadings alone by the Japs run into the millions.

"Dr. Kimura's disappearance," and Robinson's mind lingered on the word, "will bring a measure of peace to Chiang Luang. He deserves some peace.

"Kimura deserves his 'disappearance'."

Robinson read the letter from Gerry Francis quickly. He also read the enclosed clipping regarding Dr. Shiro Kimura.

It took only that brief episode to transport him back to Manila with its sadness, tragedy and all the turmoil of war with its broken and dead people. Robinson already had relegated that to the rear of his mind as he dealt with the numerous projects confronting him here. He couldn't escape the past and made no effort to do so.

His projects here involved no dead people. At least not yet, he reminded himself as he thought of the impending arrival of the container. As yet unscheduled but enroute.

He knew he'd never move mentally too far from those days and those events. But regardless of the mass of detail which confronted him here and now, he found himself eagerly awaiting his next visit to the postoffice box.

The next day he checked the mail and he wasn't disappointed. He found a double reminder of what had happened in Manila and how some of those who were fortunate enough to survive the Jap slaughter had reacted.

His first mailing of extreme interest was from Ramon Cangleonn. A combination of Cangleonn's inability to write legibly and his problems with the English language gave Robinson fits as he attempted to decipher it. "Ramon should'a been a doctor," Robinson drawled slowly, thinking of the ancient joke regarding doctor's prescription scrawlings.

However, he managed to glean from Ramon's writing the man's happiness that his task in Tokyo was concluded successfully and had been duly recorded in the newspapers of the area. The clipping he sent was in English. It wasn't identified but because the dateline of the story was Tokyo, Robinson assumed it was the newly-established newspaper there which was printed in English.

Tokyo (Overseas Press) — The body of a Japanese Army officer has been discovered by the city police of Tokyo.

Police stated the body had been recovered from a pond in Hibiya Park. They further stated they had identified the dead man as Tomika Saitoi, a former officer with many responsibilities dealing with prisoners of war during the war with the United States. The report stated it appeared as if Saitoi had tripped, hit his head on a rock and fallen into the pond where he drowned. The bruise on his head didn't indicate enough force to cause death but certainly could have rendered the man unconscious.

A review of Saitoi's service record has revealed he was a man of authority at two prisons in Manila, specifically Cabanatuan and Bilibad.

He had also been in charge of one of the hellships which transported thousands of prisoners from the Philippines to Japan for work in the labor camps there.

The first PWs to leave Camp Cabanatuan came to Bilibad where they were kept for a few days, prior to boarding the Nitti Maru on December 13, 1944.

They embarked after dark from Pier #17, Manila, for Corregidor. During that first night the identifying marks on the smoke stack were exchanged with one of the two accompanying Jap troop ships.

Saitoi was senior officer on the Nitti Maru and gave the order to change this means of identification to avoid attack by American planes on accompanying warships.

This plan was tragic for the many prisoners crammed aboard the Nitti Maru.

Evidence suggests the more than 1600 prisoners jammed into the holds of the Hellship Nitti faced horrors far more inhumane than the Death March.

When the Nitti entered the China Sea, American dive bombers had attacked, the ship now displaying the smoke stack identification mark of a Jap troop ship.

The bombs of the attacking planes nearly demolished the ship which was beached. Hundreds of the prisoners were killed and the remainder attempted to swim ashore within markers established by Saitoi. Those who floated outide these markers were machine-gunned.

Robinson put the clipping aside. Recollections of the terrible affair were still quite vivid in his mind. The fact that Saitoi's record was investigated, and that he was never held for trial, was also quite real.

"How could MacArthur or any mortal with only the objective of fairness to serve, release animals such as Saitoi. How fitting he drowned. He was released by MacArthur but the court of Cangleonn obviously holds murderers of defenseless, helpless people to a tougher standard.

"The punishment," Robinson chuckled, "was fitting."

Robinson thought he could guess who might have sent the second letter. His guess was right.

It was from Ian Greene. "What irony," Robinson mused sarcastically, "How strange. It has a story concerning a former Japanese soldier who was found dead in Tokyo. Indeed, how strange."

Then he read the letter.

"Dear Dr. Robinson:

"I thought you might find the enclosed cutting from the London Telegraph of some interest. Perhaps you'd heard of this fellow while you were posted in Manila.

"No matter. He apparently suffered some sort of seizure in Tokyo. He had been residing somewhere near Tokyo since becoming redundant after the war was settled.

"Quite surprisingly enough, he was not held accountable for some of his less than heroic deeds during the war. Your man MacArthur apparently wasn't aware of some of these 'deeds', either by this chap or some of his chums. I think MacArthur could have served with our Neville Chamberlain; seems to have that same forgiving nature. Appeasement at all costs, or something of that nature."

Robinson chuckled at Greene's reference to Prime Minister Chamberlain who acquiesced to some of Adolph Hitler's early demands before the conflict in Europe really took off.

Then he continued reading.

"At any rate, the person Ahirou, Sabroa Ahirou, right, finally has had an opportunity to answer the bidding of his Emperor. He has died for him, doing as the Emperor ordered, killing all the helpless within reach.

"The sight of this little creature swinging his sword at the neck of a prisoner, forced to a kneeling position on the deck of the Nitti Maru, shall be in my mind until death. So too, will the beheading of the other prisoners, as ordered by him. The bloody slaughter of defenseless people by this animal could never be equalled by beasts.

"Can't help but wonder if he finished his days on this earth on his knees with a firm object swung down heavily, repeatedly, on the nape of his neck, even though it mightn't inflict permanent damage, but simply to give a message to those who died. I fervently hope so.

"But again, I sincerely hope he derived great happiness from dying for the Emperor. His departure shan't be mourned by any in this area. Or by any of the survivors of the people he murdered.

"And though Ahirou has now died for the Emperor, as have many hundreds of thousands of other Japanese, it should be duly noted the Emperor is alive and well. Why not? Your MacArthur has completely absolved him of all responsibility for the killings of multimillions by his followers.

"Right. And Hitler didn't have a moustache.

"Cheers, Ian Greene."

Robinson turned to the clipping, Greene's cutting as the Brits call them.

> Tokyo, February 14 (Reuters) — Authorities today found the body of a former Japanese soldier who had been living on the outskirts of Tokyo here.
>
> The authorities said they were reasonably certain it was Sabroa Ahirou. He was a man whose war responsibility included transport of Allied prisoners aboard ships from outposts to the home island where they were committed to a brief life consisting of round-the-clock work for the Emperor's war effort. Scanty rations and rampant disease with no care contributed to brief lifetimes.

Robinson put the clipping down as it continued a review of the man's military actions. He knew most of those far too well.

Normally the reason for a letter of this nature would bring sadness to the recipient. An unexpected death. But the message carried as much joy for Robinson to receive as it brought to the person who wrote it. And it was a welcome written visit from Greene for Dr. Robinson. And so prompt too.

His mail of this day and the day previous had permitted Robinson to look more kindly on the world around him. Justice was served in its own, cruel way, although any chance of having an even score on that matter simply didn't exist.

Then he skipped ahead in the clipping to read the final paragraphs.

> The men's leader, Ahirou, actually took a few swings himself, according to a report taken from liberated prisoners after the war was over.
>
> Police medical reports state there were several marks at the back of the neck of the dead man, indicating he'd been struck many times by an object obviously without an edge which would permit cutting the flesh. None of the blows was said to have carried enough force to cause death but certainly could have rendered the man unconscious after so many blows were repeated. No continuing investigation is contemplated.

"I'm happy for the men who were finally able to do their bit in this whole mess. They will be able to rest easier in the future and enjoy what is left of their lives." That was Robinson's thought as he now turned his mind to the possibility which Booth had raised. That of getting involved with an existing clinic rather than go through the multiproblems, with its agonies, of establishing a new one.

In less than a week he was in business.

The address was on East Main Street in Medford and he was biding his time now for arrival of some equipment he wanted for what he deemed a fine clinic in need of some modernizing. He arranged for that with a couple of telephone calls.

Again, combining his preparation in Medford with the work on the house, not to mention the barn, in Ashland, Robinson's days were full. Nevertheless, he took one day for a rapid-fire trip to Redding to visit with his son and sister and brother-in-law.

"I'm all set in Medford with my clinic. Have a fairly good start on cleaning up the barn. And the house is really in good shape. The lady's done a good job of it there all these years. 'Course, she's been paid for it but as you know that doesn't necessarily mean the job gets done.

"And Robby, how's school coming? Right on top of things, I suppose."

"Not too bad, I guess, uh, yeah not too bad."

It was apparent to the doctor that his son still found it difficult to communicate with someone he readily accepted as his father, of course, but still someone who was a total stranger to him. Robinson was smart enough not to pursue that aspect too long.

In fact, he bid his adieu almost abruptly because of that, although he hadn't planned on more than part of a day in Redding.

"This is just the right distance for me to give that car a workout. And sis, I don't know who you had working on it, but it's just great. Just burned my way down here. Up over the Siskiyou Mountains like they were flat prairie-land. Without you, I don't know what would have happened to young Robby here. And my car," he added with a laugh.

He was pleased to see his son join in the laughter at the obvious attempt at light humor of what was really a serious subject, the care of Robby II all those years.

Soon he was cruising back up the highway to Ashland. Now he was more relaxed. He knew where he was headed. He knew what he was going to do and he knew where he was going to do it. He was also in charge of his destiny.

It had been many years since he'd enjoyed those luxuries.

Robinson soon adjusted from the busy days of non-scheduled work details to a more orderly day-to-day routine. Of course, his early trip to the postoffice box was a priority, although he hadn't received any additional messages from his friends in Manila or Tokyo since the first letters arrived.

His next advisory from that sector came from Gerry Francis.

Francis said: "I'm sending along this clipping regarding the disappearance of Kimura. Thought you might be interested. Really don't know how much of a search is being conducted but in view of his importance here, the newspaper people are staying close to the case. I don't know if the police share that interest or are assigning that much emphasis to the case.

"Regardless, I hope all is well with you and you're becoming adjusted to life in the States. I can assure you I'm not adjusting any better to life here in the MacArthur Regiment than I was before. Frankly, I'm hoping I can see an opportunity to get transferred out. At least to Honolulu, if not the mainland.

"Who knows? I might even be sent to that veterans domiciliary right there in Southern Oregon.

"Keep me posted on anything new developing there and I hope everything's going well for you."

Robinson picked out the clipping, curious of course, to see what had developed in Tokyo regarding the missing doctor.

> Tokyo (Worldwide Press) — Authorities here report no new developments regarding the disappearance of Dr. Shiro Kimura several weeks ago.
>
> Dr. Kimura opened and directed all operations of the experimental station in Manchuria under

orders of Emperor Hirohito. Kimura was not held for trial as a war criminal.

His activities in the Manchurian experiment plant known as Unit 731 included exposing prisoners to artillery fire and to gun shots so they could experiment with the treatment. This also included freezing prisoners to death so they could conduct experiments in treatment of frostbite.

His physicians dissected prisoners so medical students could observe pulsating organs of the still living prisoners.

Based on precisely-kept records by Kimura and his assistant director, Dr. Ryoichi Naito, the prisoners were infected with all diseases from syphilis to typhoid and other fevers to study the reactions. Their records state 3000 prisoners died just from these activities.

The records are not so clear regarding the number of experiment-caused deaths since Unit 731 opened until the end of the war.

Kimura's former associate at Unit 731, Dr. Naito, has stated he did not see Dr. Kimura the night of his disappearance and has no idea where he might have gone.

Authorities have uncovered no clues to enable them to determine whether the disappearance was the result of criminal action or whether it was of Kimura's own volition.

Military investigators also have reported no developments and the case appears closed, unless new information is received.

Robinson folded the clipping, placed it inside the envelope from Francis and placed it in his briefcase.

He mumbled as he went out the door of the post office, "No new information's likely to come out. At least not real soon. Not if I can help it."

Based on his friend Booth's estimates, he wouldn't be expecting his shipment from Yokohama for another three weeks at the earliest. He had plenty to keep himself occupied in the meantime. First priority was opening his clinic and getting acquainted in the community of Medford. Booth was most helpful in that respect. So too, was the man who'd welcomed him into the clinic, Dr. Robert Hayes.

He'd been there for years and had a general practice, which was precisely what Robinson had in mind. Things were breaking good.

In high spirits he met Booth for lunch at the country club.

"No, there's nothin' new on your shipment, Rob," Booth quickly announced as the pair entered the informal dining area of the bar. Robinson nodded as if to say he wasn't expecting any news right now.

They joined a mixed group of card players and golfers just off the course who were relaxing with drinks and a bite to eat.

There was also a bevy of ladies in the clubhouse that day and Booth explained quickly to Robinson. "It's ladies day on the course. They get first priority on tee times and then after that's all filled out, it's open play for everyone. I meant to ask, do you do any golfing?"

"Not really. At one time I had some clubs but I've never had any great desire to get involved. It requires too much time and quite honestly, I have the uneasy feeling much of my time has been spent on relatively inconsequential matters. It's high time I concentrate on some more important objectives."

A puzzled Booth kept the waiting attendant a little longer as he said, "Inconsequential? I sure as hell don't consider what you've been doing for the past six years or so inconsequential. I'd say it was a major contribution."

Bringing himself back to the waiter he said, "Sorry, I'll just have the soup and salad. How about you Rob?"

"That sounds good. I'll have the same and some coffee, please."

Directing himself to Booth's statement after the waiter departed he said, "I agree with you. That is, I agree what was done out there had to be done and I'm happy I was there and able to do what I could. What I'm endeavoring to say, and not doing a great job of it, is that as far as advancing my own career along civilian pathways, I've done nothing. And that's not mentioning that my family life is non-existent. First the death of my wife, long ago, and then the death of Lenora, the woman who was trying to help me in that damnedable Bilibad.

"On the other hand, look at you. You've got your business running right on the button. Your family's all here. Intact. You've been able to work with them, give them the attention they need. That sorta thing's what I had in mind."

Booth leaned back and agreed, "Well, I can't disagree with you on that. But I think you might want to take a look at the golf course some day with the idea of getting out and relaxing a little after you've got your show on the road, so to speak."

Robinson almost grudgingly granted that much. "Maybe I should join out here if only to enjoy the lunch and, I see a few card players. Now that I wouldn't consider wasting my time. I could use a little card playing."

"Talk to my wife," Booth immediately answered. "She lives for bridge playing and would be happy to greet you to her group. Give you a chance to meet some of her friends too."

He added, "Some of them are damned eligible too for some unattached male."

Robinson quickly raised a hand in rejection. "No, no, I mean just for the card playing. I'm not sure I'm ready for any females. Other than playing cards or some casual social event. But nothing of serious nature."

Booth could readily see Robinson was quite serious on that matter and didn't pursue it. Besides, their lunches had arrived and that silenced the conversation for the moment.

As they concentrated on the soup and salad, Robinson's mind continued on the subject on which they had touched briefly. Was he really ready to get emotionally involved with another woman?

He had thought about this precise matter a couple of times in the past. At those times he hadn't had the opportunity to determine whether he was or wasn't attuned to such pursuits. Now, when those opportunities might be available, he wondered how he would react.

His initial inclination was that he wasn't interested at all. He'd already had a marvelous wife, taken by death far too early for anyone. He'd been fortunate enough to find another woman, in vastly different circumstances, but one who would be wonderful in any circumstances. She too, had given her life, in a dedicated effort to help him. He found it difficult to forget that and frankly, he admitted to himself, he didn't want to forget it.

So the upshot of all this thinking made him seriously question whether he'd ever want to make a committment to another woman. The danger of another important relationship being torn out of this life again might lurk too strongly in his mind to permit any such commitment.

That was a consideration which Robinson knew was a gigantic block to any future involvement which might present itself. He also thought it was probably a consideration that wouldn't dissipate. It more likely would remain with him for the rest of his life.

With an effort he forced the subject from his mind.

"Good soup, Bob," he said somewhat inanely to break the silence, something Booth had chosen to observe.

Then the pair resumed eating with the usual table talk until they finished up and departed, Booth to his packing plant offices and Robinson to attend to some final details at the clinic.

Two days later Booth called to tell him his wife thought it would be great if Robinson could come to dinner the next evening.

"Just the four of us. Maybe play some bridge later on. A friend of Caroline's will join us but my wife said to tell you she's not trying to fix you up or any such thing. It's just to have you sit down to a nice home-prepared meal for a change. Okay?"

Until the last portion of the invitation came over the phone from Booth, Robinson was all set to refuse. The thought of a meal in a house with good china, napkins and all that, had a certain appeal to him that he found difficult to resist.

"That sounds good. First of all, let me check my calendar. Make certain I'm free," and then he said, "Oh hell yes, I'm sure I'm heavily booked that night. My social calendar's so crowded these days. No, you tell me when and I'll be there."

Robinson's philosophy specifying no involvement with the opposite sex was now scheduled for its first test, and it was a severe test.

Caroline Booth's friend was a young widow. Later that week he told Booth, when he asked him what he thought of her, "She's young to me but it seems as if everyone I know's young. Except maybe for Doctor Hayes and hell, he's retiring."

Her husband had been killed early in the war. He was a pilot in the European Theater of War, flying bombers out of England.

She worked for an insurance agency in Medford, had no children, and was extremely attractive and witty.

The dinner was delightful and Robinson thoroughly enjoyed the bridge hands which followed. Strangers playing bridge, at least they were strangers to Robinson, can't get too clever. They stuck to basics and unlike most bridge games Robinson had been involved in, this was basically for fun.

So the entire evening was a success.

But again, when Booth and he got together for lunch downtown and a post mortem on the evening, the inevitable questions from Booth were asked regarding his impressions of Paula Gearhart, and Robinson could only shrug his shoulders.

"Bob, you know there's not a single thing I could say about her that isn't positive. She's attractive, certainly. And she's intelligent too. Nothing flighty, although she seems awfully young. But honest to God, I find myself thinking of other people in my life when I think in terms of any sort of a makeout relationship. Does that make sense?"

Booth answered honestly. "From where I sit it doesn't make sense at all. Near's I could tell, she seemed to like what she saw in you. You're both unattached. What the hell, Robby, you're not gonna ask her to get married next week. If you want a date for dinner, or maybe get tired of me for lunch, why not take a shot at her? Just for the social companionship."

Robinson was still puzzled. "I know, I know. It doesn't make sense to you. That's why I asked you because I knew you'd be honest about it. But dammit, everytime I looked at her I kept seeing these other people. Almost everytime. It's weird."

Booth knew he was talking about seeing his deceased wife and the woman in the Philippines. He knew he was utterly lacking in any expertise to deal with a situation such as that. He said so. "Robby, I'm not one of your head shrinks. Maybe they could figure that out. Maybe you don't want it figured out. I simply don't know. But it is a little crazy, don't you agree?"

"No doubt about it, Bob. That's exactly what it is. Crazy. But I may do as you say, take her to dinner or lunch, but assuming she's interested in me, even that wouldn't be fair, now would it? She'd be expecting it to go somewhere and I know for sure it's not going any place."

Booth shook his head as they made ready to leave the little cafe. "Robby, that's your problem. Frankly, I'm glad it's yours, not mine. That's a tough one. Damned tough."

As they were headed out, Robinson said, "Bob, when your wife asks you about my reaction, play it cool. Impressed yes, but if you know what I mean. I know for sure she'll be asking."

Booth laughed. "That's a cinch. Don't worry. I'll play it cool. That you think she's nice and just leave it at that. I'll tell her you've got so damned many other things on your mind right now that it'd be difficult for you to look at any thing or any one with a very serious thought. That'll handle it."

"Thanks Bob. Appreciate it. I'll catch you later. I'm going to head out to Ashland now and check the mail and get an idea what has to happen to that barn. I've got a builder coming up to see what's needed. So I'll talk to you later," and Robinson hopped into the Ford and soon was headed toward Ashland.

When he picked up his mail, one envelope drove all thoughts of the preceding night's dinner, the woman or the luncheon chat he'd had with Booth from his mind. This particular envelope had a Manila postmark.

Robinson figured it was either Jorge or Ramon. Cangleonn again or Merrando.

It was from Merrando and as he read the stilted writing he automatically translated it to more readable English:

"Dear Friend Robinson,

"I hope your trip home was safe and easy.

"Not much has changed since you left. I've been busy and am happy with what I've been able to do. I am sending to you a clipping from the Manila Herald which was printed two days ago.

"It tells of a man you may remember from the days when you were in prison here. Some of us will never forget him. I'm sure you won't forget him.

"If I can help you here please write and tell me. I will do anything I can.

"Your comrade,
Sergi Merrando"

It took Robinson only the time to read the opening paragraph of the clipping from the Herald to restore his memory of one of the more bestial bastards the Japs had thrown at the helpless ones during the war. And also to remind him of the story he'd seen before. But it was well worth reading. Often.

> Manila, March 17 — Word has been received here of the death of Maori Mori, a onetime Manila businessman who was a captain with the Jap forces in World War and was in command of the notorious prison camp at Cabanatuan.

He decided to read on. A little more.

Captain Mori was the camp commander and was a Jap reserve officer, although his place of residence was Manila and he owned a bicycle shop here before the war. He was considered a spy for the Emperor.

Mori's death was apparently natural although the police said his medical records indicated he'd had no health problems. They have initiated an investigation.

Mori's death won't be mourned by any of the five to seven thousand men who were imprisoned at Cabanatuan Prison Camp #1, as it was known. Even though he turned over command of the camp to members of his staff, there was never any indication he wasn't totally in charge of the camp. The suffering prisoners there always held him responsible for the atrocities his guards perpetrated on the helpless inmates. The few who survived his inhumane treatment never forgave the beast."

Just reading that much of Mori's treatment of the poor devils at Cabanatuan, once again flooded Robinson's mind with the horrors he had personally witnessed there. And of the horrors created every place the Japs went.

He paused a moment and then carefully folded the clipping and placed it with the others he'd already collected.

"Someday there'll be someone who'll want to read this. And any of the others that may come along. I'll do my best to save these for them."

Then he drove slowly back up the hill to the house on Sheridan.

Once back at the house, and with the current clipping still in his hand, he decided to put together some of the vast collection of material he had ready to carry to its final resting place. He'd decided that would be the attic.

Out of the way and still readily available.

This major decision made, he grabbed a cardboard box and placed the letters received so far, along with the clippings, in the box. He now had clippings his friends had sent along from Tokyo, England and the Philippines.

As he was doing this, he realized that within his baggage he had saved enough stuff to fill several boxes and he started on that next. He had filled two boxes by the time he finished sorting out all of his collection, saving what he deemed worthy and tossing into the fireplace that which he didn't want.

He carried these two boxes up the stairs to the second floor, stacking them near the stairway to the attic. In his mind he had already assigned material such as that in the two boxes to a final resting place in the attic.

"I'll move those later," he told himself, thinking he'd probably find a foot of dust on the floor of the attic, certain the cleaning lady hadn't included that area within her province of upkeep.

With the house in good order and enough basic foodstuffs for his needs, his next thoughts turned to the barn.

Most of it was useless to him. There was plenty of room for his car but he wanted the wooden floor taken up and replaced with concrete. He'd already advised a builder-carpenter of his desires and that was on the schedule.

As he attempted to determine just what remained for him to do he suddenly realized, this was just about the end of the line. Everything was about as done as could be.

At that moment the jarring ring of the telephone brought him to attention.

"Hello," he said as softly as he could, realizing that he usually used the telephone as merely an instrument into which a person must shout to make it function.

"Robby," came the voice of Bob Booth, "your package should arrive here tomorrow. I just got a call from the San Francisco office of Transasia and they're putting the container on a truck tonight so it should haul in here tomorrow midmorning."

The response he received was remarkably calm. "Fine, fine. I'll plan on coming over to your place around noon. Maybe we can grab a little lunch before I pick up the container. Will you call me when it shows?"

"Shall do," said Booth hurriedly and added, "Gotta run. See you tomorrow."

As Booth put down the phone he looked questioningly at the instrument, wondering to himself, "What's so all-important in that damned container? Robinson made me swear to super-secrecy about it. The guy's never been to Japan, or at least hasn't told me about getting up there from Manila. Oh well, that's his business."

At the other end, Robinson's mind had immediately shifted to thoughts of a young boy in Harbin, Manchuria, his home in China. He could picture him watching his father beheaded by Japanese soldiers, his mother and sister roped into position as they were converted before his very eyes into nothing more than sex repositories for the marauding Japs. They were roped there and left for the soldiers who satisfied themselves in groups or individually on impulse as they passed the helpless woman and girl.

Chiang Luang was a young boy watching these scenes as the Japs brought hundreds of thousands of Manchurian civilians in a never-ending procession into the slaughter house the Emperor had designated as Unit 731, the medical research madhouse run by Dr. Shiro Kimura.

How fitting it would be, Robinson thought, if Chiang could be here tomorrow when he picked up the container with its despicable cargo inside.

His mind quickly returned to the present and the tasks ahead of him.

He first called a car rental company, got the location, and went on downtown to make certain what he needed was available the next morning. He wanted a large pickup with four-wheel drive.

"What I'd really like is a rig with some sort of hydraulic lift at the rear. Have anything like that?" he asked the attendant.

"Sure, it's covered too. Come take a look at it."

He assured the man it was just right and completed the paper work so he could pick it up first thing in the morning.

There was nothing more he could do on this project except try to control his own emotions as he contemplated the task awaiting him the next day.

As he left the vehicle rental agency he noticed a building supply outlet and realized they'd probably have just what he needed around the barn and house. Some work gloves. He stopped off and picked up a pair of gloves. Actually, from the standpoint of tools, the barn was a repository for a variety of tools, the majority of which Robinson couldn't imagine ever using. So he sure didn't need any more tools.

With his gloves on, whenever the container was discovered, there'd be no fingerprints to help authorities determine who had deposited it. He planned to take the container's baglike shipping cover off and dispose of it in the barn's burning barrel.

Now all he had to do was wait.

As he was driving slowly back to the house he considered his project for the morrow, hoping he'd overlooked no possibilities which could cramp his plans. Emigrant Lake was notably long, narrow and not deep, and that's the element that most concerned him. Typically, there was little or no water in the Lake at this time of the year. He had checked that from afar when he first arrived in the valley.

As he considered all the factors, he became convinced he should get out there and have a look. Just to make certain there was no problem getting on the access road, and on down to the bed of the Lake.

Impulsively, he reversed his direction, saying aloud, "I'm going out there right now and check it out again. Don't want to get out there tomorrow with that rig and then find out I can't make it through."

Even with his relatively scant knowledge of the Emigrant area, and the surrounding vicinity, he still realized that Emigrant Lake was a misnomer. Because it really wasn't a Lake at all. It was Emigrant Reservoir but had somehow acquired the name of Lake.

Regardless, it was a source of irrigation water, much of which came to the lake or reservoir by way of Emigrant Creek. At this time of year though, with the orchards irrigating heavily and with the usual heavy off-winter draw on water supply, there shouldn't be much water in any part of the reservoir. He'd find out.

It was easy to get to the reservoir. When Robinson reached the end of Siskiyou Boulevard, the prime thoroughfare through Ashland, which continued as part of the highway south to California, he waited for the turnoff to the twisting highway leading across the mountain range to Klamath Falls. He took that turnoff and after a short distance he spotted the road to the reservoir. That was Emigrant Creek Road.

From there it was a short distance to the reservoir itself.

The bank was relatively high above the bed, naturally, but a gradually descending, road-like trail afforded easy accessibility to the bed under most conditions. It was favorable at this time and Robinson even let his Ford drift along the trail for a short distance before backing up to the rim once again.

The little shack was in easy view and quite accessible.

Having found everything in order he drove confidently away and back to the steeply climbing Sheridan Street to the house, far at the other end of the area from Emigrant Lake.

All he needed now was the container and time would take care of that. He pumped himself up again, a self-assuring device he had relied on often in his twisted, difficult lifetime. By the time he reached the house he no longer had second thoughts on the project.

He knew Booth was planning on lunch and that sounded good to him too.

They met at the usual place, the country club. Strangely enough, it was Ladies Day once again, a circumstance Robinson by now had concluded was less happenstance than planned by Booth.

"You know, we can only be in the company of men or women, Robby, as we go through life. Now really, wouldn't you rather be in the company of women?"

Robinson appreciated the logic and provided support.

"They sure had the Garden of Eden figured out that way so I can't argue with you on the subject."

Robinson routinely asked Booth how things were going in the orchard business and he was happy he did so. Booth gave him a bit of information that registered strongly with him.

"Well, there's been a helluva lot bigger draw on irrigation water this year than most years. Can't tell you why. No-one seems to know. But a real shortage is developing. We'll have to watch it real close the rest of the way."

"Isn't there some additional water stored somewhere? Or is Emigrant the only source you have?"

"Oh no. There's another storage up a lot higher on the mountain. Not far from the Greensprings Highway. You know, goes over to Klamath Falls?"

"Sure, I know. What about that?"

"Well, when Emigrant gets down to bone dry they usually release some of that water from up higher. That's probably what they'll be doing one of these days. They'll have to. We're getting down to the last drop or so."

Robinson digested this bit of news, hoping this water release wasn't so imminent it could upset his plans. "When do they usually release this water?"

"Well, when it's needed. You say usually, well usually we don't need it until a little later towards summer. But I'm sure they'll be cutting it loose any day now."

That news didn't help Robinson digest his lunch any easier but he was thankful he'd rented the truck. He'd quickly made up his mind to take care of his business today.

"Bob, is that container down at your plant now? Could I pick it up later today?"

"Sure. It's there. If you want me to I can have one of the guys bring it on over to your place. Whaddya say?"

"No, no," Robinson hurriedly reassured him. "I've got a rig. Just a pickup with a canopy. I'll drop by after we leave here and pick it up if that's okay."

Booth, reaching in his pocket for a pen to sign the tab, waved away Robinson's reach into his pocket for cash to pay, said, "Never discourage a generous gesture, Robby. You know that. Besides, my credit's good here. C'mon, let's get going."

With his schedule moved ahead by a day, Robinson was more than happy to get on the road.

Robinson arrived at Booth's plant, backed the rig up to the loading dock and Bob's men brought out the container. It showed no ill effects from the trip. The cover was intact and a bit weathered but otherwise Robinson could see no problem with it at all.

"Robby, this thing's a little heavy and it's damned difficult to wrestle with. You sure you don't want one of the guys here to give you a hand."

Booth was obviously somewhat dubious concerning Robinson's ability to handle the container. "No Bob, I appreciate it but I can slide this out without a problem. Once I get it open I can take out the material piece by piece so I'm not going to be lifting it too much anyway. Thanks anyway."

"Whatever you say but you must have that thing packed full. You steal some machinery over there or what? That's gotta run over a hundred pounds."

"About the only thing to steal over there's rice and I can get plenty of that right here," bandied Robinson. "No, I've got a couple of pieces of equipment that brings up the weight. It's mostly journals of Dr. Francis' activities in Japan and ours in Manila. But I'll unload the container before I start trying to move it around much. Then I'll just burn the container. Won't be needing that again.

"There won't be a return trip for this one," he said emphatically.

Without further talk he was on his way to Ashland, thinking he must have made this trip a hundred times or so in just the brief time he'd been here. And there'd be a few more once the clinic was underway.

The container fit neatly, permitting him to have the rig closed and locked in the rear. Robinson was careful concerning that, envisioning the damned container slipping out of the rear of the truck and rolling back down that steep Sheridan Street. There were no mishaps though.

Robinson clambered into the rear of the pickup once he had it backed into the barn, having left his Ford at the car rental agency.

Once there, he began slicing up the cover of the container, no easy project in itself. It was thick and almost impervious to knife or scissors. But he finally had it cut up. Then he had to use a heavy board as a lever to pry up the container at one end, slide out the container cover at one end and then reverse the procedure to get the entire cover free and clear of the container.

Robinson, talking softly to himself, almost whispered, "The damned thing looks exactly like a coffin. Maybe a poor man's coffin but I guess that's what it's for. A damned poor excuse for a man."

He had noticed a wide-wheeled dolly among the collections in the barn and wrestled that into the truck too. "No telling what I might need out there. Just in case I have a problem with it."

Then he was on his way.

Right back out to the Emigrant Lake area, following the Greensprings Highway briefly before taking the Emigrant Creek Road. Carefully he eased the truck down the narrow trail-like road to the bed of the reservoir. He checked the surface of the bed, found a few soft, damp spots but also found a path of sorts which the officials apparently used to get to the shack.

Once there he found the door was latched but not locked, with some sort of measuring devices inside. "Hell, I guess they're for measuring the water levels," Robinson muttered, answering his own unspoken question. "They don't have much work to do now."

Carefully, he backed the truck up to the wide door of the shack. Getting behind the container in the rig, he shoved hard, with his feet braced against the front wall next to the cab of the truck. Slowly he managed to get the container moving.

Once underway, it slid more readily and he soon had it just inside the shack, actually standing upright.

It was easy after that. He just shoved it over and it plopped down on the floor of the shack.

Robinson took a look around, could see once again the clasps on the container were still intact and stepped back to view the handiwork of a few. "Here you are Doctor. Have a nice rest, and think of the millions of innocents whose lives you took. This is for them."

As he moved toward the doorway, he caught himself. He reached in his pocket for the heavy punch, picked up the hammer he'd brought along, and quickly rapped a number of holes in the top of the container.

"How thoughtless of me," he said playing theater with a cloyingly sweet tone to his voice, "of course, you'll need some air."

Then he closed the shack door, clambered into the pickup and drove back to Ashland, his mind once again full of the suffering of the millions in Asia and thinking, yea praying; May Japan, and its evil, never rise again.

Back in Ashland, he again stopped by the postoffice and once again he scored. Because he had mail from George Hartley, in Sheffield, England.

"If he writes just reasonably close to how he talks, I should be able to understand," he thought fondly, recalling the many times they had troubles communicating.

"But we always managed. Right." It sounded like an echo of Hartley talking when Robinson said that aloud.

"Dear Doctor Robinson,

"My thank you to you for all your help during Manila. I have enjoyed getting home and don't miss those places we saw together. But I hope you can visit some day here. You will enjoy it.

"I hope you enjoy the story they wrote here about the crucifixion. You may keep it. Cheers to all.

"Your comrade, George Hartley"

The clipping was from the Manchester Guardian and described in infinite detail the story which Robinson had heard directly from the distraught Hartley as he endeavored to put it out of his mind.

> Manila, Jul 24, 1946 — (Overseas Press) The body of Mosarina Moditake was discovered here today. The dead man apparently died of natural causes. He was a veteran of many years of military duty with the Imperial forces of Emperor Hirohito.

Robinson read the opening paragraph and then carefully folded the news clipping and placed it back in the envelope. He knew the rest of the story without reading it.

"I may want to read it again in the future. Just to assure myself this really did happen. That I didn't make it up or dream it some crazy night when I had a fever or something."

As an afterthought to that statement he added, "Maybe someone in the future will read it and maybe that will help others understand what really went on out there in those years. Maybe."

Once again he was availing himself of one of the outside tables at a little cafe nearby and he sipped his coffee as he again thought of those days. He reminded himself of the words of advice he'd offered to so many at his clinic in Manila: Try to put all that behind you. Missions Accomplished.

With that thought fresh in his mind he drove the rig back, settled up and had a relaxed drive home in his Ford.

He'd had a full day already and it wasn't even noon yet.

After getting cleaned up he called Booth to see if he was ready for lunch. He was still in his slack season, Robinson knew, and his friend was almost always ready for lunch.

They headed for the country club and Robinson realized he was more relaxed than he'd been for a long, long time. Thinking to himself, he realized, "Now I only have Bertoni to hear from. Everyone else has reported. It seems those who had a mission confronting them have completed it. Voluntarily so, but nevertheless completed. And they've certainly kept me informed, for which I'm thankful. I'm sure Bertoni won't be far behind."

Booth could divine Robinson's mental straying. And it seemed to Booth his friend's mind for the moment was probing more peaceful mental territory than earlier. He was relaxed, whereas when he first returned to Southern Oregon he'd been quite tense.

All of which roused Booth's curiosity to another level. What in hell was in that container? He knew he'd never find out but he had to broach the subject anyway.

"Well, Robby, didja get that big old box out to the place okay? No problems?"

His question brought Robinson back to the present situation quickly. "Uh no. No problems. It wasn't much of a chore at all. Got it up there and took the rig back again. Pretty easy project. And thanks for your help. Don't forget to let me know what the cost is on that shipping, too. I want to give you a check for that. Must have been a pretty sizeable tab."

Booth held up a hand in denial. "No problem. The shipping company owed me a favor from last year's business. They knew it and told me right from the start this was on the house. 'Course, with the war over they're back in business again and they're looking for all the friends they can find. But that's on the house."

"Ye Gods man, that must be a bundle of money they're writing off. You're sure it's not costing you anything?" an incredulous Robinson asked.

"Not a cent. I swear. Frankly, I wasn't going to charge you anyway but this way, nobody pays. Sometimes I think that's the way our business runs but you can trust me, this one's on the house."

A grateful Robinson thanked him again and they finally got around to ordering lunch. As they ordered Robinson made one thing clear. "I'm paying for lunch. So far you've been paying for everything. Now we split up the tabs and it's my turn today.

"With no arguments" he quickly said as he could see Booth readying a protest.

They had lunch, Robinson paid, and then promptly won back the price of lunch and more, with his usual good fortune at rummy.

As they departed the club, Booth to his plant and Robinson down the street to his newly found offices, Booth shouted, "Thanks for lunch. I think."

He was disappointed at the clinic simply because not all, in fact, mighty little of the equipment he was expecting had shown up yet.

Dr. Hayes offered his sympathies, using an expression which became trite during the war years, and used to explain any operational defects in any function of society, when he said, "You know, there's a war on." and then added hurriedly, "There WAS a war on."

Seeing Robinson's disappointment he continued, "The company did call and left a message. They're shipping out your material posthaste. So you'll just have to wait it out, Robby. In the meantime, if you see anything here you need, go ahead and borrow. You'll be in business pretty damned soon."

"Oh, I know it," Robinson said, almost apologetically. "In fact, I don't know why I'm so impatient. I've waited years just to get to this point. Oh well, it's not like I don't have plenty to do in Ashland. At the house and barn. I'll be there in case you need me or if someone should call."

As he arrived in Ashland, the Ford almost automatically drove to the post office for Robinson's daily checkup. Finally, the letter he'd been anticipating arrived. It was from the good friend and soldier, the burly and talkative Floyd Bertoni. "From Brooklyn, USA," Robinson could almost hear the man say.

Once again, Robinson opted for a coffee out on the patio, as he called it. In reality, the sidewalk tables.

The letter was vintage Bertoni.

"Dear Robby — My man finally got the publicity the rotten bastard deserved. Mr. Azami has now had a chance to visit his ancestors. And he was burned up. It's all right here in the Herald. They sent this to me. And you can keep it. I've got it memorized.

"Hope things are going okay with you. After things calm down we'll have to see if we can get together. Maybe get in some marching or something. Oh hell yes.

"Keep the faith, Doc. I'll see you later."

Robinson eagerly clutched the clipping from the Manila Herald. It was all there.

> Manila, March 28 — Police discovered the badly burned body of a man under a huge pile of garbage at the rear of the huge garbage dump at its Southeast Manila site yesterday.
>
> Ultimately they determined the dead man's name was Ryoichi Azami.

That was really all Robinson had to read. He knew the rest.

However, he was admittedly far more interested to note the discovery of Morobita's body in the same area, at the garbage dump, was mentioned in the story.

He also enjoyed the police spokesman in Manila, who said, "There won't be any mourners in Manila," to which Robinson added, "Or anywhere else."

Before he folded up the paper to return it to the envelope he penned a preface to it, stating "My good friend Floyd Bertoni sent this to me from Brooklyn. "Haven't the slightest idea how he came by it." He still smiled as he added, "I doubt if they have home delivery of the Manila Herald in Brooklyn. Bertoni's a good man."

He said softly, "Years from now if someone besides me ever reads this, maybe all this material will help explain a few things. Maybe."

A person reading of those days would find it extremely difficult to relate those deeds to the man known as Dr. Robinson of today.

Because Robinson's roller-coaster life gradually flattened out, becoming a more sedentary one in which he literally spent more of his time sitting than anything else.

Certainly his professional life was adhering more closely to the Hippocratic oath he had taken as he began medical practice than it had during his recent experiences. He certainly lived more closely to the professional behavior segment of the oath than he had in his fading years in the military.

He spent only fleeting moments reflecting on the missions which he and his companions had undertaken years ago. Never would he change his conviction that what had been accomplished with those missions of token vengeance certainly justified the action. It had been many years since he dumped the box with its hateful but dead passenger out at Emigrant Lake. And those racing days were hard for him to believe, particularly when compared to his slower life in Southern Oregon.

But despite the slow pace to which he easily adjusted, the time passed rapidly. Young Robinson had grown, successfully finished his schooling and gone to Sacramento where he married, had a son, not surprisingly named Wallace Robinson the Third, and was in the California state government.

Just what he did Robinson, the elder, didn't know.

"You'll have to ask my sister. She's the one who raised him and much as I don't like to admit it, she's a helluva lot closer to him than I am. Or ever will be in this lifetime."

The country club, not far from his clinic which he now headed since the death of Dr. Hayes, was a welcome luncheon spot for him, along with his friend Booth. They could enliven their otherwise boring days in their respective professional pursuits with some spirited if not talented gin rummy games.

On this day at their luncheon Booth related an interesting story, first asking if he'd seen mention of it in the local paper.

"Did you notice the little story in last night's paper?" and hearing no immediate response, Booth continued, "Seems they were replacing the automatic monitors out in the shack at Emigrant Lake."

Robinson, who was busy spooning his soup, put down the spoon to chew reflectively on a cracker when he heard the magic words, Emigrant Lake.

"No. Didn't even see the Medford paper and I didn't get around to reading the Ashland paper, either. What's happened out there?"

"Well, they found this old box inside the shack, with a skeleton inside it. They're still doing work on it, trying for an identification. That's all I read of it. Pick up a paper at the front of the club when we leave. You'll find it interesting."

"I would guess so," said Robinson. "More than a little interesting. Sounds mysterious doesn't it. Have they come up with any identity? Who is it?"

Booth just shook his head as he chewed on his sandwich, clearing his mouth sufficiently to offer, "They're still working on it I guess. Don't know why they looked in the shack. They don't, usually. Unless something should go wrong with the controls. This story was written soon after they had found the boards and the bones in the shack. Anything inside there'd be quite a mess. Right?"

Robinson nodded affirmatively to Booth's statement and question.

He was really wound up on this now. "Let's get going. I really want to see that story."

"To hell with that," said Booth. "I've told you all that was in there and we've got some rummy to play. You're into me for about twenty five bucks and you're not getting outta here until we shuffle the deck a few times."

They played for what seemed an eternity to Robinson. Despite his mind wandering away from the table to the other matter, he still added a few more bucks to his winnings.

"Okay. That does it," Booth finally agreed. "Let's go. You can grab your paper. I'm on such a lousy streak I don't know why I wanted to play in the first place."

He wanted to ask Robinson what had happened to that box he'd received via Transasia from Yokohama. But he didn't dare. It really bugged him though. He couldn't help himself. Robinson getting a big box shipped here twenty years or so ago. When they were relatively young men. Now, when they're actually in the senior citizen set at the club, they find the remnants of a box.

With a body inside.

But Robinson was non-committal and Booth had to content himself with his mind games. Neither could wait to read the paper that evening though. And to watch the television news.

Once at their own homes, both Booth and Robinson probably were the most interested parties to the story in the entire valley. The story was brief.

Authorities have learned little regarding the identity of the person whose skeletonized remains were found inside the measuring shack at Emigrant Lake yesterday.

The Sheriff said, "We did find a metal identification tag but it's in a foreign language and we haven't had it translated yet. There's little else to base our investigation on.

"One other thing, the coroner has suggested the person could be Asian but it's too difficult to make a positive statement even on that."

One other notation was of interest. The coroner stated it appeared the body was devoid of blood at the time of death. He explained how he was able to ascertain that, when hardly anything more than a skeleton remained.

"That's why I'm only saying it appears so. I can't tell, nor could anyone. It just looks that way."

From Booth's standpoint, his interest increased sharply at even the suggestion of an Oriental, or Asian, as the paper stated it. The opinion regarding the absence of blood in the body at the time the person died, or whatever, was immaterial to Booth.

Robinson just read the article, picked up an Ashland paper, and found nothing new. But he was quite happy with the way it had finally been uncovered. The Asian reference caused no flinching.

He wanted the remains found and that link established. For now his long wait was over.

Now he wanted the identification of the dead one public. Worldwide public. He wanted a young Chinese boy to either read it himself, or have the pleasure of hearing it read to him.

The continuing stories of the investigation of the mysterious finding out at Emigrant Lake occupied far more of Robinson's interest than did the clinic for the next few days.

He accepted appointments only for previous patients who he knew were suffering and required immediate attention.

His head nurse referred other callers to a different clinic, an arrangement he'd made soon after his arrival almost twenty five years ago.

However, he didn't forego his almost weekly luncheons with Booth, which is where he was the day he'd been called by the sheriff's office regarding the discovery of a body at Emigrant Lake. He was called to the telephone and responded as best he could to a man assigned by the sheriff to conduct the investigation.

"Hello, Dr. Robinson?" was the question Robby heard.

"Yes it is. How can I help you?"

"Well, I'm Deputy Silver and am taking charge of the investigation of the body of a man we found out at Emigrant, just beyond Ashland. I assume you've read of it?"

"Yes, officer, I have. How can I help you?" returned Robinson, who had been expecting a call before this time so was ready.

"Apparently, through the tags we found on the remains, this man was a doctor in Tokyo and had been assigned as long ago as 1937 to direct the activity in Manchuria. Some place where they were cutting up people, experimenting in various ways supposedly to help fight disease and so on. We've established his name as Kimura. Shiro Kimura. Does that ring a bell with you?"

"Oh yes. Although I was in Manila and never in Tokyo, Japan or in Manchuria, there's not many folks involved in medicine who haven't heard his name. Are you telling me they think that's his body? Or what's left of it?" asked the apparently astounded Robinson.

"Yes sir. If these tags were originally this man's that's exactly who it is."

"How in the devil did he get to Southern Oregon from Tokyo, which is where he was, I imagine? That's hard to believe," repeated Robinson, continuing a high level of surprise at such a possibility.

"Yes sir," responded the officer. "Hard to figure out. How could the body get all the way over here. There's only a few scraps here that might have been a box or some sort of container he might have been in but there's no way we can figure the why or the how of it all. Well, if you think of anything that might help us, I'd appreciate your call. At the sheriff's office and just ask for Deputy Silver."

"Oh you can be sure I will. But it's a mystery to me. It just doesn't figure at all."

The officer thanked him for his time and they hung up.

He walked back to the lunch room where Booth was already shuffling the cards. "What the hell was that all about? You just fake that so you don't have to give me a chance to get even?"

"That, my friend Robert, was the deputy sheriff, investigating the body, or the remains of the body they found out at Emigrant. They determined he was a Japanese doctor and they thought I might be able to help them, I certainly know the name of the guy but that's it. Never laid eyes on him. He's a bad guy. Or WAS a bad guy," he corrected himself. "Ran an experiment camp where these medics experimented, operating on live Chinese just to see the effect of different elements on the different organs. I'll shut up now. No need to spoil your lunch.

"Besides. It's your deal."

As Booth flipped out the cards, Robinson impolitely picked them up, arranged them and made ready to play, with his mind thousands and thousands of miles away but wholly at ease.

"I think the damned game's fixed," Booth growled as he paid off once again to the cool and collected Robinson. "Christ, you get questioned by the sheriff on what might be a murder and then come back here and absolutely kill me at rummy. Figure that."

When they broke up the game late in the afternoon, and Robinson was cruising back to Ashland, he stopped at the little town of Talent. He needed a few things and he shopped a super market there just a short distance off the freeway.

As he walked into the store he noticed a newspaper stand with the Portland Oregon Journal prominently displayed. The eye-catching headline across the top of the cover page did what it was supposed to do; it prompted him to buy the paper.

The headline said: Body of Japanese Doctor Found at Emigrant Lake, Oregon.

He grabbed one of those in a hurry and then hurriedly did his shopping so he could get on home and read that baby. Of course, he first stopped at the postoffice and though he knew all his comrades had checked in with him by now, he was still a little disappointed there wasn't anything for him.

Thinking it might be fun to stick around town for a time, he drove to the Elks Club in midtown. He still had an Elks Club card and figured he should use it and maybe meet some interesting folks there. Besides, he could read that story in the Journal.

As he seated himself at one end of the bar he took a look at the story. It didn't reveal anything that hadn't already been written in the local papers. It seemed to him it just gave the entire matter more credibility. Printed in some area away from the specific spot where the action was taking place. Or had taken place. He read:

> Ashland, OR — City and state officials have requested an identity confirmation by the Federal government of the remains of a dead man found in a tiny cabin South of the community.

It apparently had been placed in a box inside the tiny hut on the dirt floor of Emigrant Lake. Only remnants of the box still exist. They have identified the dead man as Shiro Kimura, a doctor.

The story continued to explain his background and essentially contained all the information which had been published locally. Robinson reached in his pocket for his money clip, which had a small knife on the side.

He carefully cut the story from the paper, folding it.

"One more for the clipping archives," he said, unaware he had ordered himself another beer as the alert bartender heard "one more" and quickly drew one more beer.

"Thanks," Robinson laughingly said and after quickly scanning the rest of the paper, discarded it on the stack of papers at a side table nearby.

Several of his fellow drinkers at the bar were talking about the body out at Emigrant Lake but fortunately none of them recognized him. He didn't particularly want to be drawn into any of the discussions of a subject that was the hottest thing under the sun at the moment in sunny Southern Oregon.

As he sipped his beer, he tried to figure out his next moves. There simply wasn't anything redhot on tap. Robinson hadn't mentioned it to anyone but he was still fuming about a clipping from the Honolulu Advertiser he'd received in the mail.

It hadn't come from any of his Manila comrades but it had been sent along to him by one of the orderlies in Manila who had been re-assigned to Honolulu.

Just the thought of it incensed Robinson, even though the article was dealing with a subject clear back in 1945. What bothered Robinson was the attitude of an individual whose duty it was to prosecute the Japanese criminals in the war crimes trial.

This specific lawyer apparently hadn't been in the service, which in itself intrigued Robinson. The lawyer was one of 16 lawyers making up the prosecution team.

The attitude of the lawyer quoted was infuriating.

Robinson could remember this one quote specifically. "For me, it was just another job."

He responded to that quote simply enough. "If you'd been through what millions had suffered because of the orders of these animals on trial you sure as hell wouldn't look at it as just another job. With a guy like that we're lucky we got any of those bastards executed. Sure not like Nuremberg."

That wasn't all though. The lawyer gave some opinions concerning the Emperor's No. 1 boy, General Hideki Tojo. Robinson almost vomited everytime he thought of the quotes by this lawyer.

"I rather liked Tojo. He was brilliant — they called him 'Old Razor Brains'.

Robinson choked as he thought of this totally absurd statement and he shuddered at the thought of his continuation. "As far as I was concerned I could have defended them as easily as prosecuted them."

Oh brother, thought Robinson. And this guy was on our side. 'Rather liked Tojo'. He'd have loved the Emperor then, Robinson said to himself.

According to the story, the lawyer was 26 when the war started but wasn't in the service. Because his wife had been badly burned in a fire, he said he was too worried about his wife to feel hatred for the Japanese criminals he tried.

It had been a spell since Robinson had read this story from the Advertiser in Honolulu but he remembered every word quite clearly. He chose not to save the article, knowing it would never be away from precise, personal recall.

"Want another?" asked the bartender.

"Thanks no, I've got to get going," said Robinson, whose desire to spend some time at the bar had been thoroughly doused by his recollection of that lawyer, who "rather liked Tojo".

How could a flake-brain like that be permitted to represent the millions of people who had been sacrificed by this animal who was prescribed by a prosecutor as "brilliant"; someone he "rather liked".

Robinson wasn't sure he'd be able to eat that evening. His insides were rolling as he continued his silent bitching about such absurd stupidity. How could anyone who had an inkling of what the Japanese had done, under the direction of leaders such as Hirohito and Tojo, possibly harbor such thoughts as this lawyer expressed. Furthermore, why wasn't he fired from the case just as soon as he made the statements.

He shook his head, trying to rid his mind of the statements.

Too bad he didn't get a chance to meet Hitler. Probably he'd think he was brilliant too but not as brilliant as Tojo, of course.

Robinson fought to forget it and decided to stop at the little cafe downtown to eat. He didn't feel up to fixing anything for himself.

The sight of food dispelled the ugly thoughts the story had placed in his mind.

The story was by Alicia Brooks, for the States News Service, and published in the Advertiser in Honolulu with a Washington dateline.

The quote "rather liked Tojo", according to the quote in the story, was uttered by Lawyer Robert Donihi. And that's not all.

"He was brilliant," continued Donihi. "They called him 'Old Razor Brains".

And the general had a sense of humor according to Donihi, the story continued, recounting how Tojo had been told by the guards in his cell, 'Hubba Hubba', a slang expression of the era meaning hustle along or hurry.

"I thought it meant 'Remember Pearl Harbor'.

This thoughtless statement, by General Hideki Tojo, the war-time prime minister of Japan and the prime leader of Japan's heartless slaughter of all who were not Nipponese, was interpreted as humorous by Donihi.

Robinson could only growl, "And this is a war crimes attorney. He thinks it's 'just another job' and says he "rather liked" the prime criminal.

Those preposterous remarks by the lawyer chosen to prosecute Prime Minister Tojo and the other murderers from Japan, as quoted in the newspaper, were now firmly fixed in his mind.

When he awakened the next day Robinson remembered only too clearly the inane statements by this barrister. The man who helped prepare a case against criminals such as the Emperor and his vicious-minded stooge, Tojo, who plotted so many of the Japanese forays against humanity.

Now that Robinson was retired and well out of it he viewed the entire mess retrospectively as if it were one gigantic and sickening marionette show. With the little characters in control flitting throughout Asia cutting the strings of the helpless people who were dominated by such as Tojo and his equally vicious underlings.

There was a major difference between such as Tojo and the subordinates. Tojo heard the words of the supreme Emperor personally.

It was clear that all the millions of followers of the Emperor heard his philosophies of Japanese superiority as the master race of all time. They followed his ruthless dictates.

But no-one ever paid the price for all the terrible crimes against the civilian populations which they invaded. Some of the leaders, such as Tojo, were justifiably executed, despite the shockingly friendly attitude of one of the prosecutors. An American.

But the people only slightly removed and others far down the ladder, and there were millions practicing these crimes for many years, weren't reached by the postwar justice as directed by MacArthur.

They were reached only by those with a mission. Such as those with whom Robinson had entered an unwritten, unspoken bond. A bond to follow a mission to punish a few of these criminals.

As the years went by Robinson realized that without these missions, some of the prime criminals of the war in the South Pacific would have gone unpunished. Otherwise, the instigator of what he called the Emperor's Killing Field in Manchuria, the good Doctor Kimura, would never have received the justice he deserved for the murders he and his associates committed in Unit 731.

Others with heinous crimes against those unable to defend themselves would never have been punished.

Thinking of his comrades, Robinson realized they collectively were few. A small group but they were right on target. They represented the belief that criminals, whether in time of war or peace, should be brought to justice and punished.

Once it became obvious the victors, the United States, didn't plan to pursue these programs of justice and sustain them down through the years, such individual action was justified and needed.

Sustaining the memory of right and wrong, as had been done in Germany, apparently would never be accomplished in Japan.

"I'm afraid there's nothing we can do about that. We're too few. We don't have a big organization to force acceptance of wrong by the ancesters of those criminals who preceded them," Robinson wryly and sorrowfully admitted to himself.

He abruptly terminated his musing of times gone by. He knew Booth would be awaiting his call regarding plans for lunch. Instead of calling, he hopped out for the quick drive to the packing plant in Medford, where Booth was waiting.

"Hey, you're in luck. It's ladies day again at the club and Paula's going to join my wife for bridge. We may be able to play a few hands of bridge, if you're interested."

Robinson shrugged, indicating he was open for anything but said, "What, you're trying to ease out of our gin rummy game? You haven't lost that much money have you?"

"No. No. We'll play gin first and if it works out we can play some bridge later. I've got to get a shot at my money you're holding. Can't believe the run of cards in our games."

"Cards?" Robinson voiced in mock surprise. "That's talent, my friend. Sheer talent. Even break on cards and then talent, pure talent, takes over."

With that pre-lunch oral sparring aside, they ordered lunch. Robinson was interested in Bob's opinion on his, Robinson's, tenure in Medford thus far.

"I don't know what you're looking for. You know how to evaluate yourself and what you're doing better than I do. You're keeping busy at the clinic most of the time, near's I can tell. You'll have to figure out whether it's what you want or not."

"Well Bob, I just wonder if I've gone about as far in this as I want to go. It's been a few years now. I'm not getting any younger. Hell, in a few years we're heading into a new century. I don't know how far into that I want to keep working, assuming I'm still healthy. That goes for you too. Right?"

"Well, sure. But I've got others in the company who'll just step in when I've had enough." He laughed and added, "They're probably wishing I'd get my butt outta there now and let them take over. With you it's different. It's a one-man show, pretty much. Anyway, that's a few years down the road. Hell, you're only about seventy or so right now, aren't you?" knowing full well Robinson wouldn't affirm any specific age.

Robinson answered with his customary dodge of the question. "Just keep in mind what Helen Hayes, the marvelous actress said on that subject: 'Age is only important if you're a cheese.' And I suppose that's true of wine also, which reminds me, I'd like a glass of wine."

As they finished their lunch and began playing cards, Robinson's mind was still on the question of how long he wanted to continue in the clinic.

All of his friends from the war had long since checked in with him, the house was still standing, as was the remodeled barn, shaped more in the configuration of a garage now, and people were constantly calling regarding the orchard property down the hill from the house. They wanted to build houses in there and Robinson knew full well that was the destiny of those acres downhill from the house.

He wasn't sure he wanted to endure the necessary upheaval for the preparation of the land and the subsequent construction there. "Let all that happen later. After I'm gone," he'd told Booth one day as they talked about the developments taking place in Ashland.

As was his way, Booth was brief and to the point.

"Let one of them put some cash on the line but with the proviso the property doesn't go anyplace until after you've checked out. And after your family has taken a look at it and pronounced it ready to go. In other words, all your private stuff outta there.

"Speaking of private stuff, I notice you're driving a pickup today. Or is that a Jeep? What's happened to the Ford."

Robinson held up his hands. "I forgot all about that. The dealer in Ashland knew someone, a collector, who wanted it. Offered me enough cash to make it interesting and the dealer made me a pretty good setup on the Jeep. As you can see, I'm really into it, I don't think. Hell, I'd already forgotten all about it."

Booth voiced his surprse. "I'll be damned. Here I thought you were all wrapped up in that convertible. Something that I figured you wanted to hang onto. Sentimental value and all that. Right?"

"Not really Bob. I had it only briefly before the war and I liked it as a car. But you know my attitude about cars. They're wheels to get you to one place or another and that's it. No, I'm happy with this rig. I think it makes more sense."

Robinson didn't think that deal and the prospect of dealing off part of the Ashland property necessarily had any significance other than straight common sense. But Booth read into those changes a definite swing toward Robinson's retreat from the practice in Medford. And he was right.

As his friend and almost only confidant in Southern Oregon, Booth listened to Robinson offer his thoughts.

"I think the drastic differences between American's punitive post-war relationship with Germany, as opposed to our almost apologetic treatment of the country which actually attacked us, Japan, had far more impact on my life than anything else in this mess.

"After all, Germany didn't attack us. Hitler was in bed with them yes, but at one time he was with Russia too. Don't get me wrong. We had to join in that battle against Germany. Britain would never have made it otherwise. But look at the record.

"We've held the Germans, and the papers refer to all of them as Nazis, but we've held them responsible for all of the horrid killing campaigns of Hitler's Gestapo and SS. We've looked at that entire nation as guilty for the crimes of Hitler's crew.

"Conversely, we've done nothing to compel the Japs even to admit responsibility for any of the horrors they created. They've never admitted any of them took place."

He looked away as he cited some shocking, cold statistics from the military.

"The official figures on deaths in Prisoner of War camps in Germany is 2%. That's probably less than the national rate of attrition in civilian, or non-war days. Whatever that is.

"But you know what the death rate for the poor devils who ended up in the Jap camps is? It's 28%.

"That damned sure isn't because of the weather. That's just PWs. Add to that the millions and millions of civilians who lost their lives to those people. How many, no-one knows but it's up there. Past Stalin's numbers. And he killed 20 million or so Jews alone."

Booth chose the pause to suggest, "Robby, remember this. We're two old men talking of things that most Americans don't realize even took place. The Japs killed more civilians than any so-called combatants in the history of the world. Not just men at war. In what our politicians and so-called historians call an honorable war. They slaughtered civilians in an inhuman manner that would make Attila the Hun cringe. Most people don't know this."

And Booth reminded him of the peace treaties. "Gotta remember the treaties. Back then we signed peace treaties with Japan waiving all claims by former prisoners of war for any reparation."

Again Robinson interrupted. "No, no. I know all that. But what about the civilians? Those who were captured and either worked to death or tortured to death or just killed for the sport of it.

"And the women who were taken for use as sex playthings by the Jap soldiers. Some of them finally got some admissions of responsibility by the Japanese government and something like eighteen or twenty thousand in compensation. That's crap. The German companies who used slave labor during the war have paid billions to survivors and their families. Why not the same with the Japs?"

Both of them were thinking the same thing. Booth spoke up.

"Can't answer that Robby. Unless it's because we do so much business with Japan no-one's got the desire to stand up and force the issue. Remember the old saying. Don't get mad at your money. You know damned well the politicians won't force anything. They get all the money they need from the poor damned taxpayers and if they need more they take more.

"And just think of all the trips, for some phony reason or another, that our politicians have had to take to Japan. I'll never understand the difference.

"And all our so-called investigative reporters. They've never written in depth of those differences. The papers don't mention it. They're writing about the Nazis, a blanket term they use to indict all Germans. They write it all the time."

Then he impatiently pushed his coffee cup to one side and said, "C'mon. Let's play cards. This talk's spoiling my lunch."

So they shuffled the cards once again.

Robinson wished once again that he could settle all his problems that readily. But he was happy to tell Booth he'd settled one of them. "I got a firm offer from two young doctors today. I've decided to accept an offer for the clinic."

"Why look so surprised, Bob?"

"I'm past 90 now. That kind of a grind is for a younger man. I don't need the money so why knock myself out. You're the same but you've plenty of people to run your operation. You could play cards out here all day."

Then he needled Booth as he said, "Of course, if we played all day, I don't know if your staff could generate enough revenue to cover your losses here."

"Go to hell and deal," returned Booth, who wasn't overly surprised by his friend's announcement. The frequency of their gin games had increased lately and he knew Robinson welcomed them as a welcome diversion from his thoughts of the past and the war.

The daily grind of the clinic simply seemed to have a greater adverse affect on him lately.

It was apparent each of them spent less time at their duties, apparent because their gin games had increased. Booth knew it was a helpful diversion from Robinson's thoughts which always seemed to concern the war.

Cards or not, Robby's thoughts were still on those treaties and before they left the table, Robinson reminded Booth of what had happened in 2000, when a number of veterans in California had sued Japanese companies for compensation for forced labor during World War II.

"Remember that? And remember what our ambassador in Tokyo said? He said they couldn't sue because the suits are banned by the peace treaty. I can quote Foley, I think his name was Thomas Foley. Yeah. That's it. The quote from the paper was 'Ambassador Thomas S. Foley joined the Japanese government in rejecting the claims' and went on from there. Imagine that. Is our memory so short that we now have government officials joining with the Japanese government, instead of condemning the treaties and the buttheads who made them. Can't forget it."

When they wrapped up the card game for another day, Robinson fumed his way back to Ashland, thinking those poor devils who'd been worked to death, thousands and thousands of them, by the heartless Japanese. And then the final insult. Their own government selling them out and siding with the Japanese government.

Still fuming with anger, he detoured past the post office by habit although his mail of late had been more of the junk variety which he tossed without opening. There was more of the same today.

On his way out to Sheridan Street for the climb up the hill to his house he stopped to have the Jeep filled with gasoline. He had in mind driving out on the other side of the valley the next morning, to the area looked over by Grizzly Peak. He'd always wanted to walk out in that area but had never taken the time.

Up at the house, he went out on the front porch to look over the valley. With his binoculars he could see the area down to Bear Creek and on up to Grizzly Peak. That's where he wanted to take a closer look. He scanned over to the south a little and there was one landmark which hadn't been changed by the influx of people or by any of the elements through the years. It was Rabbit Rock, although people who'd been up there couldn't recall seeing any rabbits in the area.

Robinson had heard someone suggest it was given its name because the outcropping's configuration resembled that of a rabbit. Even now, as he peered through the glasses at the landmark, he absolutely couldn't detect the slightest resemblance to a rabbit.

Regardless, there it was and that's where he was going to walk the next day. In preparation, he went back into the house, turned off the lights and went to sleep.

Sleep was almost immediate. He'd never had the problems of tossing and turning, probably because he was always so tired when he finally gave it up and went to bed. Thus far he'd been lucky and not forced to answer nature's calls about every four hours.

So if he got his five or six hours of sleep he was almost always ready to go. This day was no exception.

It was clear outside and he took the precaution of carrying his small knapsack, with its handy water flask inside. He'd be pretty dry, walking up the side of the mountain. As an afterthought he tossed in the binoculars.

After a stop for some tea and toast he headed south on the boulevard. He knew he could connect over on the other side of Bear Creek by heading down Mountain Avenue and soon he'd crossed the creek, turned right and had Rabbit Rock within eyeshot.

When he had driven past the fenced area he knew he could start his trek almost any place now. When he found a wide spot in the roadway, he pulled off to the side and parked the Jeep.

It was almost straight up, or so it seemed. Too much of a challenge for a lesser man. Not for Robinson, though.

He started up the hill, wisely walking along the side of the hill, slanting upwards only slightly.

A few birds were startled to find anyone walking in an area they considered their own but other than that, Robinson shared the mountain that day with no one else. No matter how slowly he paced himself, and how very gradually he eased his way up the hill, it was a tiring venture.

The solitude of it all out here became more impressive with every step. More and more he found his thoughts carrying him back to the Death March on Bataan and before that, the deliriously happy days in Manila with Lenora.

Her death brought a stronger impact to bear on him than the death of his wife and again he relied on his belief it was because the woman had risked and given her life as she attempted to help him.

All of the people who had made their way through his rehabilitation center in Manila passed through his mind, some in a more refined focus than others.

Bertoni, Cangleonn, Greene, Merrando, Hartley and the youngster, Luang. They seemed so real, probably because they shared the dedication to their unstated and unwritten but well understood missions against seven particularly putrid Japs.

All of these people's lives, insofar as he knew them, also flashed briefly into his mind with amazing clarity. Pulling these bits of history from his memory bank which spanned more than sixty years, presented no hurdles for Robinson. He remembered his first night with Lenora and the subsequent though brief period of lovely living with her as if it had happened last week.

Working with Bertoni on the Death March and later at the rehab center, the Brooklyn man's unspoken conviction he shared with Robinson that those murderers should be punished, now replayed in his mind. As did the time he spent with the two Englishmen, Greene and Hartley, as well as the two natives of Manila, Cangleonn and Merrando.

Nor could he ever forget the piteous youngster, Chiang Luang, who had suffered so horribly at the hands of the relentless hordes of Japanese who invaded his country, murdered his father and after wholesale raping of his mother and sister, murdered them also.

He paused to take a refreshing swig of water from his flask. He sat and rested, almost in the shadow of Rabbit Rock now. Though he rested, his mind was racing to catch up to the present.

The richly-deserved fate of those selected by his comrades dedicated to these missions would never leave his memory. Nor would the knowledge that supreme justice had been served by a few. A justice and responsibility which should have been accepted by the government whose cause these millions were serving and for whom they gave their lives.

Instead, the men of the missions watched as their government, the government they served, gave only token punishment to a few.

As always, Dr. Robinson kept his fury locked inside him. But he was still furious when he thought again of the failure of his government to exact payment for war sins. Not from the individuals, or the government of Japan, was payment for the acts of the criminals, as ordered by Hirohito, ever received. Nor were they ever punished.

Thinking of the experimenting doctor almost made him choke. The murderer Kimura had finally met his just due, and the increasing tension within Robinson subsided slightly as he recalled the fate of that one. The bad doctor, finally discovered a few miles from here.

But then the tension struck again. Robinson could sense the finality of it. Finally, the heart which had been broken so often and completely, couldn't sustain the body any longer. High up on a mountain he felt the horrible pain in his chest. He collapsed with only the slightest of moans. With no-one to hear.

Robinson was prostrate on the sloping side of Grizzly Peak.

The good doctor was dead, his missions completed.

Not far from where he'd helped the bad doctor find his final resting place.

Medford OR.   6 Oct. 1995

To al
    good friend and
good soldier

        Ralph

Dr. Ralph Emerson Hibbs

For mail ordering *Millions of Ghosts Plead...Don't Forget,* please forward the information as detailed below.

Cost of mailing in the USA: $1.65
Cost of mailing to Canada $1.65
Total Cost USA $19.60 each copy
Total Cost (Canada) $25.65 each copy

Increase accordingly for multiple orders.
Please submit that amount by check or money order made payable to the publisher, Hartley Press. Sorry, no COD orders. Please send your payment to Hartley Press, PO Box 2657, Gearhart, Oregon 97138. Your book will be mailed promptly.

Please send _____ copies of GHOSTS to:

Name_____

Address or PO Box_____

_____

City_____State_____ Zip _____

Phone No._____

Amount Enclosed: _____